“Goldilocks, th

With a squeal, Cara turned and started running.

In quick strides Whit caught up with her and wrapped both arms around her, lifting her clean off her feet. He pinned her beneath him as they sank into a snowdrift tall enough to bury them both.

His mouth closed over hers in a kiss that was as shocking to their systems as the snow had been just moments earlier.

She couldn’t speak. Could barely breathe. The press of that hard, muscled body on hers was doing the strangest things to her brain. Despite the layers of clothing, she could feel him in every pore. The touch of those lips on hers had the breath backing up in her lungs. Her heart was beating a wild, crazy tattoo, and she wondered that it didn’t burst clear through her chest. But she couldn’t decide if it was fear or lust.

“Ready to declare a truce?” He spoke the words inside her mouth, sending yet another series of tremors through both of them.

“Not on your life, Cowboy.”

Raves for R. C. Ryan's Novels

THE REBEL OF COPPER CREEK

"Second in the Copper Creek Cowboys series, this book is a winner. Ryan writes with a realism that brings readers deep into the world she's created. The characters all have an authenticity that touches the heart."

—RT Book Reviews

THE MAVERICK OF COPPER CREEK

"Ryan's storytelling is tinged with warmth and down-to-earth grit. Her authentic, distinctive characters will get to the heart of any reader. With a sweet plot infused with family love, a fiery romance, and a bit of mystery, Ryan does not disappoint."

—RT Book Reviews

JAKE

"A must-read...cozy enough to make you want to venture into the wild west and find yourself a cowboy...And if you haven't read a western romance before, R. C. Ryan is where you should start."

—ReviewsbyMolly.com

"Wonderful characters who quickly find a way into your heart...a glorious picture of the west from one of my favorite authors."

—FreshFiction.com

"A heartwarming tale about love, loss, and forgiveness... The characters seemed to spring to life from between the pages."

—SeducedbyaBook.com

JOSH

"There's plenty of hot cowboys, action, and romance in this heady mix of a series that will leave you breathless."

***—Parkersburg News and Sentinel* (WV)**

"A powerfully emotional tale that will connect with readers... Love a feel-good cowboy romance with a touch of suspense? Then pick up *Josh*."

—RomRevToday.com

"This story is action-packed and fast-moving... A good solid story with fantastic characters and an interesting story line."

—NightOwlReviews.com

QUINN

"Ryan takes readers to Big Sky country in a big way with her vivid visual dialogue as she gives us a touching love story with a mystery subplot. The characters, some good and one evil, will stay with you long after the book is closed."

—RT Book Reviews

"*Quinn* is a satisfying read. R. C. Ryan is an accomplished and experienced storyteller. And if you enjoy contemporary cowboys in a similar vein to Linda Lael Miller, you'll enjoy this."

—GoodReads.com

"Engaging...Ryan paints a picturesque image of the rugged landscape and the boisterous, loving, close-knit Conway family."

—Publishers Weekly

MONTANA GLORY

"These not-to-be-missed books are guaranteed to warm your heart!"

—FreshFiction.com

"Wonderful romantic suspense tale starring a courageous heroine who is a lioness protecting her cub and a reluctant knight in shining armor...a terrific taut thriller."

—GenreGoRoundReviews.blogspot.com

MONTANA DESTINY

"5 stars!...The author, R. C. Ryan, delivers an ongoing, tantalizing mystery suspense with heartwarming romance. Sinfully yummy!"

—HuntressReviews.com

"Ryan's amazing genius at creating characters with heartfelt emotions, wit, and passion is awe-inspiring. I can't wait until *Montana Glory* comes out...so that I can revisit the McCord family!"

—TheRomanceReadersConnection.com

MONTANA LEGACY

A *Cosmopolitan* "Red Hot Read"

"A captivating start to a new series."

—BookPage

"Heart-melting sensuality...this engaging story skillfully refreshes a classic trilogy pattern and sets the stage for the stories to come."

—Library Journal

Also by R. C. Ryan

Montana Legacy
Montana Destiny
Montana Glory

Quinn
Josh
Jake

The Maverick of Copper Creek
The Rebel of Copper Creek

THE LEGACY OF COPPER CREEK

R. C. RYAN

FOREVER

NEW YORK BOSTON

Forever
Hachette Book Group
1290 Avenue of the Americas
New York, NY 10104
www.HachetteBookGroup.com

Printed in the United States of America

First Edition: July 2015
10 9 8 7 6 5 4 3 2 1

OPM

Forever is an imprint of Grand Central Publishing.

For my beautiful family, always so loving and supportive.
And for Tom. The love of my life.
Always.

THE LEGACY OF COPPER CREEK

Prologue

Copper Creek, Montana—2002

"Where do you think you're going?" Bear MacKenzie looked up in surprise as his fourteen-year-old son, Whit, headed toward the mudroom of their ranch house carrying a blanket roll, his bulging saddlebags tossed over one shoulder.

"Up to the highlands."

"All by yourself?"

"I'm going with Brady."

At the mention of the ranch foreman, Bear shook his head. "Brady Storm's the finest worker I've ever known. But he doesn't need to play nursemaid to some green kid while tending the herd."

"In case you haven't noticed, I'm not a kid, Pop." Whit didn't even break stride.

"Hold on now." Bear was out of his chair and heading after him, stopping Whit at the back door. "You see that snow out there, son? It may be just starting here, but up in those hills it could already be five feet deep or more. You could be stranded up in that range shack for weeks."

The boy shrugged. "So?"

"What in the hell will you do up there all that time?"

"Same thing I do here at home. Instead of barn chores, Brady and I will be making repairs on the shack and checking on the herd."

"And at night?"

"Maybe we'll get roaring drunk." Seeing his father's red-faced reaction, he was quick to add, "I've got a deck of cards, some board games, and a couple of books, Pop. I'll have plenty to keep me busy."

Bear studied his younger son, who had grown increasingly withdrawn since his older brother, Ash, had left after a particularly nasty fight. No one had heard from Ash since, and with each passing month, Whit had begun spending more and more time up in the hills with the herds.

Bear turned to his wife, who had listened to the entire exchange in silence. "I hope you can knock some sense into your son's thick head."

Willow bit back the smile that curved her lips. Whenever Bear got his anger stirred, the boys became "her" sons.

"I think Whit's head has been knocked enough. Let it be, Bear."

Temper flared in Bear's eyes. "You don't care that your kid could be trapped in the hills?"

"He's ready for whatever comes his way, Bear. A blizzard isn't going to rattle Whit any more than it would throw you off stride."

"We're a family. He should want to be here with his

parents..." Bear looked at his wife and then at his own father, Maddock MacKenzie, seated in his wheelchair, stirring something on the stove. "With his grandfather."

Willow kept her smile in place. "Maybe he needs a break from all of us."

At her words, her father-in-law, Mad, turned to shoot her a knowing look.

"That would be my guess, too, lass." To his son he added, "A lad of his age needs some space. Especially now that Ash is gone. Let the lad flex his muscles, son."

Bear threw up his hands. "You're both nuts."

At the back door, Whit called, "See you."

The door slammed behind him as he ran to the waiting truck, driven by Brady Storm. He tossed his things into the backseat, and they started away, hauling a horse trailer. If the snow in the highlands was too deep to navigate, they would abandon the trailer and ride their horses the rest of the way up the mountain.

Brady glanced over. "Why the long face?"

"Another fight with Pop."

"What was it this time?"

Whit scowled. "He thinks I'm some kind of baby who can't take care of myself in a storm. He thinks I should want to spend my time at home with him."

Brady's tone was low and conversational. "Your dad knows you're no baby, Whit. He knows for certain you can handle whatever nature throws at you. I've seen the pride in Bear's eyes when he brags that his sons are tough and independent. But it has to gnaw at him whenever he feels you're abandoning him."

"I'm not Ash."

"No, you're not. But just remember that Ash hasn't

even left word where he's settled. And now you're taking every opportunity to put as much distance between yourself and your father as possible."

"And why shouldn't I? I'm sick and tired of Pop's temper. There's never any praise for what I do right, but there's plenty of hot temper and curses and fists when I mess up."

"I know, son. But I know this, too—Bear loves you and Ash with every ounce of his being. Every time you leave, he thinks he's losing you the same way he lost Ash. And though he loves you and wants you to stay, he doesn't know how to say it without sounding too soft. All he knows, all he's ever known, is how to use his voice and his fists as weapons. And though he's tamed the wilderness and turned it into one of the most successful ranches in Montana, he doesn't know how to tame his own nature."

"So I should just stick around and take it? Is that what you're saying, Brady?"

"I'm saying that Bear sincerely believes that the only way to succeed in this harsh land is to be tougher than everyone else. He's told me a hundred times or more that that was the first lesson his own father had taught him. He's just doing what he was taught to do. But you can change things."

"How? By resorting to my fists to show him how much tougher I am?"

Brady watched the plume of snow in his side mirror, searching for the words this wounded kid needed to hear.

"There are other ways to be tough, Whit. Look at your mom. Strangers may think she's all soft and pretty, but she's the strongest woman I know. She counters your father's temper with words, not fists. That's because she's smart and steady and not at all bothered by his knee-jerk reaction to the problems of life. She sees the tender side of Bear MacKenzie that he doesn't want the world to see. So try to bide your time, son, and figure out how to get him to show you that side of his nature. Okay?"

When the silence stretched out between them, Brady turned. Whit was staring out the side window. In profile, his jaw was clenched, his brow furrowed. His fists, held tightly in his lap, revealed the depth of his misery.

Growing up was always hard. Growing up a MacKenzie caused its boys to become men before they were ready.

Brady Storm knew a thing or two about that.

CHAPTER ONE

MacKenzie Ranch—Today, Early Spring

Whit MacKenzie pushed the last of the hay from the flatbed truck before parking at the mouth of Stone Canyon, where he'd left his horse tethered. Satisfied that the cattle milling about in the snow had enough to keep them alive for the duration of the blizzard that had come roaring in across the mountains, he mounted Old Red, his favorite roan gelding, and headed toward the range shack in the distance.

The cabin was one of several spread out along the farthest perimeters of the sprawling, thousand-plus acres that made up the MacKenzie ranch. These cabins had been built in remote locations to accommodate the wranglers who tended the giant herds of cattle that summered in the high country. Equipped with a wood-burning fireplace, a generous supply of logs, and enough canned and dried food to last a month or more, it was the perfect shelter from the unexpected spring snowstorm that had already dumped eight feet of snow and didn't look as though it would end any time soon. Besides the snow that blanketed these hills, there was the wind, howling like a monster, creating giant snowdrifts that slowed horse and rider's pace to a crawl. Whit found himself wishing he'd brought along a snowmobile instead of Old Red as he faced into the blizzard, pulling the brim of his hat low before hunching deeper into his parka.

He'd spent all of his life here in Montana. Whether the temperature soared to a hundred or dipped to twenty below zero, Whit MacKenzie knew no fear of the elements. Snow in April or September and wildflowers popping up before spring had a chance to melt the frost were as natural as breathing.

Despite his parka and wide-brimmed hat, he couldn't ignore the bone-chilling cold and the snow lashing his face like shrapnel. The thought of a warm shelter and the bottle of good scotch he would splash liberally into his coffee as soon as he settled in had him smiling. After nearly twenty hours of never-ending work, his body was desperate for sleep. He couldn't wait to slip out of his frozen clothes and into one of those thick blankets that covered the bunk beds.

Some cowboys couldn't bear the isolation of the hills, preferring instead to share a longneck and a bowl of gut-burning chili at Wylie's Saloon with the rest of the wranglers from neighboring ranches. That, and the promise of a quick tumble with one of the hot chicks who waited patiently in town for the weekend rush, was all they needed to get them through another week of endless chores.

For a loner like Whit, time away from his big, loud

family was as necessary as food. And as tempting as one of his grandfather's steaks cooked to perfection on the new grill he'd had installed in the ranch's giant kitchen. Without question, Whit loved his family. His mother, Willow, and grandfather, Mad. His brother Ash and Ash's wife, Brenna; his half brother Griff, who he'd never met until this past year; and Griff's new bride, Juliet, and her two little boys, Ethan and Casey. Ever since the murder of their father, Bear MacKenzie, the family had drawn even closer. But maybe because of their closeness, he cherished his alone time more than ever. Especially now that both Ash and Griff had gone all lovey-dovey, obsessed with their wives, and in Griff's case, two adopted sons. It was, Whit thought, one more reason he was never falling into the love trap.

In the lean-to that abutted the cabin, he unsaddled Old Red and toweled him down before filling troughs with feed and water. Grabbing up his rifle and saddlebags, he trudged around to the door of the range shack and leaned a shoulder into it. Just as he did, he caught the unexpected whiff of wood smoke.

Inside, he dropped the saddlebags and rifle on the floor before turning to secure the door.

"Move a muscle, you're dead."

He felt the press of something hard between his shoulder blades at the same instant he heard the whispered words.

"What the hell...?"

"I said don't move."

It was too late. On his lips was a snarl of rage as he turned to face his attacker. The beam of light from a flashlight momentarily blinded him. He lashed out with a fist, sending the flashlight clattering to the floor. "You'd better not miss on your first shot because there won't be a second..."

Now that the blinding light had been deflected, the words died in his throat. The weapon was a broom handle. And the one holding it was a woman, wrapped in a blanket, thick blond hair tumbling over her shoulders and down her back in a riot of tangled curls. Her eyes, more green than blue, were wide with absolute terror.

His blood was too hot to cool, despite what he saw. In one smooth motion, he knocked the broom aside, then pulled away the blanket to assure himself she wasn't hiding a weapon underneath.

Too late, he realized his mistake. There was no weapon, and no way she could be hiding anything. Beneath the blanket he saw only the tiniest bikini briefs and a nude lace bra. And an expanse of pale firm flesh that had his throat going dry as dust.

Her eyes blazed, and he could have sworn he felt daggers aimed straight at his heart.

Her words were pure ice. "Okay. You've looked long enough. You make one move toward me, Cowboy, I'll rip your head from your shoulders and feed it to the wolves."

It was the sexiest voice he'd ever heard. Low, sultry, breathless. *Sheer bravado?* he wondered. *Or calm, cool anger?*

Never in his life had Whit backed away from a fight. And though the MacKenzie temper already had him by the throat, the look of her, like a cat poised to pounce, had laughter bubbling up instead of the expected anger.

"You and what army, honey?"

She tossed her head, sending that wild mane flying.

"I'm not your honey. And if you think I'm just going to stand here and let some lecherous drifter..."

His hand shot out, gripping her wrist so firmly her head jerked back and her eyes went wide with undisguised terror.

"I warned you..." Her words died in her throat when he dragged her close.

"I heard you." His voice was little more than a growl. "Now I'm warning you. I'm tired. And I'm mad as hell. You're trespassing on my land. This is my range shack. You have one minute to explain why I shouldn't throw you outside in that blizzard and let the wolves have a tasty little meal tonight."

When he released her, she rubbed her sore wrist while backing away. "First I need my clothes..."

"Don't bother on my account." With a half grin of appreciation, he watched as she turned away and snatched at a makeshift clothesline strung across the upper bunk, retrieving a pair of denims and a plaid shirt.

Whit couldn't help admiring the air of dignity about her as she slipped into the jeans and covered herself with the shirt, buttoning it clear to her throat before turning to face him.

He picked up the discarded flashlight and set it on the small kitchen counter, and noted the way she put the distance of the room between them, while her gaze darted to his rifle on the floor, then back to his face.

"Don't even think about it," he warned.

She stood, ramrod straight, her head high, her chin lifted like a prizefighter.

He watched her through narrowed eyes. "I didn't see a vehicle outside. And the only horse in the lean-to is mine. How'd you get up here?"

"I... walked."

"From where?"

"A friend's ranch."

"This friend have a name?"

"It's none of your business."

"Okay. We're done." He tossed his parka over the back of a wooden chair and, carrying his rifle with him, stormed across the room.

Turning his back on her, he sat on the edge of the lower bunk and eased off his boots with a long, deep sigh, grateful that she already had a fire burning on the hearth.

She was so startled, she started toward him, then froze. "What are you doing?"

He never even looked up. "Making myself comfortable... in my cabin."

"But you can't..." She paused and tried again. "Look, I know you said this was your place and—"

"It is my place. And I'm here for the night."

"Can't you just go back to your ranch?"

He did look up then, his eyes reflecting the weariness he was feeling. "In case you haven't noticed, there's a blizzard raging out there."

"Are you calling this little storm a blizzard?" She stalked to the door and pulled it open. A wild gust of wind snatched it from her hand and sent it slamming against the wall. Within seconds, snow billowed inward, dusting the floor at her feet.

With a look of disbelief, she stared at the alien landscape outside. Everything was buried beneath mountains of snow. With great effort, she forced the door shut and locked it before turning to face him.

"I'm sorry. I didn't realize..." She took in a breath. "I know I should leave, but I don't see how I can."

Whit shrugged. "Looks like we're stuck with each other until it's safe to travel."

He crossed to the small kitchen counter and dumped bottled water into a coffeemaker, along with a measure of ground coffee from a package, before setting it on a grate over the fire. Soon the little cabin was filled with the wonderful aroma of brewed coffee.

"Want some?"

At her nod, Whit filled two cups and opened the bottle of scotch, pouring a liberal amount into his coffee.

"Want a splash of this?"

She shook her head.

"Suit yourself." He handed her the cup and leaned a hip against the small wooden table as he took a long, satisfying drink.

As the warmth snaked through his veins, he looked up to see her watching him.

Though he was far from feeling human, he managed a smile. "My name's Whit. Whit MacKenzie."

"Cara Walton."

"We'll talk in the morning, Cara Walton. I'm afraid if I don't crawl into that bunk right now, I'll be asleep on my feet."

He drained his coffee and placed the empty mug in the sink before crossing to the bunk beds.

The blankets on the lower bunk were mussed, indicating that his uninvited guest had been sleeping there. No matter. He didn't have the energy left to climb to the top bunk.

There was no energy left for modesty, either.

Without a thought about the woman, he shucked his wet denims and plaid shirt, tossing them over the back of a chair to dry.

"Sorry, Goldilocks. I'm reclaiming my bed. You'll have to make do up there." He nodded toward the upper bunk.

Rolling beneath the covers, he lay the rifle beside him, closed his eyes, and fell into an exhausted sleep.

Cara stood across the room, reeling from the assault on her senses. First there had been the sudden appearance of this stranger in the dark of night and their terrifying scuffle.

She rubbed her wrist. He could have easily snapped her bones like twigs. She should be grateful to still be standing.

She began pacing. What were the odds that somebody would stumble on this cabin in the middle of nowhere? Not just somebody, but the owner. Wasn't this just her luck? And why should she be surprised? Everything that other people took for granted seemed just out of her reach. In the past year, when she'd thought things were turning around, even the simplest things had been flipped upside down. All her dreams, all her plans snatched from her grasp. She knew she ought to be feeling scared, vulnerable, overwhelmed. Instead, all she was feeling was a deep well of anger.

She turned, crossing her arms over her chest. She'd thought this little cabin in the middle of nowhere might be her sanctuary, at least until she could sort out her future. And now this cowboy shows up just in time to send her packing yet again.

She bit her lip as she watched and listened to the man in the bunk. Her bunk, she thought with a rush of annoyance. She couldn't believe he was actually asleep. One minute he'd come rushing in like a tornado and the next he was out like a light. But at least that gave her time to think. To plot her next move.

She'd heard the wind howling outside the cabin, of course. But she'd been so sound asleep, she'd never bothered to get up and check on the weather. Who would have predicted a blizzard in early April? Judging by the amount of snow she'd spotted out the door, it could be up to the roof by morning.

That little trick of Mother Nature's would require a change of plans. She couldn't just slip away while the intruder slept. That meant she might be forced to spend a day or more in these tight quarters with an arrogant, hot-tempered cowboy.

She finished her coffee before turning toward the bunks. First things first. She would sleep while he was sleeping so she would be fresh in the morning and better able to stay one step ahead of him.

As she switched off the flashlight and climbed the rustic ladder to the upper bunk, she smiled grimly. Wasn't it just her luck to be trapped in the wilderness with a stranger, who, if that introduction was any indication, had a nasty temper and the muscles to back it up.

Chapter Two

As was his custom, Whit awoke instantly. Without moving, he took a moment to gather himself. The mattress of his bunk wasn't nearly as soft as the one at home, but he'd slept on worse. In his years with the herd, he'd often slept on the ground, cushioned only by his bedroll. If a man worked hard enough, he could sleep anywhere, under any conditions.

He heard the soft sigh of the woman in the bunk above him and the slight movement as she rolled to her side. Cara Walton. He could smell her in the blanket. On his pillow. A really pleasant scent. Not the sweet, cloying perfume favored by some of the girls in town, hoping to overcome the smells of sweat and horses and wet leather that pervaded Wylie's Saloon. He breathed it in and found himself grinning. Delicate. Like wildflowers on a spring morning.

Not that he was going to be fooled by that scent. This

was no delicate flower. He didn't care what she smelled like. And he wasn't going to let himself think about that amazing body he'd viewed under the blanket she'd worn like a suit of armor.

Who was Cara Walton, and what in the hell was she doing way out here?

Just how long had she been holed up in this range shack? As far as he knew, none of the wranglers had used this place for months, not since the herd had been rounded up last autumn.

She'd appeared genuinely terrified about sharing this space with him, and yet she'd put up a good fight. A good actress? Or an act of desperation? Whatever was going on with her, he'd figure it out sooner or later.

He'd been too weary to hear her story last night. In truth, he could barely recall sliding into the bunk. He'd been dead on his feet and ready to collapse.

But today was a new day. And after a good night's sleep, he was a new man. He'd grab some grub and about a gallon of coffee, and then he'd be ready to deal with the weather and the woman, both of whom seemed full of surprises.

Cara awoke to the wonderful aroma of coffee. After the night she'd put in, tossing and turning in the upper bunk, she felt vaguely disoriented as she pulled the covers over her head. Then, as she heard the door slam and felt the quick rush of cold air that shivered over her, she sat up with a start.

The cowboy. Whit MacKenzie.

She'd gone over and over again in her mind the story she would tell him. By the time she'd finally given in to sleep, she was satisfied that it would work.

She descended the ladder and hurried into the tiny bathroom to prepare for the day while he was outside.

She'd never showered and dressed in such haste, but since coming here she'd learned that there was nothing like freezing cold water to turn a shower into a torture chamber. She would have taken a pass today, but she wanted to look casual and disinterested by the time the cowboy walked in.

She glanced at her reflection in the mirror over the sink and shuddered. With no makeup, and no way to dry her hair, she looked like something out of a horror flick. Not that it mattered. She certainly didn't need to impress this backwoods bozo, even if he was good looking. But, she cautioned herself, she needed him to believe her.

She winced before muttering, "Yeah. That's my story and I'm sticking to it."

She stepped out of the bathroom just as the door was opened on another blast of frigid air.

Whit's arms were filled with logs. He used his hip to nudge the door shut before crossing to the fireplace and depositing them on the hearth, where he knelt to add more logs to the already blazing fire.

When he was done, he stood and wiped his palms down his pants before turning. "Hey. Morning, Goldilocks."

His obvious good humor caught her by surprise. His use of that stupid nickname, however, had her smile turning to a frown. "If I'm Goldilocks, I guess that makes you one of those smelly old bears."

When she got no reaction from him, she added, "I see you've been busy."

He nodded as he removed his parka and hung it on a hook by the door. "The first rule of ranching: Start your chores early if you want to stay one step ahead all day."

"And you like staying ahead of the game?"

Another quick nod. "You bet. It's a MacKenzie law."

He walked to the tiny kitchen and hauled powdered eggs and canned ham from a cupboard before rummaging around in search of utensils.

She found herself staring at the ripple of muscle beneath the sleeves of his shirt. "Is there something I can do?"

"Not unless you can cook."

"I cook a little. Enough to get by." She bent down and retrieved a skillet. "How do you like your powdered eggs?"

"Any way you can fix them." He retrieved a loaf of bread from his saddlebags. "I'll make the toast."

Cara set the ham in the skillet on a rack over the blazing fire. Then she began stirring powdered milk, water, and half a dozen different ingredients into the egg mixture before pouring it into a second skillet.

A short time later the little cabin was filled with the most wonderful, mouthwatering scents.

Whit carried a plate of toast and jelly to the small wooden table before pouring two mugs of coffee. He handed one to Cara and watched as she sliced the steaming ham before turning the bubbling egg mixture onto a second plate.

He carried the ham while she carried the eggs. He held her chair before taking the seat across from her.

She was caught off guard by that little touch of courtesy. It wasn't at all what she'd been expecting from the owner of this cabin, who'd found a squatter taking up residence.

Whit filled his plate and tucked into his breakfast. He didn't say a word for long minutes while he emptied his plate, then filled it a second time and emptied that as well. Finally he lifted his coffee to his mouth before smiling.

"You lied."

Her hand bobbled and coffee sloshed over the rim of her mug. "What's that supposed to mean?"

He met her worried look. "You said you cook enough to get by. After tasting those eggs, I'd say you do a lot more than get by. Anybody who can turn powder into something that tastes like heaven is a miracle worker."

She relaxed and gave him a smile. "Actually, I've done a good bit of cooking."

He nodded and stabbed at a last bite of egg. "Where'd you do this cooking?"

"A little town called Minerva, Montana. Ever hear of it?"

He shook his head.

"Neither has anybody else. Minerva's so small, if you hiccup, you miss it."

"Do you?"

"Do I what?"

"Miss it?"

She sat back, fiddling with her spoon. "I used to think that if I could just get out of Minerva, I'd never look back."

Whit watched her. "Copper Creek isn't much of a town either, but I'd miss it if I left."

"Then you're one of the lucky ones. When I left Minerva, I promised myself I'd never be back."

"Where'd you go when you left?"

"All over Montana. College, then jobs at a dude ranch, and finally a job at a ski resort."

He chuckled. "I guess you were eager to leave Minerva but not the state of Montana."

"Maybe I'm a country girl at heart."

She set aside the spoon and looked up to find him watching her a little too carefully. "Tell me about your ranch."

He sipped his coffee, aware that she was trying to change the subject. "It's big. We raise cattle. It takes a whole lot of work. What else would you like to know?"

She noted his sarcasm. "Did you grow up here, working the ranch?"

"Yeah. My grandfather had a ranch next door. After his accident, he moved in with us and merged his land with ours."

"What kind of accident?"

"A truck on a slippery road. It flipped, and by the time he was rescued, he needed a wheelchair."

"That sounds tragic."

"It's not a tragedy if you deal with it. Mad deals. He's always dealt with whatever life throws at him."

"Mad?"

"Maddock MacKenzie. He's Mad to everyone."

She chuckled. "Just as long as he isn't mad *at* everyone."

"Sometimes he is. There's a lot of bluster in the old man. The MacKenzie family is known for a hot temper. But once you get past that, he's got a heart of gold."

"Is that true of all of you?"

He shook his head. "Just the others. I'm the heartless one. But Mad..." Whit grinned. "Despite his sharp tongue, he wears his heart on his sleeve."

"So you don't mind having your grandfather living with you?"

"Mind?" He grinned. "When he moved in, he took

over the kitchen from our long-time housekeeper, Myrna Hill." Whit arched a brow. "You'd like her. The two of you have something in common. You're both good cooks. But so is Mad. He's self-taught, and he makes a mean pot roast."

That piqued Cara's interest. "So there's more than you and your grandfather and a housekeeper? How many does he cook for?"

Whit paused. "Let's see. My mom and two brothers and their wives, plus little Casey and Ethan. They're my newly acquired nephews. Our ranch foreman and any of the wranglers who are spending the night in the bunkhouse. Oh, and any friends or neighbors who happen to stop by. Most of them arrange a visit in early evening so they're sure to be included in our supper plans."

"So many people. Sounds as though the MacKenzie ranch is a pretty popular place." She paused. "You didn't mention a father."

Whit's smile faded. "He's dead. He was shot almost a year ago. The coward who shot him in the back hasn't been found yet. But he will. We intend to see that he pays for what he did."

"I'm sorry." She stood and began gathering up the dishes, aware that her question had struck a nerve.

Whit surprised her by rounding the table and taking the dishes from her hands. "You cooked. I'll clean up."

He carried them to the sink and filled it with dish soap and hot water from a kettle he'd warned over the fire. Without a word, Cara removed a clean dish towel from a stack in a drawer. Stepping up beside him, she began drying the dishes and setting them in their proper cupboards.

Standing this close, she became even more aware of

him. Of the muscled arms as he washed each dish. Of the size of his big, work-worn hands. Of the way he towered over her. Her head barely reached his shoulder. "I bet you don't wash dishes at home."

He grinned. "You'd win that bet. The kitchen is Mad and Myrna's territory, and they guard it jealously. None of us would ever dare to intrude."

"Do you know how to cook?"

He glanced over. "I won't ever starve. But it's pretty basic stuff. Steak and eggs. Toast. Coffee. When I'm up here in the hills with the herds, I don't much care what I eat as long as I have something that fills me up."

"What do you do when you're way up here, away from civilization?"

"Play poker with the wranglers. But I prefer being alone so I can think. Watch the stars. Read."

Her head came up sharply. "You read?"

He gave a wry laugh. "From the expression on your face, I guess that means you figured I'd just look at the pictures."

She joined in his laughter. "Sorry. I didn't mean to imply anything. But I didn't think reading was something a cowboy would enjoy."

"This cowboy loves it."

"So do I. Sometimes I just want to get away from people."

"To read?"

She nodded. "I love it, too. But sometimes I just want to write."

"What do you write?"

"Just... stuff." She turned away, ducking her head.

He drained the soapy water and dried his hands on her

towel before starting across the room. "I'm going outside to get another armload of firewood. It doesn't look like this storm is going away any time soon."

Cara simply stared at his retreating back.

He hadn't asked her how she happened to be here, or where she was going, or anything about her personal business except where she'd been born.

Strange. And as if that wasn't enough, he'd been relaxed, fun, and a real gentleman.

Not that she was complaining. She would take this Whit MacKenzie over last night's angry version any time.

Still, it wouldn't do to let down her guard. From the look of him, she had the impression that this rugged cowboy could go from sweet to snarling in the blink of an eye. And she didn't want to be on the receiving end of the MacKenzie temper he'd boasted about.

Cara decided that two could play this game.

As long as he was making nice, so would she.

CHAPTER THREE

Whit swung the ax and felt the blade bite into the log. It felt good to breathe the frigid air deep into his lungs while he worked up a sweat. The smooth, easy rhythm of chopping firewood allowed his mind to work overtime.

The nervous, jumpy-as-a-cat female he'd encountered last night was gone this morning, replaced by a composed, rather pleasant woman. She hadn't lied about being able to cook. Anybody who could take powdered eggs and turn them into a feast had a gift for cooking. Still, though she may have passed the cooking test, she had yet to pass thc truth test.

He'd thought about grilling her over breakfast, but he'd been sidetracked by the surprisingly good food. Now, fortified, he figured he'd let her stew while he took care of the basics. Once he laid in a supply of firewood and checked on Old Red, he'd find a way to engage her in an in-depth conversation. And she had better offer him a plausible explanation for what had brought her here, to the middle of the wilderness.

As far as he could figure, she had to be on the run. If she turned out to be an ax murderer, he'd turn her in to the authorities. If she was running for her life...He grinned. He'd still turn her into the authorities. For her own good.

When he'd chopped enough wood to get them through the day and night, he made his way to the lean-to and filled Old Red's troughs with feed and water.

Then he lifted as many logs as his arms could hold and trudged through waist-high snow to the door of the cabin.

Inside, he breathed in the scents of wood smoke and coffee and found himself smiling as he deposited the firewood on the hearth. Turning, he wiped his hands on his pants.

"You look happy, Cowboy."

He glanced over at Cara, who was filling two mugs with fresh coffee.

"I am."

"I don't know too many men who would be happy spending hours in snowdrifts, chopping wood."

"Then you don't know too many ranchers." He hung his parka on a hook by the door before crossing to the tiny kitchen area. "This is one part of my life that never gets old. My herd is safe and well fed. I've got food and shelter and a warm fire. Add to that a pot of fresh coffee"—he lifted his mug in a salute to her—"and life couldn't get much better."

"Is your life always this simple?"

He thought about that while he drank. "It's not complicated. Whether I'm up in the hills or working on the ranch, my life revolves around my family and the whims of the weather." He fixed her with a steady look. "How about your life? Simple or complicated?"

She looked away. "Not as simple as yours, I guess. But not very complicated."

"So hiding out in the middle of nowhere, in a cabin that belongs to strangers, is your idea of not very complicated?"

She turned and met his look. "Score one for you, Cowboy."

He drank again and topped off his mug before crossing to the fireplace. "I'm not looking to score points. I'm looking for the truth. You said you were born in Minerva and moved around the state. Where's your home now?"

"I...don't actually have one at the moment."

"Where were you living before coming here?"

"In a condo at a ski resort."

"It's a big state. Where, specifically?"

"Ghost Mountain. A...friend's place."

Whit raised a brow. "Pretty pricey digs. You must travel with some high rollers." When she didn't respond, he frowned. "How did you happen to go from Ghost Mountain to Copper Creek?"

"I was on my way to see someone."

"And you just happened to get sidetracked along the way? How did you get to these highlands, with no transportation? And what are you doing way out here in the middle of nowhere?"

"So many questions." She took in a breath and crossed the room, settling herself in one of the chairs in front of the fire. She drew her knees up, wrapping her arms around them. "I got up here to...*your*"—she emphasized the word—"cabin by walking. Of course, there was no snow, so it wasn't as impossible as it sounds."

"How long ago?"

"I've been here eight days now."

He nodded, his face a study in concentration.

Seeing it, she gave a puzzled frown. "You don't seem surprised. What's that look about?"

His mouth relaxed into a grin. "At least I know that much is the truth." Before she could ask more, he added, "The trash can out back is full of empty cans and boxes. When my wranglers stay here, they have orders to carry the trash home with them, so it isn't tossed around by wild critters. And a few minutes ago you knew where to find clean dish towels. You knew exactly which cupboard held the various plates and bowls. You didn't learn that in a day."

She swallowed, even more aware than ever that she wasn't dealing with some brainless hick.

"So you've been here for eight days, after climbing to the highlands. Did you have a destination when you started?"

She looked away. "No."

"But you were in a hurry to get as far away as possible. What were you running from?"

"Not what. Who." Her voice lowered. "I'm running from a man."

"An angry lover? An ex-husband?"

"No."

"Who, then?"

"I don't know his name."

"Uh-huh." He folded his arms over his chest. "Okay. What do you know about Mr. No Name?"

"Not much, except that he's evil and I believe if he finds me, he'll do his best to keep me from telling what I saw."

"What did you see?"

"I didn't actually see him do anything wrong, but I heard him threaten another man."

"Threaten what?"

"To make him sorry if he told what he knew."

"Did Mr. No Name say what the other guy knew?"

"No."

"Who was the man Mr. No Name threatened?"

"I don't know."

"Where did this happen?" His tone lowered with annoyance. "And don't tell me you don't know. It's beginning to sound like an old-time comedy act."

She almost smiled before biting her lip. "Just outside a town called Red Rock."

Whit nodded. "I know Red Rock. About a hundred miles from Copper Creek. Where were you and these two men when you overheard this threat?"

"I was standing on a rancher's porch, hoping to ask directions. I was lost, and my rental car's GPS system quit on me. The door between the porch and kitchen was open, and two men were standing in the kitchen. One was white-haired and wearing overalls and a plaid shirt. I figured he lived there. Thc other was wearing a suit and tie and certainly didn't look like a rancher. The white-haired man was upset about something and started calling the other man a thief and a liar. That's when Suit-and-Tie grabbed him by the front of his plaid shirt and said he had two choices—keep his mouth shut and take the money or go to the police, who would never take his word over that of a man of the law. But if the old man tried to report him, he would find himself the victim of a 'terrible accident.' His words, not mine."

"What did you do while all this was being said?"

"I was upset. I started to turn away, and both men heard me and stepped apart. I ran to my car. When I got there, I realized that Suit-and-Tie had run after me. Just as I started to drive away, he grabbed at the open window of my car and caught a handful of my hair. I looked over and saw his eyes, and I was so scared I floored the gas pedal and drove away. But he saw my face. He knows what I look like. And I know, without a doubt, if he sees me again, he'll do whatever he can to keep me from repeating what I saw and heard."

Whit's voice was as calm as hers was agitated. "And you know all this because...?"

She shook her head. "You don't understand. I saw his eyes. They were...they were pure evil. So evil, I think he'd even kill me to keep me quiet."

"And how did all of that happen to bring you here?"

"I was driving as fast as I could through Red Rock, where I got stopped by a police officer for speeding. When I tried to tell him why I was going so fast, I had to pass a Breathalyzer to prove I was sober."

Whit grinned. "I'm not surprised. It's a hell of a farfetched story. What was his reaction?"

"He told me Suit-and-Tie couldn't be a lawman around there. He was the only officer in Red Rock besides the chief, and neither of them wore a suit and tie in their lifetime, except to weddings and funerals. Then he calmly told me that if I wanted to protest the fine, I could hire a lawyer and appear the following week before a judge."

"So you paid the fine."

She nodded. "I didn't see that I had any choice. I couldn't spend a week in Red Rock."

"Why?"

"I had to get out of there. I was afraid that Suit-and-Tie was tailing me."

"Tailing you? I guess that proves one thing. You watch a lot of cop shows on TV. All right. You paid your fine. By check?"

"Cash. It took almost all I had left, and then I got out of town as fast as I could."

"And then?"

"I was looking for a place to spend the night when I saw Suit-and-Tie again. He drove past while I was waiting for traffic to clear, but when he spotted my car he turned around. I saw him in my rearview mirror and knew I had to disappear. I drove like a maniac until I lost him. Then I turned onto a dirt lane and just kept driving until I ran out of gas."

"At which point you started walking up a mountain until you found this place?"

She got to her feet and began to pace. "When you say it like that, it sounds stupid. But honestly, I was so afraid of seeing those evil eyes again, that's what I did. The dirt road I was following led to an old abandoned ranch. When I realized there was nobody around to help me, I just left my car where it was and called the car rental agency to tell them the approximate location of their car. They said there would be an additional fee on my credit card for picking up the car. I figure by the time they're through with additional fees, my bank account will be maxed out."

"And you got here by . . . ?"

"Walking. I just kept walking up these hills. And here I am."

Whit studied her before biting back a smile. "That's good, Goldilocks."

Her head snapped up. "Good?"

"You tell a whale of a tale."

"But you don't believe it."

"Not a word of it. But you told it really well."

"Thanks." She gripped her hands together and gave a sigh of annoyance. "I had all night to rehearse."

"Yeah. That's what I figured." He carried his mug to the coffeepot simmering over the fire and filled it before turning. "Okay. So you're here for whatever reason, which you don't care to share with me, and now that you've been found out, what's your next move? Is there a Plan B?"

She shook her head. "I don't have one."

He glanced out the small window, where a curtain of snow was falling. "I'm sure by the time we're able to leave, you'll figure it out." He managed a lazy smile. "All that work has me revved. How about a game to pass the time?"

She had the look of a deer in the headlights before she composed her features and shot him a glare guaranteed to freeze a man's blood. "Sorry. I'm not into games, Cowboy."

When he realized her misunderstanding, he muttered, "You must have been hanging out with some pretty bad dudes." He crossed to a cupboard and held up a deck of cards and a board game. "I was talking about poker or Scrabble. You play, don't you?"

She looked so relieved, he couldn't help smiling.

"I played when I was a kid."

"Even better. Let's start with Scrabble." He took a seat at the wooden table and opened the board before digging into a bag for a handful of letters, laying them out in front of him. "How about a penny a point?"

"I don't have any money left."

"It doesn't matter. I'd be happy to accept your IOU. It'll make it more interesting." He studied the letters. "Take a seat. First one able to make a word gets to start."

As she sat and reached into the bag of letters, a slow smile touched her lips and she grabbed a pencil and pad of paper. "It's not that I don't trust you, Cowboy, but just for the sake of honesty, I'll keep score."

"Suit yourself. I should warn you, though. I'm considered something of an expert around the bunkhouse."

"Oh, I'm sure those brainy cowboys are a real challenge." Her tone was as smug as his.

Whit stared at the board as Cara carefully laid down her last letters. "What's that?"

"Abacus. It means—"

"I know what it means. How'd you get another *A*?"

"I just dug one out."

He looked down at the *X* and *Z* in front of him. He'd been hoping for a vowel, and now the bag was empty. "I guess I'll have to declare you the winner. Again."

"Let's see." Cara began tallying up the points before looking over with a triumphant smile. "You owe me seven dollars and twenty-five cents."

"If you don't mind, I'd like to check those figures." He circled around the table and bent over her shoulder.

As he did, she breathed him in and felt a quick little flutter of nerves. For the past hour she'd been forced to sit across the table from him, watching those midnight blue eyes narrow in concentration or crinkle with joy whenever he came up with an impossible word. She'd been absolutely enthralled at the range of emotions that crossed that rugged, handsome face. And it was handsome, made even more rugged with the growth of dark hair on his cheeks and chin.

"All right. The numbers tally."

He dug into his pocket and counted out the money, dropping it on the table in front of her. "You play this game like a pro. I thought you said you hadn't played since you were a kid."

"What I said was I played this game when I was a kid. I've also been known to pass the time beating boyfriends at it when they started thinking they were smarter than me."

He shook his head. "I'll give you this. You've got a way with words, Goldilocks."

"You're not bad yourself, Cowboy. I expected you to be easy, but it was a challenge just to keep up with you."

"Uh-huh." He chuckled. "Goldilocks, any time you'd care to sharpen your vocabulary, just let me know."

"You do the same."

He stretched his arms over his head. "All this competitiveness has made me hungry."

She looked over, trying not to stare at those long, lanky legs accentuated in the faded denims and that muscled torso and flat stomach. "Tell you what. We could play one more game, double or nothing. The loser makes dinner."

He shot her a look of surprise. "You never quit, do

you? Especially since you're on a winning streak." After a moment's hesitation, he nodded and took the seat across from her. "Okay. Loser makes dinner."

They bent over the board, each studying the letters they'd fished out of the bag.

"I'll start." Whit set out the word *sexy*.

Her eyes rounded. "An *S* and a *Y*. You're good, Cowboy."

"Maybe I'm inspired by my opponent."

She looked up sharply. "I'm not sure how to take that."

"You're the one who's good with words. Are you going to tell me you don't know you're sexy?"

She felt her cheeks grow warm.

A moment later she laid down the word *hot*.

His smile grew before he set down the word *body*.

She couldn't stop the grin that tugged on her lips. "Is this some kind of message?"

"You can't blame a guy for trying."

She set out four letters that spelled *uh uh*.

He looked at the words, then into her eyes, crinkled with laughter. "Nice try, but that's not a word."

"It is when I say it firmly. Read my lips, Cowboy. Uh-uh."

Despite the laughter, she felt his gaze narrow on her mouth. Though he remained perfectly still, she could feel a shaft of heat slice through her veins.

Silence stretched between them.

Finally he leaned back, reminding her of a sleek panther eyeing its prey. "Okay, Goldilocks. I'll give you a pass. But just this once. And only because you're making the game a real challenge."

An hour later, Whit pushed away from the table. His

tone was more than a little grumpy. "Since I'm cooking tonight, what's your pleasure?"

"Why don't you surprise me?"

"You surprise me, Goldilocks. You're good."

"Thanks. You're not bad yourself. A few more lessons, and you might even manage to be a challenge."

A challenge? While she took her time putting away the board and letters, Whit studied her backside as she reached into the cupboard.

He didn't even mind losing. He'd just spent the most enjoyable hour sparring with a woman who continued to intrigue him.

Who the hell are you, Cara Walton? And what delicious mystery are you hiding?

Chapter Four

Cara pulled a wooden rocker in front of the fireplace and lifted her feet to the raised hearth, basking in the warmth of the fire. It had been fun beating Whit MacKenzie at his own game. He'd been so smug. So sure that she would be an easy mark.

Of course, she'd had to work really hard to keep her mind on the game. Having an opponent who was rugged, gorgeous, and smart was a real distraction. She'd never met a man who could come up with so many suggestive words. She actually liked the fact that he'd been such a surprise. Not at all what she'd thought he would be.

Even though his presence here was forcing her to change her plans, she had to admit she felt a lot safer having him around. He might not believe her story, but in a duel with Suit-and-Tie, she'd put her money on Whit MacKenzie.

Anybody who could spend hours in the snow chopping

wood, listen to an unbelievable story about a mysterious villain with evil eyes, and then calmly start a board game was either as cool a cowboy as they came or an empty-headed fool. And though she'd like to believe she was dealing with someone she could outthink, she knew better. She'd already detected a sharp mind underneath that spill of shaggy dark hair.

Which is why, while he'd been outside chopping firewood earlier, she'd made a rash decision.

What did Gram love to say? Truth was stranger than fiction.

Even though she'd known her story would be tough to swallow, she'd decided to forget about the lie she'd spent the night concocting and had instead told him the truth. Or at least as much of it as she could. In truth, she was already beginning to doubt what she'd seen and heard. She'd been in such a state of anxiety when she'd fled Ghost Mountain that she was sure every stranger she encountered was out to harm her. Maybe, with her life in such turmoil, the whole thing had been blown completely out of proportion. But she'd really tried to tell this cowboy as much as she could.

So much for honesty. Now he thought she was some crazy, half-baked lunatic who deserved to be locked up for her own good.

And there was no one to blame but herself.

She'd stumbled into a hornet's nest, and with every turn she was bound to get stung again and again. But hey, she'd been stung before. Too many times to count. Gram used to say adversity made you stronger. Cara wasn't so sure of that. With each stumble, she was finding it harder and harder to get up.

Still, she had to try if she were to ever reach her dream.

Maybe it was time to put childhood dreams aside and get real. Look where all her dreaming had taken her.

Whit MacKenzie had asked her what her Plan B was. She needed to have one, and she needed it soon.

It was her last coherent thought before the warmth of the fire defeated her, and she let her head fall back as she drifted off to sleep.

Whit rummaged through the cupboards. There were cans of ham, tuna, and corned beef, as well as boxes of rice, noodles, and freeze-dried potatoes. Enough staples to feed an army of starving wranglers.

His fingers encountered paper, and he retrieved an envelope. On the front of it was written the words: *I hope this covers the food and shelter I took without permission.* A signature, *Cara Walton*, was scrawled as an afterthought. Inside were neatly folded bills that totaled fifty dollars.

What a funny little thing she was. Such a contradiction. Fearless enough to break into a shack in the middle of wilderness, yet scrupulous enough to do something so unexpected in order to make it right. She had apparently used the last of her money to pay for her room and board.

Whit glanced over to see Cara lean her head back. Within minutes her breathing was slow and easy.

He tucked the envelope back in the cupboard where he'd found it, reluctant to let her know that he'd uncovered her secret honesty.

Goldilocks was asleep, and it wasn't even in a soft Baby Bear bed, but a hard, wooden chair.

No wonder. It must have taken her hours to put together that whopper of a lie about No Name. It sounded like the plot for a great who-done-it. And he wasn't buying a word of her fiction.

But he had to admit that he'd enjoyed hearing her recite it. Of course, she could probably recite the month's grain prices and he'd enjoy it just as much. It wasn't just that low, sexy voice. Or those deep, soulful eyes that a man could happily drown in. Or that killer body with the face of an angel. But all of it together in one fabulous package was enough to make a man overlook the lies and just enjoy having her around. If, he reminded himself, a man was looking for trouble. Because this little Goldilocks was trouble with a capital *T*. And he was smart enough to avoid the obvious trap.

With a vengeance, he opened a can of this, a box of that, allowing a vague recipe to form while his thoughts returned again and again to his strange visitor. Though it made no sense, he had to admit he was enjoying her company. He'd come here hoping for a little solitude from his very big, very raucous family, and here he was actually looking forward to this intruder's next surprise.

Part of her appeal was her easy acceptance of the situation. She'd quickly come to terms with the fact that she would have to share this space until the blizzard blew over. And once she'd satisfied herself that he wasn't a bully or a rapist, she'd actually become a model roommate. She was smart and neat and fun to be around. He especially enjoyed her clever mind and quick wit. And next time he wanted to play a game to pass the time, he'd suggest poker instead of a word game.

Hey. A guy was entitled to win some of the time.

Of course, he could think of a much more satisfying

way to pass the time. But first, he'd have to find a way past that wall of mistrust she kept around her.

He'd always loved a challenge. And this challenge came wrapped in a gorgeous package.

He was actually smiling as he dug out a heavy iron skillet and several sturdy pots and pans.

Cara felt a touch on her shoulder and came instantly awake.

Whit was bending close, his eyes on hers as they opened. He shot her one of those quick, charming grins. "Wow. In the blink of an eye you went from Sleeping Beauty to Goldilocks. I wonder which one I'll be having lunch with."

Still reeling from the rush of heat from his touch, her head came up sharply and she was forced to struggle to ignore his lips, mere inches from hers. "The Wicked Witch of the West if that food doesn't taste as heavenly as it smells."

He smiled and, as if testing her willpower, leaned in even closer, brushing a lock of hair from her eyes. "You've got a quick mind, Goldilocks. Barely awake and already trading insults."

"Just trying to stay one step ahead of you, Cowboy."

He remained there, so close she could feel herself sweating, before he got to his feet and crossed to the fireplace, where he set slices of bread slathered with thick slabs of ham and cheese on a wire rack over the hot coals. Sitting back on his heels, he stirred some fried potatoes and onions in a skillet.

Watching him, Cara muttered, "I hope you know what you're doing."

In his best John Wayne drawl he said, "Don't you worry your pretty head about my cookin', little lady. Everyone in these parts knows that Whit MacKenzie makes the best gall darned skillet taters in all of Montana."

"Skillet taters." She nodded. "I like the sound of that."

"You writing a cookbook?"

"Something like that. Actually, I've been dreaming of having a book published for most of my life."

"What kind of book?"

She chewed her lip, aware that she'd revealed more than she'd intended. Now she was forced to plow ahead. "An illustrated children's book about a girl growing up in a small town and her imaginary friend, who is really a magical flying horse."

He thought about that a minute. "Sounds like something every kid dreams about. I always wished I could fly. What's the title?"

She wrinkled her nose. "I've played with so many titles, you can have your pick. *Adventures with Arac. The Great Horse Caper*. And my favorite, *Arac and Her Magic Horse*."

He laughed. "And you think they're original?"

"Yeah. I hear you. But whenever I think about titles, I get stuck."

"So, your amazing brain can't come up with a simple, catchy title?"

"I could always call it *Home on the Range*."

He rolled his eyes. "Were you planning on growing a bushy beard and signing autographs from a rickety wooden wagon?"

That had her laughing. "Yeah. I guess it's a little too corny."

Whit used a hot pad to remove the skillet from the fire and place it on the wooden table set for two. "I made coffee if you'd like some."

"Thanks. I'll get my cup." She stood and stretched before crossing to the table.

"You looked really comfortable in that chair."

"It was a perfect nap. And what a great way to wake up."

"You mean, seeing me next to you?"

"I was talking about this." She spread her hands to indicate the fried potatoes and ham-and-cheese sandwiches, melted to perfection, laid out on the table.

"The story of my life. I come in second to a ham and cheese."

She was laughing as she turned. "Want some coffee?"

"Sure."

She filled two mugs before taking her place across from him. As she bit into her sandwich, she couldn't help the sigh of pure pleasure. "Oh, this is even better than it looks."

"Thanks, I think." He grinned at the compliment before taking a bite of fried potatoes. "Hey, for something that came out of a box and was freeze-dried, these aren't bad either."

Following his lead, Cara spooned the potatoes and onions onto her plate and tasted.

As they enjoyed their meal, Whit glanced over. "Now, about your book. What are you planning on doing with it?"

She blushed. "That's one of the things I need to figure out. So here I am."

"You're up here hiding from the world to figure out your life?"

She stared hard at her plate, avoiding his eyes. "It's really hard to let go of a lifetime dream. But a...person recently let me know that I'm only fooling myself if I think I'm good enough to be a published author."

Whit arched a brow. "Could this person be a guy?"

Her head snapped up. "I didn't say it was a guy."

"You didn't have to. Now, about the book? How did it come about?"

Cara was relieved. She would much rather talk about the book than about the guy who'd caused her to question her long-held dream. "I grew up in my gram's house in Minerva. She was strict and tough, but she taught me how to read and write and to work hard to follow my dreams. And though she was tough, she loved me unconditionally. And when I finished high school, she pushed me to search for every tuition grant available so I could be the first in my family to go to college."

"And did you?"

Her smile was quick and bright. "Yeah. At first I did it for Gram. And later, for myself."

"I bet she's proud of you."

Her smile faded. "Gram passed away while I was in Cheyenne."

"Do you have any other family?"

Cara shook her head. "I never knew my dad. My mother was only fifteen when she had me. She left me with Gram and I never saw her again until I was twelve. Gram got word that she died somewhere in Wyoming when I was seventeen."

"I'm sorry."

"It's all right. When Gram told me the news, it was like hearing about a stranger. But my grandmother's passing really hit me. That's when I realized I was all alone and I'd have to figure things out for myself."

"Like your book?"

"Yeah." Her eyes danced with a sudden light. "Want to see it? It's really just a collection of my childhood notes and drawings."

Before he could answer, she pushed away from the table and rummaged under the pillow of the upper bunk. Turning, she held out a handful of yellowed, lined notepaper.

As he studied them, Whit looked over at her. "You drew these as a kid?"

"Yeah." She turned away. "Pretty silly, right?"

"Silly? Not at all. You know something, Goldilocks? I'm no expert, but I'd say you've got real talent."

For a moment she was so stunned by his words that her eyes filled, and she was forced to blink rapidly before turning to him. "That's what I used to tell myself. And I wanted so badly to prove it. But lately I've been thinking that I've allowed this foolish childhood dream to take over my life."

He caught her hand, sending heat pulsing along her arm. "Dreams are never foolish. They're what feed our souls."

For a moment she was speechless, not only by the fierceness of his words, but also because they touched a place deep in her heart.

When he released her hand, she wiped furiously at her eyes, surprised that he'd made her cry. "Anyhow, that's all behind me now."

"Hey." Instinctively he was on his feet and gathering her close. "No tears."

His words, muffled against her hair, sent shivers up and down her spine. "They're not." She sniffed. "I never cry." Sensing her battle with her emotions, Whit tipped up her chin. "Of course you don't. There's probably a leak in the roof." With unexpected tenderness, he wiped at a tear with his thumb.

For the space of a heartbeat she went very still, knowing he was going to kiss her.

He actually lowered his head before suddenly moving back a space.

With studied casualness he remarked, "Okay, Goldilocks. You've been lazy long enough."

"Lazy..." She couldn't seem to get her bearings. One second he'd been ready to kiss her; the next he was calling her names.

He touched his rough palms to her cheeks. "I chopped wood and made your lunch. Now it's your turn to pull some weight around here."

She slapped his hands away.

Pleased, he tossed her a dish towel. "I'll heat some water over the fire, and I'll wash while you dry."

Her tears, he noted with satisfaction, dried as quickly as they'd started.

With this woman, he'd take temper over tears any time. Because there was something about this fierce little female, with so many layers of mystery, that did strange things to his heart. And though he could happily tease her all day long, what he really wanted to do was spend his time kissing that gorgeous, pouty mouth.

CHAPTER FIVE

Hearing the ping of an incoming text on her cell phone, Cara paused to read it. Her brows knit together, and she swallowed loudly before tucking the phone in her pocket.

Whit poured hot water from a kettle into a small plastic tub he'd set in the sink. "So, what did you do at Ghost Mountain?"

"Do?"

"Your job. At the pricey ski resort."

Cara was silent for so long, he figured he'd overstepped his bounds.

When she finally spoke, the words were strained, as though she were fighting to remain emotionless.

"I started out as a waitress."

"You quit college?"

She shook her head. "I got through. Barely. But I had so much student loan debt, I was taking every job I could just to get by. Besides, working at the resort gave me a place to live."

"What about your grandmother's place in Minerva?"

"Sold for back taxes." She scrubbed a plate.

"Okay. So you were a waitress."

"And then I was moved up to hostess and then manager of food operations."

"That's pretty impressive. Why aren't you still working there?"

Whit saw the way her hands stilled. "I...needed to get away by myself."

"You left a good job to drive across the state to Red Rock and then, after your encounter with No Name Suit-and-Tie, you end up here in the wilderness? Okay, Goldilocks. Something's going on. Are you in some kind of trouble?"

She swallowed. "Not the kind you're imagining."

He tugged on a strand of her hair, trying to keep things light. "You can read my mind?"

She stepped back, away from his touch. "I didn't steal anything. I'm not wanted by the law. But I..."

"You what?"

She twisted the dish towel around and around in her hands. "I really made a mess of things. There was a guy..."

"Lover?"

"Jared Billingham."

"Billingham." Whit looked over. "How do I know that name?"

"His father is the owner of Ghost Mountain Group."

Whit snapped his fingers. "That's it. I've seen the name on billboards and commercials. Hotels, condos, vacation villas. And, of course, that fabulous ski resort. So you were swimming with the big fish."

She gave a wan smile. "I turned out to be the biggest fish of all."

"So you and Jared..." Whit handed her a soapy mug. "You were a couple?"

She nearly bobbled the mug before catching it. "Yeah. My best friend, Mary Alice, used to refer to him as Prince Charming. Looking back, I think he chased after me because I was the only woman who never bothered to drool over him. He could have had his pick of really beautiful women, who made it clear they were available. Instead he chose plain old me."

"Plain? If you think that, you haven't looked in a mirror lately."

Instead of laughter, or even a smile, she shook her head. "I didn't think I could ever fit in. He knew the right wines, the gourmet foods. I thought he really was the perfect gentleman. But it was all fake. The charm. The quiet, polite manners he showed the world..."

"I take it Prince Charming morphed into something else."

"I didn't even realize at first what was happening. His jealousy, his controlling nature, were subtle. He'd scold me for spending too much time talking to one of his friends, or even to one of my girlfriends at work. But then it got worse. I found him picking up my cell phone and checking all my messages. One night after work, when I spotted him watching me during my entire shift, seeing who I talked to, who I laughed with, I told him I'd had enough. I didn't want to see him anymore."

"How did that go?" Whit saw the way her lower lip quivered.

"I guess I expected him to be angry or hurt. Instead, he was icy calm as he told me I was terminated immediately. He demanded my keys, my badge, and my uniform and asked security to escort me from the property. I asked about my belongings. He told me they would be waiting for me at the condo. I'm glad now that I took Mary Alice along with me to pick them up. They were in a box on the front porch. And he was sitting on a bench, waiting. Knowing Mary Alice could overhear, he simply told me that he felt sorry for me. That I was a fool who had allowed my silly childhood dream of writing to take over my life. That my promotions hadn't been earned because I was such a good worker or so smart but because he'd arranged them, in order to show me just how much power he wielded. And that, with the snap of his fingers, he could take it all away. But, he told me, whenever I came to my senses, he would be willing to take me back."

"He sounds pretty impressed with his own importance."

Cara nodded. "He'd kept most of his speech cold and polite. But when Mary Alice picked up the box and walked toward the car, he grabbed my arm and told me that unless I grew up and came back to him, he would make my life a living hell."

Whit's hands fisted at his sides. "So you were running from Jared before you ran into No Name in Red Rock."

She nodded. "I just wanted to get away. I had a rental car, a credit card, and a little cash, and no destination until I landed here."

"That text." Whit nodded toward her cell phone. "Did it come from a friend or . . . ?"

"Jared. He doesn't know where I am, but he's still sending threatening texts."

"Threatening?" Whit's eyes narrowed.

"Telling me what he'll do to me when he finds me."

"A really nice guy." Whit's tone was low with fury.

"Yeah." She began to pace. "I'm sorry I dropped all this on you. It's been eating away at me. But now, if you don't mind, I'm going to look around for something physical to do. Otherwise, I'll just have way too much time on my hands. And that will lead to another pity party and I've had enough of those." She draped the towel over the edge of the sink.

Whit thought a moment before nodding. "I agree. If you're going to share this place, you need to earn your keep, Goldilocks. I'm going to chop more firewood. You can stack while I chop."

She glanced at the flimsy jacket hanging on a hook by the door. "When I started out on this little odyssey, I was wearing that. I don't think it'll do much good in the snow."

He indicated a door on the far wall. "You'll find plenty of parkas, boots, and work gloves in that closet."

"Now you tell me."

"I figured you'd had time to explore every nook and cranny."

She crossed the room. "I missed this one."

"Afraid you'd find a dead body or two?"

"Hey. I figured it was possible, the way my life has been going lately." She managed a wry smile as she crossed the room.

A few minutes later, as he headed toward the cabin door, he saw her emerge carrying an armload of winter gear.

She looked over. "I'll join you outside in a few minutes."

He chuckled. “Judging by all the stuff you’ve got there, it may take a while.”

He slid his arms into a parka and strolled out the door. Minutes later, as he picked up the ax and started to work, he thought about Cara. He frowned. He seemed to be doing a lot of that lately. He was spending entirely too much time thinking about her.

At least now he understood why she’d been so jumpy at their first encounter. He lifted the ax high above his head and brought it down, biting deep into the log. She expected every guy she met to be like Jared Billingham, out to get whatever they could, by any means necessary.

He had the satisfaction of watching the log split in one quick slice. It wasn’t a fist in Billingham’s face, but it was the best he could do. Any man who would manipulate a woman and then try to crush her dreams in order to control her deserved much more than a fist.

Cara Walton could fuel any guy’s fantasies. It wasn’t just the angel face and the model’s body. There was also that combination of sharp brain and sophistication mixed with a dash of innocence and simplicity that was intriguing.

He brought the ax down again and again, enjoying the hard, physical release.

The door opened and the woman who’d been on his mind stepped into the snow and started toward him.

“I feel like Nanook of the North.” She was grinning from ear to ear.

He was relieved to see the smile back in her eyes. “You look like my nephew Casey when his mother puts him in a snowsuit. It’s like a straightjacket and he can barely move. Can you bend those arms?”

With a laugh, she walked stiff-legged and stiff-armed in his direction. "What arms? Are there arms under all these layers?"

He was laughing as she bent down and, without warning, scooped up a handful of snow before taking aim. It hit him squarely in the face.

His smile turned into a look of surprise before he set aside the ax and filled both hands with snow. "Goldilocks, that was a declaration of war. And you don't stand a chance."

Seeing what he planned, she ducked, and the snowball he tossed landed harmlessly on the bark of a tree behind her.

"A certain cowboy needs to correct his aim." She scooped up more snow and sent it flying toward his head.

Before she could blink, a handful of snow landed on her cheek and found its way down the collar of her parka. Just as she brushed it aside, she looked up to see him racing toward her.

With a squeal, she turned and started running.

In quick strides he caught up with her and wrapped both arms around her, lifting her clean off her feet. In one quick motion, he scooped up snow and lobbed it right at her.

"Oh, you'll pay for this, Cowboy." She was still wiping away the snow when he bent down and filled his hands with more.

Seeing that, she dropped to her knees and did the same.

"Not on your life, woman." Whit leapt on her, moving so quickly she was pinned beneath him, and they sank into a snowdrift tall enough to bury them both.

He grabbed some snow and held it up menacingly.

"You'd better apologize for that sneak attack, Goldilocks, or your face is going to freeze."

She held up both hands in a sign of surrender. "Whit. No. I've had enough."

Laughing, he tossed aside the snow. When he looked down at her, he realized too late that it had been a mock surrender. Laughing, she tackled him and rubbed a snowball into his face, forcing him to eat a handful of snow.

"Quite the little actress, aren't you? Now you've done it. I won't be fooled again by your cheating."

"I wasn't cheating. I was using war strategy."

"Here's your strategy." Straddling her, he smeared snow over her face just as she did the same to him.

They both froze in place, laughing so hard they could barely catch their breath.

"I love the devious way you think, Goldilocks."

"You mean, the same way you do?"

"Yeah." Whit leaned close enough to touch his forehead to hers. And immediately realized his mistake.

Up close, her face was glowing and her lips, pursed in a perfect little pout, filled his line of vision.

"I think I've found a way to end this war."

Seeing the way his gaze burned over her lips, she understood his intention and tried to turn her face away.

He reached up and caught her chin so that she could do nothing more than watch as his face slowly descended toward hers.

"You'd better declare a truce, Goldilocks."

"Never." The word was forced from her suddenly dry throat in a low, drawn-out whisper.

"Oh, I do love a challenge. Don't say I didn't warn you."

His mouth closed over hers in a kiss that was as shocking to their systems as the snow had been just moments earlier. A kiss that sent tiny spears of fire and ice dancing through both their veins.

"Ready to declare a truce?" He spoke the words inside her mouth, sending yet another series of tremors through both of them.

This wasn't at all what she'd expected. Where Jared's advances had been deliberate and calculated, this seemed more like an accidental seduction.

Still, she couldn't speak. Could barely breathe. The press of that hard, muscled body on hers was doing the strangest things to her brain. Despite the layers of clothing, she could feel him in every pore. The touch of those lips on hers had the breath backing up in her lungs. Her heart was beating a wild, crazy tattoo, and she wondered that it didn't burst clear through her chest. But she couldn't decide if it was fear or lust.

"I'll take that for a no." His mouth roamed her face, pausing to nuzzle her chin, her cheek, the curve of her ear, where he whispered, "Did you know you have the most amazing mouth?"

"And you..." She was suddenly terrified as his arms came around her, pinning her to the length of him as he returned to her lips.

At first it was merely a quick kiss. But then he kissed her again, long and slow and deep until her sudden gasp alerted him that the dynamics had just changed.

If he'd meant this to be a friendly kiss or, at the most, payback for her sneaky attack, it had become something quite different to a girl who'd just escaped a painful encounter. This would feel more like a threat than play.

At her gasp, Whit rolled aside and took in a long, frigid

breath of air before getting to his feet. Reaching down, he caught her hand and helped her up.

"Hold still." He had to fight the sudden urge to gather her close and kiss her until both their heads were spinning.

Instead, he turned her and brushed snow from her hair and backside before lowering his hand and holding it stiffly by his side. "You might want to go inside and get out of those frozen clothes."

"So you can call me a quitter? Not on your life, Cowboy." She flounced away and began picking up logs. Seeing him standing as still as a statue, she called over her shoulder, "What are you waiting for? Did your brain freeze? You promised to chop the firewood, and I promised to carry it inside." She lifted her chin, determined to hold on to her dignity. "At least one of us is doing her job."

"You know what, Goldilocks? You've got a wicked-sharp tongue." He picked up the ax and set another log in place before splitting it in one clean cut.

As she walked toward the cabin carrying an armload of logs, he paused and watched the sway of her hips, the haughty toss of her head.

Was this another act? Hadn't she been at all affected by his kiss? Or had she been so hurt by her encounter with Jared that she expected the worst from all men?

He gave a thoughtful frown.

He'd been right to think she was trouble. And if he wasn't careful, by the time he was able to leave this place, he might be in a whole pile of it.

Chapter Six

"Something smells great." Whit deposited an armload of logs on the hearth.

He'd spent another hour or more chopping wood, working off the restless energy brought on by the close proximity to his uninvited cabin mate.

Cara looked from the table where she was cutting thick squares of something in a skillet. "I found a can of salmon and decided I'd like to do something with it."

"If it tastes half as good as it smells, I may be forced to admit you're a cooking genius."

"Careful. I may hold you to that." She walked to the fireplace and removed a cookie tin on which she'd toasted narrow strips of bread crusted with bubbling Parmesan cheese.

Whit rolled his sleeves and washed his hands before filling two glasses with ice-cold water.

He winked as he took a seat at the table. "The one thing we have up here is plenty of freezing water."

"As I discovered when I took my first shower."

"I'll bet that was a shock." Whit helped himself to one of the squares of salmon and a strip of the Parmesan toast.

After his first bite, he looked over in surprise. "Wow. This is even better than it smells. What is this?"

"Salmon loaf. Gram used to make it, and I tried to duplicate it as much as I could. I made bread crumbs, and instead of fresh onion I used onion salt. A little Worcestershire sauce, some hot pepper sauce, and whatever I could find in those cupboards."

Whit polished off the first slice and helped himself to a second, larger slice. "Maybe you ought to think about writing a cookbook to go along with your illustrated children's book."

That had her scowling. "You must be hallucinating. You're beginning to sound like I used to, when I believed in my pipe dream."

"Hey, Goldilocks. Every success has to start with a dream. Why not yours?"

While he polished off a third slice of salmon loaf, she sat back with a thoughtful look. She wished she'd never told him the truth. It was easier giving up on her dream when nobody else knew about it. But right now, even though she was convinced that her dreams would never materialize, she couldn't help feeling a quick tug at her heart over his words.

She glanced toward the blazing logs. "When I first got here, it was mild enough that I didn't even need a fire at night. When the temperature started dropping, I was glad for the meager pile of logs. I never dreamed this area would be hit by a blizzard." She sipped her water. "I wonder what would have happened if you hadn't come along.

All I had was that thin jacket and enough wood to see me through the night. I'm wondering now if I could have managed to chop enough wood to keep from freezing."

"Good thing you didn't have to find out."

"Yeah." She crossed to the fire and placed the coffeemaker on the grill set over the logs. Within minutes the little cabin was filled with the wonderful aroma of coffee.

Whit watched the ease with which she'd managed to do the difficult things that would have been so simple back at his ranch. Things that seemed more in line with his grandfather's early years. Cooking over a fire. Taking an ice-cold shower. And all without complaint.

"I think, if I hadn't come along, you'd have managed just fine on your own, Goldilocks."

"Well, I suppose I could always burn the furniture." She shot him a sly smile. "Though I'm not so sure you and your family would be sympathetic."

"No doubt about it, Mad would have had the law on your trail." He opened a cabinet door and retrieved a deck of cards. "Since you beat me so badly at word games, how about a few hands of poker?"

"Can't stand losing?" She grinned. "Okay. Deal the cards and I'll pour two mugs of coffee."

When she returned to the table, she placed a plate of delicate butter cookies to one side. "I found a sealed tin of these in the pantry. Gram used to bake something like these every Christmas." She reached for one. "Not that I expect them to be as good as Gram's."

Whit popped one into his mouth as he picked up the cards and studied them. After his first bite, he raised a brow. "Hey, these are good."

Cara nodded. "Almost as good as Gram's. What are we playing for? More pennies?"

He thought a minute. "Tell you what. My feet are still frozen. I say the loser has to give the winner a foot bath and foot massage." He looked over with a gleam of laughter in his eyes. "Deal?"

Cara wrinkled her nose before glancing toward his worn boots dripping beside the door. "It's a good thing I'm going to win. I'd hate to have to get up close and personal with feet that have been stuck in those smelly boots all day."

As he took a sip of coffee and reached for another cookie, his grin deepened. "Goldilocks, this smelly old bear is going to thoroughly enjoy beating your…hide."

"You're so full of yourself." She topped off their cups before picking up her cards.

For the next few hours, as they drank the entire pot of coffee and emptied the plate of butter cookies, they went through hand after hand of poker, their voices and laughter growing with each win and loss.

While they played, Cara asked endless questions about Whit's family, which he happily described to her, explaining about Ash and his childhood love, Brenna, and Griff, the brother he never even knew about until his father's sudden, shocking death.

"And now Griff's bride, Juliet, has two little boys? How do you like being an uncle?"

"That's the best part about acquiring more family. They've got Mad wrapped around their fingers. And they say the darndest things. My mom has discovered the joy of being an instant grandmother." He gave a quick shake of his head. "In truth, our ranch has turned into a land of sugar and spice, with those two females added to the family. Sometimes I just have to get away by myself, to remember how it used to be."

"Spoken like a guy who seems determined to remain a bachelor."

"You got that right. The female wasn't born who'll lead me down the garden path." Whit had the smug look of a man holding a winning hand. "Okay, Goldilocks. We've each won ten games. This is the one that will tell the tale. Has the lady been enjoying beginner's luck? Or is she actually a card shark hoping to swallow some poor, unwitting fish?"

"Wouldn't you like to know?"

He grinned. "How many cards?"

She returned his slow, easy smile with one of her own. "None. I'll play these."

His eyebrow lifted just a bit as he discarded two cards and took two from the deck.

After glancing at his cards, he gave her a long look. "I'll give you a chance to up the ante. How about the loser throwing in a back rub along with that foot massage?"

The corners of her lips twitched. "I think I'd enjoy that a whole lot. Okay. You're on."

He gave a slight nod of his head. "Ladies first."

She made a grand sweep of her hand. "I'll let the loser go first."

"Suit yourself." He lay down his hand, displaying three aces and two kings.

Cara stared at them for long seconds, her confident smile fading as she lay down her cards.

"Why, Goldilocks, you poor little thing. I can see why you were looking so smug. Ordinarily three queens and two deuces would be worth a king's ransom. Unless, of course, you're playing Whit MacKenzie." He stretched his arms high over his head and gave a mock sigh. "I guess I forgot to tell you I'm considered the luckiest poker player who ever set foot in Wylie's Saloon in Copper Creek."

"You're lucky, all right. But you had to draw two cards to beat me."

"A win is a win. Besides, all's fair in love and poker."

As she pushed away from the table and warmed a dishpan filled with water over the hot logs, Whit peeled off his socks and rolled up the legs of his faded denims. Then he settled himself into the rocker, all the while whistling a happy tune.

A short time later, Cara placed the steaming pan of water on a towel and poured a liberal amount of liquid soap.

"I hope it's warm enough."

"I could always add a dash of hot sauce."

"Woman. A hot cowboy like me doesn't need help from a jar of sauce."

He dipped a toe, then a foot, and then both feet. "It's perfect."

"I'll let you soak those smelly feet before I attempt a massage."

"Coward." A huge smile split his lips. "I'll let you know if the water gets too cool."

"I'm sure you will."

She walked away and started a second pot of coffee before filling the plate with more cookies.

When she offered him one, he shook his head. "I've had enough. But when the coffee's ready, I'll have a splash of whiskey in mine."

"I guess you're hoping to be warm inside and out."

"A man can never be too hot." He was humming as she moved around the kitchen, storing the cookies, putting away the last of the dinner items in the small pantry.

When she handed him a steaming cup of coffee laced with whiskey, Whit lifted his feet from the tepid water and settled them on the towel she'd provided.

She looked over. "You've had enough?"

"More than." He indicated a second chair. "I'm ready for my foot massage now."

"Is there any lotion I can use?"

He pointed to the tiny bathroom. "There's a tube of cream we use when our skin cracks from the sun and wind. I guess that ought to do the job."

She returned with it and lifted his feet to her lap as she sat and began massaging the cream into the soles of his feet.

She looked at him in surprise. "Your skin's soft. How can a cowboy who's on his feet all his life in tall leather boots have such soft skin?"

"I come from good stock. How about you, Goldilocks? Aren't your feet soft?"

"Not as soft as yours."

"You may have to let me rub your feet later." At her look, he added quickly, "Just so I can compare."

"Is that what you have in mind?"

"I don't think you want to know what's in my mind, Goldilocks. Especially right at the moment."

She ducked her head and bent to her work, her hair drifting forward.

Whit sipped his coffee and watched her through narrowed eyes. He liked looking at her when she was unaware. At times like this, there was a sweetness, a serenity about her that had him smiling.

She looked up. "I guess, from that smug smile, you're enjoying this."

"You'll never know just how much, Goldilocks."

She laughed. "At least all that soap and lotion keeps you from smelling like Papa Bear."

"That's good." He took another long sip of coffee laced with whiskey. "Because right now I'm not feeling much like a bear. But I am feeling like a king in his castle."

"Just so you realize I'm not the king's wench."

That had him laughing out loud. "Damn. And I was so hoping I could get you to do my bidding."

"You've got about five more minutes of pampering, Your Majesty, and then your bubble is about to burst."

"Have you forgotten my back rub?"

It was clear, from the look on her face, that she had completely forgotten.

To her credit, she bit back the words that sprang to her lips and merely gritted her teeth in silence.

Whit gave a sigh. "My feet feel as soft as a newborn calf's hide."

"And that's no bull."

At her little joke, he huffed out a chuckle before allowing his head to fall back.

Soothed by the feel of her hands on his feet, and completely relaxed from the warmth of the fire and whiskey, he dozed.

Cara felt the change in Whit as he slipped ever so slowly into sleep.

Her hands slowed their movements. She studied his

face. He had the rugged good looks of a man who labored outdoors. Tanned skin. A firm jaw. Straight nose. Perfectly formed mouth.

She allowed her gaze to roam that face, those lips, and her heartbeat suddenly quickened at the thought of that mouth on hers.

That surprise kiss hadn't been at all like most kisses. But then, she thought, Whit MacKenzie wasn't like most guys she knew. Even though he was handsome, he didn't seem aware of his looks. And though he'd caught her in a very vulnerable situation, he hadn't used it against her as some might have.

Not that this cowboy was any kind of saint. But at least when he'd realized that his kiss had been out of line, he'd had the decency to step back and give her some space.

He may not be a saint, but he was fun and easy to be around. And that couldn't be said for every guy she knew.

Speaking of fun...She had a sudden thought. What would Whit MacKenzie's reaction be if he awoke and found his toenails painted candy-apple red?

She crossed to the hooks by the door and dug through her purse until she found the small bottle of polish. She worked quickly, eager to finish before he awoke.

When she was done, she returned the bottle to her purse and took her seat at his feet, just as she felt him beginning to stir.

Chapter Seven

"Okay, Goldilocks." Whit's eyes blinked as he struggled to wake. "I guess I've had enough. Now it's time for that back rub."

Cara let his feet drop to the floor.

He crossed to the bunk and slipped off his plaid shirt before stretching out on the blankets.

Cara squeezed lotion into her hands and began smoothing it over his skin. The minute her hands touched his flesh, she felt the heat rise to her cheeks. She was grateful Whit couldn't see her face. This was infinitely more awkward than she'd expected.

Determined to keep things light between them, she muttered, "I hope Your Majesty approves."

"Mmm." It was all he could manage.

When the silence stretched out, Cara glanced at his face. "Are you asleep again?"

"Hmm?" Whit feigned sleep, though in truth, the feel

of those hands on his bare flesh was sending shock waves coursing through him. He may have been nearly comatose earlier, but now he was suddenly, shockingly awake and alert.

"There's something wrong with this picture," she said accusingly. "Here I am, slaving over a back rub while you're the picture of contentment."

"I wouldn't exactly call it contentment, Goldilocks. It's more like electricity. And if you're not careful with those hands, I may blow not just a fuse, but a transformer."

"That might be fun to watch." She poured lotion into her palm and began rubbing it over his shoulders.

He sighed and clenched his hands, causing the muscles of his upper arms to tense and bunch.

Fascinated, Cara rubbed the lotion down his arms, then up and over his back, before moving her hands along his sides.

"Careful, Goldilocks."

The sensual thrill racing along his spine had him reaching out without a thought to the consequences.

In one quick movement, he rolled over, keeping both of her hands in his. Before she could react, he dragged her down until her body was pressed firmly to his.

Her mouth was open in surprise, until it met his.

"Whit..." She whispered the word inside his mouth, inflaming him even more.

His hands moved over her back, drawing her fully against him, making her achingly aware of his arousal.

Even though she tried to push away, his hands lifted to frame her face while he kissed her with a thoroughness that had them both gasping for air.

Her hair fanned forward, tickling his naked flesh, adding

to his heightened awareness. "God, you taste good, Goldilocks. Mind if I taste a little more?"

"No, Whit. Don't..."

At the alarm in her voice, he went suddenly still.

His gaze sharpened as he caught the fear in those green eyes before she blinked and looked away.

"Sorry." In one swift movement, he rolled her aside and got to his feet. "Blame it on the fact that I wasn't in control of my senses."

That's when he caught sight of the red on his toenails. "What the hell...?"

Cara couldn't help herself. Despite the combination of fear and sexual tingle still racing through her veins, she burst into gales of laughter while backing away from him.

"I think every cowboy should have candy-apple-red toenails at least once in his life."

She waited for his furious reaction.

With a howl he was across the room, grabbing her in a bear hug while convulsing with laughter.

For long minutes they stood together, shaking with laughter at the absurdity of what she'd done.

He pressed his forehead to hers. "I should have known you wouldn't just let me get away with all that pleasure without making me pay."

"Oh, Cowboy, you so deserved it."

He was still laughing as he dipped his head and kissed her.

"Mmm. You taste so damned good, Goldilocks. I wish..."

He lifted his head and realized that she'd gone as still as a statue.

His expression altered suddenly. "What the hell is

wrong with me? When am I going to get it through my thick head...?"

He released her and stepped back. Within moments he was across the room, slipping into his shirt and stepping into his boots before drawing on his parka.

Without even taking the time to say a word, he opened the door of the cabin, sending a chill through the room. The door slammed behind him.

And all she could hear was the crunch of his footsteps on the frozen snow as he stormed into the night, muttering every rich, ripe oath he could think of.

Dazed, Cara climbed to the upper bunk and lay there shivering under the blankets.

What was happening to her? Hadn't she just taken a terrible emotional battering at the hands of an arrogant jerk? Hadn't she come here hoping to hide and lick her wounds?

On top of that, wasn't there a stranger out there who'd looked angry enough to want her dead?

How, then, did she willingly fall into another stranger's arms and play sexy games with him, feeling as if she were somehow safe with him?

Though she'd fully intended to guard herself and her emotions with Whit MacKenzie, there was something about him that made her forget all her good intentions.

Somewhere between the easy humor and the warmth of his lips, she was feeling lost and confused.

Take that kiss. It was just a kiss. But almost from the moment his mouth covered hers, she'd become caught up in the pleasure of that hungry mouth moving over hers. A mouth that knew exactly how to give pleasure. And those hands. Those strong, work-roughened hands that held her as gently as if she were made of fragile glass. And that body pressed to hers. A perfect male body that made her think of things better left forgotten.

She'd felt herself falling into him. And wanting what he offered.

Dangerous thoughts, she knew. But she couldn't seem to control them whenever she got too close to him.

Maybe it was his zany sense of humor. How many men would have laughed it off when they found their nails painted red? It had felt so delicious to finally be able to laugh about something, after all the misery she'd endured.

She lay awake for what seemed an hour or more before the door to the cabin was opened.

She pretended to be asleep while he prowled the cabin, drinking the last of the coffee splashed with scotch and then brooding in front of the fire.

Sometime later she heard Whit pry off his boots and climb into the lower bunk.

At last, hearing his soft, easy breathing, she fell into an exhausted sleep.

Whit lay in his bunk, his mood darker than the night. He'd come close to something he wasn't proud of. Here was a young woman fresh off an incident so traumatic she was willing to hide in a shack in the middle of wilderness, and he'd practically ravished her.

The last thing Cara needed right now was some guy coming on to her while she was feeling trapped and all alone, far from civilization.

He'd planned on staying another couple of days, but

since the snow had melted enough to open up some trails, the wisest thing they could do was get out of here and back to a place where an abundance of noisy, busy people would make it impossible to think about what he was thinking about right now.

The woman in the bunk overhead. All the things he'd rather be doing with her than lying here thinking.

Just knowing she was there had him sweating.

He punched his pillow and turned on his side. Even a woman as tempting as Cara Walton was no match for the distractions of the MacKenzie ranch and its cast of characters. If there was ever a place where she'd be safe, from him, from the world, it was there. And maybe, if he was able to persuade her to stay awhile, she could regain her faith in herself and her dream.

It was the least he could do to make things up to her.

Cara awoke to the sound of the cabin door closing. A minute later she heard the distinct bite of an ax splitting a log.

She sat up and looked around in alarm. It wasn't even dawn yet. She felt as though she'd just fallen asleep. Why in the world was Whit working at this impossible hour of the day?

With a sigh, she scrambled from her bunk and into the freezing bathroom. Within minutes she'd endured another frigid shower and was dressed.

By the time Whit strolled in with an armload of logs, she had canned ham sizzling over the fire, along with an egg concoction that smelled heavenly.

"Good morning." She moved aside so Whit could deposit the logs on the hearth.

"Morning." He stepped away and hung his parka on a hook by the door, avoiding her eyes.

She took note of the distance he kept between them. It could mean only one thing. He regretted that hot little scene last night. She should, too, but in truth, she couldn't get it out of her mind. The way she'd felt when he'd kissed her. The way she fit in his arms, all snug and safe. The fire that had built inside her with every touch, every kiss.

"You're up early." She carried the skillet to the wooden table.

"Long day ahead of us."

"Us?" She looked up as he washed his hands and started toward the table.

"Yeah. The temperature climbed overnight, the sun's just coming up, and there's enough snowmelt that the trails are no longer deadly. I figure it's time we headed down to my place."

"You're inviting me to your ranch?"

"Unless you'd rather stay up here all by yourself."

She ducked her head to hide her relief. "If you're inviting me, I'm accepting. Just until I figure out where I'll go next."

He helped himself to ham and eggs and toast. "You're welcome to stay as long as you want."

"I would think your family will have something to say about that. I'll bet another body in that already overcrowded mob might be as welcome as a skunk at a picnic."

He fixed her with a look. "Once you meet my family, you'll understand. They like crowds. The more the merrier. After just a day or two, you'll feel like one of us."

Feel like one of us.

Impossible, of course, but the way he said it had her feeling suddenly hungry.

She heaped her plate and dug in. "What time are we leaving?"

"As soon as we pack up."

She managed a smile. "That will take me all of a minute. In case you've forgotten, I came here with just the clothes on my back."

He bit back a grin. "Remember all the garbage and litter that's been produced? We leave nothing behind for the critters."

"Of course." She sat back and sipped her coffee. "How could I forget?" She glanced at the overflowing garbage bag. "How does all that fit in your saddlebags?"

"Easy. There's a pit behind the lean-to. I'll burn all I can and carry home what can't be burned."

"Now you tell me. I was feeling guilty for creating so much litter."

He winked. "That was the idea, Goldilocks."

Her heart gave a little flutter at that wink. What was it about this cowboy that he could make her so happy with something so simple?

Whit made a final check of the cabin before climbing into the saddle. He leaned down and eased Cara up behind him.

She marveled at the strength in his grip.

"Warm enough?"

Her voice was muffled against his shoulder. "Yeah. Thanks for the use of the parka."

"I'm glad you found one that fit you."

"Well, it's big enough to fit around two of me," she said with a laugh. "But at least it's warm."

"You'll need it. At least until we reach a lower level." He glanced skyward. "But there's no snow in those clouds."

Old Red moved easily through the melting snow.

Cara wrapped her arms around Whit's waist, feeling again that odd little tingle at the mere touch of him. She was grateful for the width of his shoulders shielding her from the wind.

As they moved leisurely down the snow-covered hills, Cara took the time to study the glorious landscape.

"Oh, Whit. This scenery is so pretty. Do you ever take the time to appreciate what you have?"

"Yeah. It's great, isn't it? I know this part of the country is off the beaten track, and it took the genius of Mad and Pop to see all that it could become, but I never take it for granted. This is the only place I'd ever want to be."

"I don't blame you. If I had all this land, I'd never want to leave."

Her words, muffled against his shoulder, had him studying the land with sharper interest. "I do love it. But sometimes I forget to appreciate just how much it cost my father and grandfather to carve out this ranch in the middle of wilderness."

Halfway down the hills, they moved past the snow line. The trail ahead of them was bright with spring grass.

Whit brought their mount to a halt. He slid from the saddle before helping Cara down.

"Why are we stopping?"

"I don't know about you, but I'm too warm." He removed his parka and stuffed it into the already filled saddlebag. Cara removed hers and tied the sleeves around her waist.

From the opposite saddlebag, Whit removed a bottle of water and uncapped it before handing it to Cara. She drank, then offered it to him. He drained the bottle and returned the empty to his bag.

Cara grinned. "The no-litter rule."

"You bet." He pulled himself into the saddle and helped her up behind him.

Their horse started off along the grassy route with a spring in his step. With the snow behind them, Old Red seemed eager to reach the familiar food and shelter he knew would be at the end of their trail.

Now that the weather had gentled and the sun was high overhead, Cara found herself achingly aware of the muscled thighs pressed to hers and the lean, chiseled body encircled by her arms.

"You're awfully quiet back there."

"Just enjoying the scenery." A grin split her lips the moment the words were out of her mouth.

Scenery indeed. Whit MacKenzie could easily pose as a personal trainer for one of those famous workout places scattered across the country.

She thought of Jared, the arrogant man who had tried to impress her with his wealth and his family's success. He spent a fortune to have a toned body—showcasing his strength and masculinity even though he didn't possess either.

She swallowed back her feelings of resentment at Jared's cruel treatment. She needed to put the past behind her and move forward.

The only problem was, she had no idea where forward might be. Where did she go from here?

There wasn't much time to ponder before she spotted signs of civilization far below. Barns, outbuildings, corrals and fences, and then the house, half hidden behind the shadow of huge barns. As the house came more sharply into view, she saw the long, graceful sweep of three stories of stone and weathered wood that looked as ageless as the hills surrounding it.

They approached from the back, along an asphalt landing strip that led to a huge barn. Through the open door she spotted a plane. Before she could ask about it, their horse picked up his pace, heading directly toward a second, smaller barn.

Inside, Whit reined in his mount and helped Cara down before unsaddling Red and tossing the saddle over a stall door. Unfettered, the gelding hurried over to a food trough and began munching.

A tall man in faded jeans and plaid shirt with the sleeves rolled to his elbows stepped out of an adjoining stall and shoved back his hat, revealing white hair and a tanned, handsome face. Seeing Whit, he hurried forward to welcome him in a bear hug.

"How's the herd, Whit?"

"I left them in Stone Canyon. Dumped a ton of hay from the flatbed and left it there, too. Old Red and I hunkered down during the blizzard at one of the range shacks."

The man's lips split into a wide smile when he spotted Cara standing to one side. "I see you brought back a souvenir."

"Brady, this is Cara Walton. Cara, our ranch foreman, Brady Storm."

If the foreman had questions, he was too polite to ask them. Cara's palm was engulfed in a large calloused hand. "Hello, Cara."

"Brady. It's nice to meet you."

"Cara will be staying with us for a while."

"Well, then." Brady tipped his hat. "I'll see you inside at supper." He carried a pitchfork across the width of the barn and carefully hung it on a hook before selecting a shovel and stepping outside.

"Come on." Whit slung his saddlebags over his shoulder and turned toward the house. "Time for you to meet the family."

CHAPTER EIGHT

Hey, Mad." Whit paused in the doorway of the mudroom, where he'd hung his saddlebags and wide-brimmed hat before prying off his boots and washing his hands at the sink. "I see your scooter finally came."

At the sound of Whit's voice, the old man turned a sleek red electric scooter from the stove to face his grandson. "That it did, laddie. Isn't it dandy? And just look at how easy it is to operate." He turned the scooter this way and that at the touch of a button. "Where has this thing been all my life?" He rolled closer. "You've been gone long enough, laddie. Got socked in by that blizzard up in the hills, did you?"

"Yeah. Dumped a ton of snow up there. But it's melting as fast as it fell." Whit turned, revealing Cara behind him. "Mad, this is Cara Walton. Cara, my grandfather, Maddock MacKenzie. Everyone calls him Mad."

"Well. Hello, lass."

"Hello, Mad." She continued to hang back until the old man extended his hand, forcing her to step around Whit and accept his handshake.

Whit indicated the small, plump woman just entering the kitchen. "And this is Myrna Hill. Myrna, this is Cara Walton."

"Lovely to meet you, Cara." Myrna placed a stack of neatly folded dish towels in a drawer before offering a hand.

"So, lass." Mad chuckled. "Did you fall from the sky with the snow?"

Cara laughed in delight. "I like that better than the truth. Mind if I use that explanation?"

"Not at all." The old man waited a heartbeat before asking, "So where did you meet my handsome grandson?"

"Handsome?" Whit puffed up his chest with a sly grin. "That's a new one, coming from you."

Myrna huffed out a breath. "Ira Pettigrew told him just yesterday that you remind him of Mad, and the old fool has decided that the two of you are the best-looking ones in the family."

"And isn't that the truth, lad?" Mad threw back his head and roared.

Instead of joining his laughter, Whit's look sharpened. "What was Ira doing here? Does he have some news about Pop's murder?"

"Sorry, lad. No. He was just clearing up some facts with your mother."

Just then, Willow walked into the room and hurried over to hug her youngest son. "Did you get enough time to yourself during the blizzard?"

"Not much." With his arm around his mother's shoulders, Whit turned to Cara. "Mom, I'd like you to meet Cara Walton. Cara, my mother, Willow."

"Mrs. MacKenzie."

"Please, call me Willow. How very nice to meet you, Cara."

"I invited Cara to spend some time here. I hope that's all right."

Willow squeezed his arm. "You know you never have to ask. Your friends are always welcome here." She glanced at the clock on the wall. "If you'd like to show Cara to a guest room upstairs, you'd better do it before everyone gets here." She turned to Cara to explain. "Once the whole family gets here for supper, it tends to become sheer bedlam. So I'd advise you to unpack and settle in before supper."

Cara glanced at Whit, hoping he could explain her lack of luggage.

"Cara's traveling light, Mom. There's nothing to unpack."

Willow paused only a beat before turning to the young woman with a bright smile. "No problem. Until you can get into town and pick up a few things, you can certainly find whatever you need here. The guest room is fully stocked with toothpaste, shampoo, and even a computer, if you need to contact anyone."

"Thank you, Mrs.... Willow. That's very generous of you."

"Cara, while you're here, please make yourself at home."

The back door opened and tall, handsome Ash MacKenzie and his wife, Brenna, hurried inside. While Ash held the door, Brenna tugged on a leash and their pup Sammy burst inside and hurried over to lick Mad's hand.

"See who he runs to first?" Obviously delighted, the old man bent down to scratch behind the pup's ears.

"That's because you always slip him food under the table. Sammy knows exactly what he's doing."

"And who butters his bread. Or in this case, who cuts him chunks of prime rib."

Whit kissed his sister-in-law's cheek before handling the introductions. "Cara Walton, this is my brother, Ash, and his wife, Brenna, and their baby, Sammy."

"Hello. It's nice to meet you." She shook hands before bending down to rub Sammy's head.

He rewarded her with a long, wet kiss.

As she straightened, the door opened yet again and another handsome cowboy stepped inside carrying a little boy, while his wife and her older son followed.

"Hey, Griff. Juliet." Whit stepped forward and hugged Ethan before taking the younger one from his brother's hands. "And Casey. I've only been gone a couple of days, and you got bigger."

"I'm a big boy now, Uncle Whit," little Casey said.

"You're two, right?"

"Uncle Whit." The boy's eyes went wide. "You know I'm free." He held up three fingers, causing Whit to chuckle at their little joke before setting Casey on his feet.

"Cara Walton, meet my other brother, Griff; his wife, Juliet; and their sons, Casey and Ethan."

After greeting the adults, Cara dropped to her knees in front of the two little boys. "Hello, Casey and Ethan. I know how old you are," she said to Casey. "How old are you, Ethan?"

"Efan's six." Casey held up six fingers. Then, before he could say more, he caught sight of Sammy across the room and let out a shriek as he raced toward the puppy.

Whit caught Cara's hand. "My mom warned you. It's about to turn into bedlam here. Come on. I'll show you your room." He turned to his grandfather. "How much time do we have until supper?"

"An hour, more or less."

"Good." Whit grinned. "I might spend the entire hour under a hot shower."

"This is your room." Whit opened the door and stood aside to allow Cara to precede him.

She stared around with a look of wonder. "This is the guest room?"

"One of them. We actually have four more. And we need them when the whole family decides to spend the night."

"Do they do that often?"

"Probably not as much as they'd like. With ranch chores, it's hard to stay away from their own places very often. But if the weather takes a turn, it's nice to know they can all bunk here comfortably."

"This is way more than comfortable." She looked around at the big bed covered in a down comforter, with a soft heather throw at the foot. Across the room was a floor-to-ceiling window allowing a magnificent view of the hills, dotted with cattle. In front of the window was a desk and chair and, atop the desk, a laptop computer.

A huge flat-screen TV stood on a long, sleek cabinet, and to one side was a lovely upholstered chair.

Whit crossed the room and opened a door to reveal

a bathroom fit for royalty. Dove-gray tile floor led to a white marble countertop, a glass-enclosed shower big enough for half a dozen, and a tub that looked so inviting, Cara nearly wept.

She turned to Whit, who was watching her reaction. "Oh, Whit, this is so much more than I could have dreamed. I can't wait to fill that tub with precious, wonderful, warm water. I thought I'd never be warm again."

"I know what you mean. But remember what Mad said. We have an hour. Then we'll have to return to the chaos downstairs."

As he stepped from the room, she was laughing. "After a long bath, I'll be ready for anything."

Cara leaned her head back against the towel she'd folded behind her neck. After the time spent in the hills, this place was paradise. The bathroom was steamy from the tub filled to the top with hot water.

Willow had made good on her promise. Everything Cara could want or need had been stored in the elegant glass-fronted cabinets. From shampoo to toothpaste to bubble bath to lotions, she had her choice of the best.

She lifted an arm from the water and started to laugh. "I've turned into a prune."

With a sigh, she stepped out of the tub and wrapped herself in a fluffy towel. After drying off, she made her way to the bedroom, expecting to put on the filthy clothes she'd worn on the trail.

To her surprise, her clothes had been washed and carefully folded atop the dresser.

"Myrna?" she wondered aloud.

Of course. That sweet old woman had heard her say

she had no luggage and had generously taken it upon herself to make certain she wouldn't be embarrassed by wearing soiled clothes.

She slipped into her underthings that were now whisper-soft and then into the plaid shirt and faded denims she'd been living in for so long. They not only felt clean, but they also smelled sunshine fresh.

After towel-drying her hair, she ran a brush through the springy curls that were already spilling around her face and shoulders. A glance at her watch told her there was no time to fuss.

At a knock on her door, she hurried over to find Whit, freshly shaved, his hair still glistening with droplets. He was wearing fresh denims and a plaid shirt and a smile that deepened when he took a long, slow look at her.

"You clean up nice, Goldilocks."

"You're not bad yourself. You've gone from hairy, smelly Papa Bear to a handsome cowboy."

"Handsome? Why, little lady, it seems you and my grandpa think alike."

At his terrible imitation of an old-time cowboy, she chuckled. "Don't let it go to your head, MacKenzie. I'm sure by tomorrow you'll be back to looking more like Papa Bear."

He caught her hand. "Come on. Time to face *la familia*."

As they descended the stairs, they could hear voices raised in laughter. Above the din came the shrieks of two little boys chasing after an energetic puppy, while Juliet could be heard cautioning the boys to slow down before someone got hurt.

"Every mother's famous words," Whit said in her ear.

"It means her patience is wearing thin, and if they don't slow down soon, she'll be the one putting the hurt on them."

When they stepped into the kitchen, both Whit and Cara were laughing so hard, they failed to notice the way the entire family was studying them.

From his vantage point across the room, Mad winked at Brady Storm, who was sharing a beer with Ash and Griff.

Brady merely grinned and took another swig of beer.

Both men noted the way Whit was holding Cara's hand. Realizing they were the object of interest, Whit released her hand and asked, "I see beer, lemonade, and milk on Myrna's tray. What's your pleasure?"

"Lemonade." As Whit made his way to the counter, Cara headed toward Myrna. "Thank you," she said quietly.

Myrna straightened and placed a tray on a hot pad. "Oh, don't you look fresh."

"And all thanks to you." Cara ran a hand over the crisp sleeve of her shirt. "That was so kind of you, Myrna."

"I'm happy to do it. When I was a girl, I traveled to some of those range shacks, hauling meals to the wranglers. They were pretty primitive. I doubt they're much better now."

"They're shelter from a storm, and for that I'm grateful."

"And now you have even more shelter. I hope you'll enjoy your stay."

Whit crossed to them and handed a frosty glass of lemonade to Cara. "What secrets are you two sharing?"

"If we told you, they wouldn't be secrets." Cara smiled at Myrna before following Whit across the room to join the others, who were arguing everything from the wild weather to the latest news in town.

Cara stood back listening and found herself thinking that all these strangers and all these raised voices were just about the sweetest sounds she'd ever heard.

"Okay." Mad turned his scooter from the stove. "Supper's ready. Let's get to it while it's hot."

Still discussing ranch and weather news, the family moved easily to the big farm table, where Mad and Myrna were busy setting out steaming platters.

Whit led Cara to the far side of the table and held her chair before sitting beside her.

With Willow and Brady at one end and Mad and Myrna at the other, the rest of the family filled in on either side, with Ash and Brenna alongside Whit and Cara and Griff and Juliet on the other side, with Ethan and Casey between them.

Before anyone could say a word, little Casey reached out a hand to his mother and brother and watched as the others around the table followed his lead and reached out to those on either side.

The little boy turned to Cara. "Now that me and Efan—"

"Ethan and I," his mother corrected softly.

"Oh, yeah. Now that Efan and I have a daddy and all this big family, we're learning to say a blessing." He lifted pleading eyes to Cara. "Do you know any blessings?"

"I might know one or two. I lived with my gram, and she insisted that we always say a blessing before eating."

The little boy looked relieved as he turned to his mother. "Can Cara say the blessing tonight?"

"I think that would be fine." Juliet nodded toward Cara.

Her cheeks bright pink as she felt the others watching and listening, she clasped Whit's hand and said the words she'd always said at home. "Bless this food, and all of us here to enjoy it."

Oh, Gram, she thought. *I can hear your voice, saying these very words*. A feeling of warmth flooded through her. As though Gram had just wrapped her arms around her and pressed a soft kiss to her cheek. And why not? Hadn't Cara believed that her grandmother would always be around to watch over her? Somehow, in the past year, she'd lost her faith. But now, here in this room, with these good people, she experienced a flood of happy memories.

As an afterthought, she added, "And bless those who are no longer with us, but who live forever in our hearts."

When she looked up, Willow was blinking rapidly. Cara had forgotten for a moment about this family's terrible loss, still so fresh in their hearts and minds.

She felt a quick sizzle of alarm until Mad called, "Well done, lass. I couldn't have done better myself. Now pass the potatoes."

CHAPTER NINE

Whit." Ash helped himself to a sizzling steak from the platter before passing it on. "You haven't heard the latest gossip about Luther."

In an aside, Whit explained to Cara, "Luther Culkin is the scourge of Copper Creek. If there's trouble, you can be sure Luther's part of it."

"And probably the ringleader," Ash added. "Anyway, Luther got liquored up and decided it would be fun to help himself to some of Rita's carrot cake. At three in the morning. So when he gets to her shop and finds the doors locked and the lights out, he just figures why not smash a window and let himself in? After all, in Luther's world, rules are meant to be broken. When the alarm went off, Chief Ira Pettigrew got the call to investigate. He was mad as a hornet when he found Luther drunk and sitting on the floor of Rita's shop, protesting his innocence. Luther claimed somebody else broke in and he was just staying there to protect Rita's baked goods until somebody could come and lock it up."

Cara asked innocently, "If there weren't any witnesses, how did the police chief know he was lying?"

"I guess the first clue," Ash said with a wink to the others, "was Luther's hands were covered with carrot cake and gooey frosting."

"That would do it for me," Willow said with a laugh.

"But there's more." Ash was enjoying his story now and laughing between every word. "Ira noticed a bag on the floor beside Luther, who was still too drunk to stand. Inside the bag was another carrot cake. I guess Luther figured he'd save himself the trouble of coming back during regular business hours and buying something for his sweet tooth tomorrow."

"So how long will Luther be in jail this time?" Whit asked.

"He got out the next day."

When Whit shot him a look of surprise, Ash rolled his eyes. "Rita refused to press charges. Talk in the town is that she has a history of being attracted to troublemakers. Her last husband lost their ranch to a gambling addiction and had to declare bankruptcy. That's why she opened the shop, hoping her skill as a baker could keep her head above water. I just hope she doesn't lose her head, and her profits, to Luther."

Mad shook his head. "They say there's someone for everyone."

Ash merely grinned. "There were some in town who thought that about us." He leaned close to brush a kiss on Brenna's cheek. "I was the town bad boy for leaving, and Brenna was a fool for taking me back."

At Cara's arched brow, Brenna leaned over to pat her hand. "Remind me to tell you about it sometime."

Mad helped himself to a second portion of steak and garlic potatoes, liberally covered with mushroom gravy. "I don't think I told all of you about old Abe Parson over in Red Rock."

At the mention of the town, Cara's head came up sharply.

"Isn't he the rancher who sold you that bull that broke through a fence and ran clear to the highway?" Ash paused to look over at his grandfather.

"That's him. When the bull ran away again, poor Abe had to buy him back just to save face. Turns out that bull was determined to live out its life on Abe's ranch. Though Abe and I weren't close, we kept in touch."

"What about him?" Willow looked across the length of the table toward her father-in-law.

"Got himself killed. A single bullet in the back."

At that, there was a collective gasp around the table. Everyone, without saying a word, was thrust into the moment when they'd first heard about Bear.

Brady asked the question that was on everyone's mind. "Do the state police think there's any connection between Abe's murder and Bear's?"

Mad glanced at his daughter-in-law, seeing her look of shock and pain. "Ira was on it as soon as he got the news, hoping it might be the answer we've been waiting for. He spoke directly with the police chief in Red Rock, who said he'd interviewed Abe's nephew. Apparently the nephew had assumed he'd inherit the ranch. He was furious when he learned that he'd been disinherited."

Willow sighed, the only signal that she'd had another hope dashed.

Ash gave a slow shake of his head. "This nephew must have been a real thorn in Abe's side to get that kind of treatment. I wonder if he'd been mistreating or neglecting the old man. Has he been arrested?"

"Not yet. The police are calling him a 'person of interest,' but there were no other relatives, and Abe had no known enemies, so I'd say it's pretty open and shut. It wouldn't be the first time a family feud heated up and the relative flew into a rage and shot one of his own."

Willow mused aloud, "I wonder how the nephew learned that he'd been disinherited?"

Mad shook his head. "I don't know. Maybe Abe wanted him to know, in order to make the punishment even harsher."

"That could be." She set aside her fork. "Who will inherit Abe's ranch now?"

Mad shrugged. "Ira wasn't sure, but he said Abe had recently written his lawyer into his will."

"I'm glad it won't have to go to auction." Willow glanced around the table at her family. "There have been too many ranches falling into bankruptcy lately."

"You can say that again." Out of habit, Mad slammed his hand down on the arm of the scooter, as he'd always done on his wheelchair, and the scooter lurched backward with a jolt, before Mad managed to bring it under control.

That tiny incident broke the tension and had everyone laughing.

Looking sheepish, Mad shot a look around the table. "Guess I need some practice on this thing."

Juliet was quick to soothe. "You're doing amazingly well, Mad. You and your wheelchair were together a long time. But now this scooter is allowing you precious freedom."

"That it is, lassie. That it is." His smile was back as he turned to the others. "Since Juliet has been working with me, she thinks I'm ready to ride old Scout again. And she even thinks I'll be able to fly, as soon as I have a bit more therapy."

"Oh, Mad." Willow rounded the table to give him a hug. "That's wonderful news." She turned to Juliet. "Now that you're a certified therapist, you've been an angel of mercy to spend so much time helping Mad."

"And to celebrate..." Myrna was out of her chair and passing around thick slices of chocolate torte layered with a rich cream filling and milk-chocolate frosting.

The older woman paused beside Cara's chair. "A big slice or a smaller one?"

Cara forced herself out of her thoughts and managed a smile. "Nothing, thanks. I think I've eaten more tonight than I have in days."

"You don't cook, lassie?" Mad paused with his fork halfway to his mouth.

"She's a great cook, Mad." Whit was quick to defend her. "You know the kind of boxed and canned stuff we stock in the range shacks? She could open a box of this, a can of that, and turn it into a feast fit for a king."

"You don't say?" Mad winked at Brady, who turned to study Whit and Cara more carefully. "Sounds like your stay up in the highlands wasn't all hard work and dreary nights, lad."

Whit flushed and happened to catch Brady's look, which changed from surprise to sudden insight.

Brady wasn't the only one who was aware of something deeper here.

Willow, watching her son's body language, surprised

the others by saying, "Cara, if you don't need to be anywhere soon, I hope you'll agree to stay on here awhile."

"Oh, thank you. I'd...love to. But only if I can earn my keep in some way." She glanced at the two little boys seated between Griff and Juliet. "I'm really great with children. Maybe I could be a nanny?"

Juliet exchanged a loving look with Griff before turning to Cara with a smile. "It's wonderful to know I can count on you in an emergency, Cara. But the truth is, Griff and I love being with the boys all the time. When they're not out in the fields with Griff, they're in the barn with me while I do my therapy classes."

Cara looked over with interest. "What kind of therapy?"

"I call it horse therapy. It began with a group of veterans learning to use disabled muscles by riding gentle horses. Now it's grown into something much more. Griff and I call our place Hope Ranch, and we've opened it to anyone with a desire to improve their lives by riding, roping, and even learning to drive handicap-ready equipment."

"Which is why I'm now ready to ride my old horse again," Mad added. "I've been working with Juliet for over a month, and my life has improved so much, I feel like a young man again."

"That's wonderful." Cara turned to Juliet. "You must be so proud of your work."

Griff reached over to squeeze his wife's hand.

Juliet beamed. "I'm proud of all of us. We've come so far."

Myrna, who'd been enjoying her torte in silence, suddenly asked Cara, "How would you feel about helping me here, especially in the kitchen?"

Everyone turned to look at her.

Mad raised a brow. "Are you thinking of kicking me out of my own kitchen?"

Myrna smiled. "I'm thinking, since you're going to be riding Scout and taking the plane up soon, you won't have time to be a full-time cook anymore. And with all my household chores, I'd welcome some help, especially in the kitchen." She added slyly, "Especially since Whit boasted that she's some kind of magician with food."

Mad clapped his hands. "Say yes, lassie. I'm more than ready to turn over my apron. And heaven knows Myrna will be lost without someone to take my place."

"Praise heaven for small favors," Myrna deadpanned before turning to Cara. "Though I hate to ever admit when Maddock MacKenzie is right, this time I'll give him his due. I'll be lost without some help, Cara. It would mean a lot to me."

Everyone turned to Cara, whose smile was answer enough.

"Thank you for that vote of confidence. I hope I won't disappoint all of you."

Willow stood and hurried around the table to embrace the young woman. "Cara, don't you worry about disappointing us. Having you here will make such a difference." She then turned to her father-in-law and bent down to kiss his cheek. "I'm just delighted that you're reclaiming your life."

"Aye, lassie." His voice was rough, and he was forced to swallow before saying, "I never thought I'd see this day. But thanks to Juliet's bullying, I'm learning that anything is possible, as long as we have the will to work for it."

Myrna walked up beside Cara and placed a generous slice of torte in front of her.

Cara blinked. "I thought—"

Myrna interrupted. "Now it's a true celebration. I hope your appetite has perked up some. Welcome to the family."

With a laugh of delight, Cara dug into her dessert.

Cara and Whit climbed the stairs together. When she stopped at the door of her suite of rooms, he surprised her by asking, "Mind if I step in?"

Seeing the wary look that stole over her, he held up a hand. "Just for a minute."

"Okay." She opened the door and he stepped inside behind her before closing it and leaning against it.

"Is it just a coincidence that your wild story, which you claimed you'd dreamed up overnight, was set in Red Rock?"

She looked away.

He touched her hand, then, feeling the familiar sexual tingle, just as quickly withdrew it. "I'm not trying to scare you or intimidate you, Cara. And I'm certainly not accusing you of lying. It's just..." He took a breath. "It's just that your story was so improbable, I immediately dismissed it as your clever way of holding off any more questions." He paused, watching her reaction. "Then, when I learned about your treatment at the hands of Jared Billingham, I thought I understood why you were running scared."

He saw the shudder that passed through her at the mention of her wealthy tormentor and hated himself for having to bring it up again. As gently as possible, he said,

"Just tell me. Was your story about the encounter in Red Rock fact or fiction?"

Her voice was little more than a whisper. "Fact."

"All of it?"

She looked at him then. Stared fully into his eyes, and her own were filled with such misery, he could feel his heart aching for her.

"I think so. At the time I was so scared, all I could do was run. Now, when I look back at it, I wonder how much of it was real and how much of it was"—she shrugged—"my crazy imagination."

He hadn't meant to, but seeing her like this brought out his need to soothe. To protect.

He gathered her into his arms and pressed his lips to her temple. Against a tangle of hair he whispered, "I'll talk to Ira. Tell him what you saw, or think you saw. Maybe that will be the end of it. Or maybe he'll want to talk to you."

He felt her pull back. In her wide eyes, the fear was back.

"Don't worry, Cara. I don't want you to worry about a thing."

"But I do. I will. What if he thinks it's the ravings of a silly female? What if—"

Whit lowered his head and kissed her. It began as an attempt to reassure her. A simple touch of mouth to mouth. But the moment they came together, everything changed.

His big hands dragged her closer. So close he could feel every quivering breath she took.

He took the kiss deeper, hungry for more, until it became a desperation that had him digging his fingers into her hair, while his eager, avid mouth roamed her face, kissing her cheek, her ear, the curve of her brow. As he brushed his lips over her eye, he felt the moisture of tears.

He lifted his head. "I'm sorry, Cara. I'm so rough. I didn't mean..."

His tenderness was her undoing, and the tears streamed down her cheeks.

Burying her face in her hands, she turned away from him. "Now look what you've done. I never cry. And I've cried more tears since meeting you than I've cried in my lifetime."

Desperate to soothe, he laid a big hand on her shoulder. "I'm sorry. I'll go now. Please don't cry anymore."

She turned and clutched his sleeve. "I'm not crying because..." She swallowed. "This isn't about..." She blinked rapidly to stem the tide. "I guess it's just everything. Being afraid, and then finding you, and your wonderful family, and..." She dropped her hand to her side. "This is all so new to me. I'm so mixed up. I just need some time to get used to... kind people."

He touched a hand to her cheek.

"Okay. Good night, Cara."

He opened the door and turned back to her with a half-smile. "I'm glad you're staying."

Before she could say a word, the door closed and he was gone.

Alone in her room, Cara was too agitated to settle. She walked to the window and stared at the hills, veiled in darkness. Over their peaks, a full moon glowed bright orange in a midnight sky.

Earlier, listening to Mad's account of the old rancher

who'd been shot, she'd experienced a deep feeling of dread. Could this be the same old man who'd been threatened by Suit-and-Tie? Or was she allowing her writer's wild imagination to steer her in the wrong direction?

Her gram always used to say that Cara was either blessed to escape into an imaginary world of adventure or cursed to see monsters and villains around every corner. And it was so true.

She'd covered all her childhood fears by conjuring an imaginary girl and her horse who could fly around the world, saving those in need. In time, she'd begun to believe she could go anywhere, do anything, and no harm could touch her.

This past year had been a challenge. But meeting Whit, and now his family, gave her hope for a fresh start.

She wrapped her arms around herself and began to pace. Oh, how she hoped the killer of that old man in Red Rock had been the rancher's nephew. Then she would be able to breathe freely again, knowing the man with the evil eyes had been magnified in her mind.

Hearing the silence settle over the household, she began undressing and getting ready for bed.

For so long now she'd been feeling adrift. But now, knowing she could stay here in this isolated place, surrounded by this large, noisy, loving family, she was beginning to believe she could actually relax and enjoy life for a while. Just until she figured out where to go from here.

So much had happened to her. The painful incident with Jared had shattered her confidence.

Witnessing what she thought was a deadly threat to both that old rancher and to her had her running scared.

Having Whit storm into that cabin in the middle of nowhere had been, for her, the final straw. And then, after blowing in like the blizzard raging outside, he'd turned into a fun, funny, interesting companion.

Companion. The very word had her shivering as she climbed between the covers.

Whit MacKenzie was hot, sexy, and the greatest temptation she'd ever had to fight. If it hadn't been for her experience with Jared, she might have welcomed his attentions and acted on them. But she was still sorting out way too many things right now and questioning her own judgment.

She intended to take things one baby step at a time.

Still, it would be so easy to give in to the pleasure he offered.

She fell asleep dreaming about rolling around in this big, soft bed, making mad, passionate love with the sexiest cowboy she'd ever known.

Chapter Ten

The sun was just rising when Brady sat on the backhoe and began working the big claw through layers of mud. Whit stood at the gaping hole in the ground with a shovel over his shoulder.

"Okay, son. That's as far as I can go without doing damage. Give it a try."

At Brady's shout, Whit dropped into the deep hole and began shoveling the last layers of muck before looking up. "It's broken."

"That's what I was afraid of." Brady climbed down and jumped into the hole beside Whit. "We're going to have to set a whole new pipe in here before this entire road collapses."

Whit nodded. "And we'll have to work fast. There's more rain coming."

Brady dug out his cell phone. "Ridley. Brady Storm here. How soon can your guys deliver a ten-inch culvert?"

He listened before saying, "Yeah. It's our main road out to the highway, and with more rain coming, I need this now."

In an aside to Whit, he muttered, "It's not looking good."

He listened some more before saying, "Great. Thanks, Ridley. I owe you."

He dropped his phone back in his pocket. "They'll be here before supper. They're thinking around three or four o'clock. So for now, it looks like we may as well clean up and see about having some breakfast."

"I've been thinking about food for hours."

Brady clapped a muddy hand on Whit's shoulder. "I know what you mean, son. The days start early on a ranch."

As they walked toward the barn, Brady said casually, "Your girl's a cute little thing."

"She's not my girl." Whit paused. "I mean... we just met."

"And spent some time together up in the hills."

"Well, yeah. She was squatting there..."

Brady stopped and turned to face him. "She was living there? In the range shack?"

Whit nodded. "Yeah. Actually she was hiding out."

"Is she in some kind of trouble?"

"She got herself into a jam with a smooth-talking guy."

"Where's she from?"

"Minerva."

Brady squinted his eyes. "I know of it. Smaller even than Copper Creek. Spit and you're through it."

Whit started grinning. "Yeah. That's how Cara described it. Anyway, she was holed up in our shack and I guess I gave her quite a scare when I showed up out of the blue."

"Yeah. That face of yours would be enough to scare any girl senseless."

Whit punched Brady's arm. "I managed to turn on the charm."

"I just bet you did. And now what? How long is she staying?"

"I don't think she has any place to go."

"She's homeless?"

"As far as I can tell. She grew up with a grandmother, who's now dead."

"Parents?"

Whit shook his head. "Her ma's dead. Doesn't know her father."

Brady took his time digesting that. "But she's still standing."

"Yeah. And damned independent. She left this in the cupboard up at the range shack." He handed over the envelope.

Brady read the note, then counted the money inside. "Fifty-seven dollars and twenty-five cents? Isn't that an odd amount of money?"

"She'd put fifty in first. I think that was all she had left, and she intended to leave it there when she left. Then she beat me at Scrabble for seven dollars and twenty-five cents and must have added it when I wasn't looking."

Brady smiled at Whit. "I'm liking that young woman more all the time."

"Yeah." Whit returned the foreman's smile as he tucked away the envelope. "A lot of strikes against her, but, like you said, she's still standing. And determined to earn her way. I guess that's what I like about her, too."

"You?" Brady shot him a knowing look. "That may be one of the things you like about her now, but I'm guessing long before you learned about her background, you happened to notice a whole lot more. Like those dimples when she smiles, and those big green eyes, and—"

"Okay." Whit lifted both hands. "Just so you know, she may be easy to look at, but she's also a really good person."

"You don't have to convince me, son."

The two men were both grinning as they stowed their gear in the barn and headed toward the ranch house.

Myrna stepped into the kitchen and filled a drawer with clean towels. "As soon as I finish parceling out this first load of laundry, I can give you a hand, Cara."

Cara looked up from the stove. "Don't worry about it. I've got everything handled."

The older woman paused to give her a long look. "I heard you up before dawn."

Cara laughed. "Actually, I was up most of the night, thinking about what to fix for my first meal."

Myrna walked closer and put a hand on her arm. "I know you're feeling a bit anxious, but it's all going to be fine. Everyone is so pleased that you're staying on here."

"That's sweet of all of you. But after that buildup by Whit, I have a lot to prove."

"This isn't a test. You shouldn't worry about passing or failing."

Cara gave her a gentle smile. "Thanks. I needed that."

The older woman gave her a long, stern look. "Who did that to you?"

Cara took a step back. "I don't know what you mean."

"I mean that lack of confidence." Myrna caught her hand. "Somebody made you feel like you aren't good enough."

Cara held her silence.

Myrna blew out a breath. "Okay. Whatever happened, you can overcome it. Listen to me, child. Whenever you start to doubt yourself, just remember this. Your best, done with good intentions, is always good enough."

Cara ducked her head. "Thank you."

When she looked up, she saw that Myrna was already heading out of the room with another armload of freshly folded clothes.

When Whit and Brady stepped into the mudroom and started peeling off layers of mud-soaked boots and parkas, her heart did a somersault.

She busied herself at the stove to keep from staring at Whit as he washed at the big mudroom sink.

Just seeing him made her day brighter.

"Hey." Whit stepped into the kitchen, followed by Brady.

"Good morning. There's coffee and juice if you'd like."

"Coffee." Whit crossed to the sideboard. "About a gallon of it."

"I'll second that," Brady said with a laugh.

Cara poured two steaming mugs and handed one to each of them.

The two men wrapped their hands around the mugs, breathing in the warmth of the kitchen.

"Mmm. This is good." Whit took a long drink. "It might say spring on the calendar, but somebody forgot to mention it to Mother Nature. It's freezing out there."

"I'll say." Brady sauntered toward the door. "I'm taking this with me. I'll have it gone before I hit the shower."

"Me too." Whit shivered. "If I don't get out of these wet things soon, I'll turn into an ice cube."

The two men left the kitchen and climbed the stairs.

When she was alone, Cara let out a long, slow breath. She was going to have to work overtime to keep from glowing every time she caught sight of Whit. There was something about that tall, muscled cowboy that just flat-out made her always want to grin like a fool.

When she saw Myrna walk in and stare at her, she turned away and pretended to be busy with something on the stove. But in truth, she was thinking about Whit upstairs, peeling off his wet clothes and stepping naked into the shower.

"You must be working too close to that stove," Myrna remarked. "Your cheeks are bright red."

Cara lifted her hands to her cheeks. What was happening to her? She had never before let a guy take over her thoughts this way.

"I was whisking some eggs."

"Good. We're having scrambled?"

"I thought maybe omelets. With fried potatoes and ham."

"Even better." Myrna pulled a fresh apron from a drawer and began tying it around her ample middle. "What can I do to help?"

"Maybe you could start with orange juice."

"I'm happy to make it."

Cara laughed. "It's already made. I was thinking you might enjoy taking a breath and having some juice at the table while I finish making the toast."

Myrna accepted a foamy glass from Cara's hands and settled herself at the table. "Now this is something I haven't done in the morning in more than thirty years."

"Then it's time you started pampering yourself."

"Pamper. Huh." Myrna huffed out a breath.

But as she sat watching Cara move easily from the stove to the counter to the sink, she was wearing a smile. Maybe, just for a minute, she would do exactly that.

Mad and Willow were just pouring coffee when Whit and Brady stepped into the kitchen.

Mad looked over at them. "I heard the backhoe's engine while it was still dark outside. Something wrong?"

"Just your usual early spring routine." Brady helped himself to coffee. "I think it's a rule of the universe that just when the rains begin, pipes break and roads wash away. Those pipes never burst in the middle of summer, when the job would be easy."

Whit helped himself to coffee and gave a laugh. "At least the two of us smell a whole lot better now than we did an hour ago."

"Another rule of the universe," Mad said with a chuckle. "If you're going to crawl around in the mud, you're not coming up smelling like a rose."

"Speaking of good smells..." Whit glanced at Cara, filling platters. "Whatever you're fixing, my stomach is already growling with hunger."

She turned and carried a heaping platter to the table. "Then dig in. I think I made enough for an army."

As the family gathered around the table, the talk continued about the broken culvert and the need to get it replaced as soon as possible.

Brady held the platter while Willow filled her plate. "Ridley Collins agreed to pull some strings and get the pipe delivered before supper. He thinks it will get here around three this afternoon. If he's as good as his word, I'll owe him big-time. They usually need at least a week to fill an order like ours."

"So, it looks like we won't be heading up to the hills today?" Willow tasted her omelet and glanced up suddenly. "Oh, Cara. This is heavenly."

Mad took a taste and arched a brow. "I see you're as good as Whit said, lass. What did you add to these eggs?"

"Mushrooms. Peppers, red and yellow, for color. And a dash of Tabasco sauce."

"Tabasco?" Mad grinned. "I'm going to remember that."

As the others around the table filled their plates and remarked on the great food, Myrna turned to Whit. "What will you do until the pipe arrives?"

Whit shrugged. "My time is yours, Myrna. What do you need me to do?"

She gave him a sly smile. "You may want to think about driving Cara to town to buy a few things."

Cara looked up in surprise. "I don't need—"

Myrna went on as though Cara hadn't interrupted. "Belle's shop over in Copper Creek has everything a girl could want. Denims, simple shirts, pajamas, and even underthings."

Cara's face flamed as Mad said, "That'll teach you to allow Myrna to do your laundry, lass. Don't think she doesn't remind all of us when our personal items are in need of replacement."

"And you're lucky I pay attention. There are some

here"—she turned to stare directly at Mad—"who would end up naked as the day they were born if I didn't look out for their wardrobes."

"You're not the only one, Mad," Willow said with a gentle smile. "Just last week Myrna reminded me that if I didn't soon replace my favorite jeans, I'd feel saddle and a lot of very cold air on my backside."

That had everyone laughing.

"All right." Whit helped himself to seconds. "If you're willing, Cara, we'll go right after breakfast."

Knowing everyone was watching and listening, Cara managed a demure smile, though in truth, she wanted to do a little happy dance. "I guess I'd better agree, or I'll face being shamed into it by Myrna."

The old woman sat back with a look of smug satisfaction.

CHAPTER ELEVEN

Whit drove the ranch truck to the back porch and held the door for Cara. Once inside, they rolled along the curving road that led to the highway.

"That was a great breakfast. I noticed that everybody had seconds and Mad had a third helping."

That had Cara grinning. "Do I detect a note of relief in your voice?"

He laughed. "Hey, Goldilocks. I never had a doubt you'd charm the entire family with your cooking."

"I wish I had your confidence."

He reached over and caught her hand. "The first day's always the hardest. From now on, it'll be a piece of cake."

"Speaking of which...what's your favorite? Chocolate, vanilla, carrot, spinach?"

"Spinach cake?"

He was still holding her hand, and she could feel the

heat moving through her veins. “I just wanted to see if you were listening.”

“When you talk, I’m listening.”

“Careful. That’s bound to make me feel powerful.”

“Good. It’s time you realized your importance.”

She eased her hand away and looked over at him. “Are you trying to send me a message?”

At his raised brow, she added, “Myrna suggested to me this morning that I needed to have more confidence in myself.”

Whit lowered the window and let the fresh breeze in. “Don’t let Myrna’s looks fool you. She’s sharp as a tack and knows how to read people. She’s also one of the kindest women I know.”

“How long have you known her?”

“All my life. She was here before I was born. Like Brady, she was never too busy to listen to my problems. No matter how crazy things got around our place, she always had time for me.”

“I wish I’d had people like that in my childhood. I guess that’s why I’m drawn to Myrna.”

“She likes you, too.”

“How do you know?”

He shook his head. “With Myrna, you know. She doesn’t put on airs. She’s honest and direct. If she sees something out of line, she’ll let you know.”

He looked over. “You realize, of course, that she set us up.”

“Set us up? For what?”

He chuckled. “The minute she heard Brady say that the pipe wouldn’t be delivered until later today, I could see the wheels turning in her head. She decided that we need some time away from the family. The 'what' is whatever we want to do with that time." He wiggled his brows like a mock villain. "So what do you say, little lady? Want to get us a case of beer and a hotel room?"

"I think you'd better get your brain engaged in another direction, Cowboy. Let's just get me to Belle's. Then we'll talk about really sexy things like a pair of denims and a couple of shirts for the ranch cook."

"You really need to put some romance in your life, little woman."

"Uh-huh."

As they started into town, he was grinning like a fool. "It's a good thing you didn't jump at the chance of beer and a hotel room."

"Why?"

"Because there isn't a hotel in town. The closest thing is a ranch bed-and-breakfast."

"So you were just testing the waters, so to speak?"

He winked as they slowed to a crawl on Main Street. When Whit pulled into a parking slot, he pointed. "There's Belle's. Want me to go with you?"

"While I pick out underwear? I don't think I'd be comfortable with that scene."

"You forget. My first glimpse of you was in that very sexy thong. And somehow, I just can't get it out of my mind."

"Well, enjoy the memory, Cowboy."

"Oh, I do. Often." He handed her a credit card. "Use this."

She stared at it and then at his face. "I have my own."

"You said your abandoned rental car probably maxed it out. Just to be safe, use this." When he saw that she was about to argue, he added, "You can pay me back later."

"Okay." She blew him a kiss as she began crossing the street. "Where will I find you when I'm finished?"

"Don't worry. I'll find you."

Whit waited until Cara stepped into Belle's before heading down the street.

He opened the door to Chief Ira Pettigrew's office. Ordinarily, Ira's wife, Peggy, was manning the reception desk, but today the chief was alone.

He looked up. Seeing Whit, he walked around his desk to shake hands. "Hey, Whit. What brings you here?"

Whit returned the handshake before sitting across the desk from the chief. "I'm just back from the highlands, and Mad was filling me in on the shooting over at Red Rock."

Ira nodded. "Nasty business. I was hoping there would be a connection to your daddy's shooting, but Red Rock's chief thinks it's pretty apparent that old Abe's nephew is the shooter. A family feud that got out of control."

"That's what Mad said." Whit tapped a finger on the arm of his chair before saying, "I've got something to tell you."

As quickly as possible, he relayed the story that Cara had told him. When Whit was finished, Ira steepled his hands on his desktop. "If you don't mind bringing her here, I'll ask the sheriff in Red Rock to fax me a photo of the deceased, to see if she can identify him as the rancher she saw."

Whit nodded. "If he is, then what?"

"Sheriff Hack may want to have a talk with her."

"Today?"

Ira considered. "One step at a time, Whit. Let me talk to Todd Hack over in Red Rock and see if he has a good, recent photo of Abe Parson. By the time your young lady is finished shopping, I'll try to get a better handle on the matter, and then we'll decide whether or not Sheriff Hack will want to interview her."

Whit nodded. "That's fair." He stood and offered his hand. "Thanks, Ira."

"You're welcome. And thanks for coming in with this information. It may be something, or it may be nothing at all."

"I'm sure you'll figure it out." Whit walked to the door and turned. "Now I just need to find a gentle way to let her know I've talked to you about this."

"I suggest you feed her." The chief patted his thick middle. "Everything seems better on a full stomach."

"I'll keep that in mind, Chief."

Cara walked out of the shop carrying several bulging, handled bags. As soon as she stepped out the door, Whit was there to relieve her of her burden.

After stowing the bags in his truck, he caught her hand.

She glanced at their linked hands, enjoying the quick sizzle of heat. "Where are we going?"

"To pay a call."

Something in his tone had Cara holding her silence.

They walked leisurely along the street and up the hill toward a church, where bells were just tolling the noon hour. Instead of going inside, Whit led her around the back and through the ornate wrought-iron gate announcing the Copper Creek Cemetery.

They strolled among the headstones until they came to

a grave marked with a small flat stone etched simply with MURDOCH (BEAR) MACKENZIE.

Whit removed his wide-brimmed hat before dropping to one knee. "Pop, I'd like you to meet Cara Walton."

Cara knelt beside him and ran a finger over the flat stone.

Seeing it, Whit explained, "Mom didn't want some big, ornate marker like these." He swept his hand to indicate some of the hundred-year-old crosses and angels and towering obelisks marking some of the nearby graves. "So she's ordered an engraved marble bench. That way whenever we visit, we can just sit in the sunlight or snowflakes and talk awhile the way we always did."

Cara's eyes widened. "Oh, I love that idea."

"Yeah. Me too. We all agreed it was the right thing for Pop."

They remained that way for long, silent minutes before Whit got to his feet and helped Cara up. He slapped his hat against his leg as he turned away. "Bye, Pop. See you later."

It was so simple, and yet so intimate, Cara felt the sudden sting of tears as they walked from the cemetery and down the hill.

Whit paused. "How about some lunch?"

She nodded. "All right."

"You have a choice. There's the Boxcar Inn, with family-friendly food like club sandwiches and homemade soup." Whit pointed to the train boxcar parked in the center of town. "Or Wylie's, home of gut-burning chili and fries or a burger guaranteed to drip juice down the front of every diner's shirt."

"That all sounds too good to miss. Wylie's."

"Wylie's it is." He caught her hand. "I'm warning you. Order a tall glass of ice water along with whatever other beverage you want. You'll need it."

They were still laughing as they stepped inside the smoky room, where the smell of grease on a grill hung heavy in the air.

Whit breathed deeply. "This is the place I call my second home."

Just then a woman with orange spiked hair and a voice like a foghorn caught him in a bear hug. "Whit MacKenzie. Now my day is complete."

He hugged her tightly before saying, "Nonie Claxton, I'd like you to meet Cara Walton."

"Walton, huh?" Without missing a beat, she said, "You one of those who used to say, 'Good night, John Boy'?"

"Yep. Walton's Mountain. Of course, that would make me about sixty, wouldn't it?" Cara asked.

Nonie gave a throaty laugh. "She's smart. I like her, Whit." She gave Cara a long look. "You're not from around these parts."

"Minerva."

"Never heard of it. What're you doing with this bad boy?" She caught Cara's arm and said in a loud stage whisper, "Watch yourself, honey. This one's got all the right moves."

"Is that so?"

"He's a heartbreaker. Ask any woman in Copper Creek. From sixteen to sixty, they've all fallen for him at one time or another."

"I'll keep that in mind."

Nonie turned to Whit. "Park yourselves, and I'll be right over."

Whit led the way through the crowded tables to a booth in the back. Minutes later Nonie arrived with two tall glasses of ice water and a longneck beer.

"Figured I'd save myself a little time. This is what you wanted, right, Whit?"

"That's right." He turned to Cara. "What'll you drink?"

She eyed the beer and said, "I think ice water is fine."

Whit ignored the menu tucked between the salt and pepper shakers and the ketchup and mustard. "What's the special today?"

"Wylie's famous gut-burning chili."

Whit nodded. "I'll have that."

Nonie turned to Cara, who said, "I'll have the same."

"I'll give her this," Nonie said to Whit. "She's either crazy or very brave."

"I guess you'll just have to find out." Whit winked before she turned away.

She returned a short time later and served them two bowls of chili and a tray of assorted cheese, chips, crackers, and onions.

Whit added a little of each to his bowl and dug in.

Cara did the same.

After her first taste, she reached for the glass of water and took a big drink. "You weren't kidding."

"Told you." He looked over, spotting her watery eyes. "You going to survive?"

"Oh yeah." She dug in and managed to empty her bowl while Whit was already tackling his second bowl.

"You're really a glutton for punishment."

"I'll have you know I have a superior palate."

"And who told you this giant lie?"

Whit grinned. "Wylie himself."

"Oh. That explains it." Cara sat back, sipping the last of her water.

When he'd polished off his second bowl of chili, Whit drained his beer. "While you were shopping, I paid a call on our police chief, Ira Pettigrew."

Cara visibly tensed.

"I thought I'd share your story with him. I know I should have asked your permission, but I figured it was easier to ask forgiveness than permission."

She shot him a frosty look. "Wipe that smirk off your face and tell me what Police Chief Ira Pettigrew said."

"That he'll put in a call to the chief of Red Rock and make a decision whether or not to interview you."

She folded her hands primly on the table.

Whit couldn't help teasing her a bit. "Well, at least he didn't rush over to Belle's and put the cuffs on you for withholding information."

She couldn't hold back the grin that curved the corners of her mouth. "Well, there is that."

He reached across the table and put his hands over hers. "So, you're not mad at me?"

She went very still, absorbing the tingle. Nerves? Or a sexual awareness that was beginning to sharpen each time Whit touched her? "Maybe a little."

He tightened his grasp on her hands. "Woman, you're killing me."

Nonie swooped down on them and began piling their dishes on her empty tray. "You're not going for a third, Whit honey?"

"Not today."

She glanced pointedly at his hand over Cara's. "Yeah,

that's what happens when a cowboy's with a pretty girl. The heart wins out over the stomach every time."

She was still chuckling at her little joke as she placed the check on the table and walked away with a full tray.

"Come on." Whit peeled off some bills and dropped them on the table before catching Cara's hand and leading her to the door.

Outside, he kept her hand in his until they reached the police station.

Inside, Chief Pettigrew looked up with a smile.

"Chief Pettigrew, this is Cara Walton."

They shook hands and the chief indicated a chair. "Good timing, Whit. This just came over the fax."

He handed Cara a grainy black and white photo of an old man in a starched white shirt and clean denims. "According to Sheriff Todd Hack over in Red Rock, this is the most recent photo of the deceased, taken at a church picnic last summer. Is this the man you saw?"

Cara nodded. "I only caught a glimpse of his face, but I'm sure this is the man."

He handed her a second photo of a young man with shaggy hair and a crooked smile. "Do you recognize this man?"

She shook her head. "I've never seen him before."

"This isn't the man you saw with Abe?"

"No. I'm sorry. Is he the suspect in the killing?"

"That's right. Abe's nephew."

"I guess my information isn't important, then."

"That's up to Sheriff Hack in Red Rock." Ira placed both photos on his desk before looking at Cara. "I'll give this information to him and see if he wants to pursue it further. If so, you may have to make the trip to Red Rock. Are you all right with that?"

Cara glanced at Whit, who nodded. "You just let me know, Ira, and I'll drive Cara there."

"Good." The police chief shook their hands and remained standing until they were out the door and heading toward Whit's truck.

Once there, Whit held the door and helped her to the passenger seat before circling around to the driver's side.

On the drive home, he was whistling a happy tune while Cara worried the cuff of her plaid shirt. She ought to be concerned about being interviewed by the sheriff in Red Rock, but she found herself thinking instead that she was beginning to like having her hand held. It wasn't something she'd had much experience with, but it was altogether too pleasant to ignore.

She turned to Whit. "Do you think we'll have to drive to Red Rock?"

"Will you worry about it if we do?"

She shook her head. "Not really. I can only repeat what I saw. And if the sheriff there is half as nice as Chief Pettigrew, I'll be fine with it. But I hope it's over, and they have the guilty man in custody. Then I'll be done with it for good."

"I hope so, too." He glanced around. "What did you think of our town?"

"It's bigger than Minerva. And cleaner. And I enjoyed lunch at Wylie's." Her eyes danced. "Nonie's a character. And she really likes you."

"Nonie Claxton likes every man who's ever walked through the door of that saloon."

"No. She may be attracted to every man, but she really likes you. It shows."

"Because I'm easy to like." He reached over and turned on the radio.

And as the truck ate up the miles, Cara found herself relaxing in Whit's pleasant company as they both hummed along with Willie, singing about being on the road again.

CHAPTER TWELVE

Myrna waddled into the kitchen with an armload of folded laundry and breathed deeply. "I swear, Cara, something smells like heaven."

Cara looked up from the counter, where she was chopping vegetables for a salad. "I found a beef roast in the fridge. Since most of the meat is in that giant freezer, I thought I'd cook the roast tonight before I plan menus for the rest of the week."

"I can't wait to taste it and see what you've done to make it smell so good." Myrna began placing clean towels neatly into a deep drawer.

Seeing it, Cara said, "You keep everything in such good order, Myrna. Just like my gram taught me."

"Did she live near you, honey?"

Cara shook her head. "I lived with her."

"Where were your folks?"

"I never knew my dad. My mother never married him. And she left me with Gram when I was a baby."

"Is your grandmother still living?"

"She passed away while I was in college."

"I'm sorry, Cara. It's hard to lose the people we love."

Cara continued working while Myrna walked away to fetch another load of laundry. As Cara chopped and sliced and diced, she couldn't keep from comparing Myrna with her grandmother. Both women were hardworking, simple, and direct. But being simple didn't mean being uninformed. Though Gram never judged the daughter who had chosen a honky-tonk lifestyle over motherhood, she'd urged her granddaughter to make wise choices.

Wise choices. That mess with Jared Billingham was of her own making. She'd convinced herself that a handsome, charming, and very rich boss would have only her best interest at heart. And even when she'd recognized his controlling nature, she'd looked the other way. It was only when he'd mocked her dream that she'd been forced to face what he really was. A selfish, manipulative man concerned with his own pleasure. What had Gram always said? *You have a right to your dreams, girl. But you have a duty to earn them.*

She wouldn't soon forget that lesson again.

If this was her second chance, or possibly her third or fourth chance, she would do it the right way. She would earn it. And not by hoping the MacKenzie family would somehow send all her troubles packing. This time, she would stand strong, and she would do the right thing, no matter what.

As she mixed up a batch of dough and placed a tray of rolls in the oven, she caught sight of Whit and Brady strolling from the barn, laughing together, covered from head to toe in mud.

Just the sight of Whit, so filthy and so obviously happy, had her heart doing a little dance.

He was so strong, so sure of himself. So comfortable in his own skin. She would have labeled him a man's man, except that Nonie's words reminded her that he was also extremely comfortable around women of any age.

"Hey there." Whit poked his head in the doorway. "Something smells great."

"I bet it smells a whole lot better'n us," Brady added with a grin.

"Yeah." Whit motioned to Cara. "Don't come near us. We smell like we've been working in a sewer."

Brady laughed. "We have been."

"Yeah." Whit shucked his boots, his hat, and his mud-streaked shirt before strolling shirtless through the kitchen. "If you weren't here," he called over his shoulder, "I'd've shucked these pants, too."

Cara rolled her eyes. "Thank heaven for small favors."

When both men had gone to their rooms, she thought again about the differences between Whit and the man who'd so badly used her.

Though Whit was a tough cowboy, he seemed almost old-fashioned in the courteous ways he treated her.

Jared Billingham had been willing to hurt anyone, to shatter anyone's dreams, simply because he thought he was above them.

Cara had no doubt that Whit MacKenzie would be willing to help anyone, no matter the cost to him, while remaining true to himself and his values.

As she returned her attention to dinner preparations,

she vowed she would never forget the difference between a spoiled child and a real man.

By the time Whit and Brady descended the stairs, hair still glistening from their long, hot showers, the kitchen and gathering room were crowded with the entire family.

Griff and Juliet and their boys, Ethan and Casey, had flown in with Mad, after he'd spent the day at their ranch.

Ash and Brenna arrived with their pup, Sammy, who wriggled in excitement the minute he spotted the two little boys. They ran off, teaching him to fetch their ball, amid shrieks of delight.

Willow returned from the barn and hugged everyone in greeting before heading up the stairs for a quick shower.

By the time she returned, the others were gathered around the fireplace, with longnecks or glasses of wine or soda. Cara set out a fancy platter of crackers and spinach-and-avocado dip, along with a tray of cheeses.

While they discussed the crazy weather, the number of calves being born early, and the fact that Mad could now go almost anywhere with ease since the introduction of his new scooter, Whit walked up beside Cara.

"Looks like another big score for you, Goldilocks."

She glanced over to see him holding the tray and platter. Both were empty.

"I'm glad they enjoyed it."

"I don't know if *enjoy* is the proper description. They inhaled it."

She laughed at his little joke.

"Do you have any more?"

She shook her head. "That's it. But I do have dinner ready, if you'd like to let everyone know."

Breaking through the chorus of voices, he called, "If anybody's interested, supper is ready."

There was no need to announce it again. As if drawn by invisible strings, they all moved to the table, taking up their accustomed seats as the conversation continued without interruption.

As Myrna began carrying platters of roast beef swimming in gravy and a bowl of creamy potatoes, the conversation slowed as they helped themselves.

Cara placed a basket of hot rolls in the middle of the table, followed by a family-sized salad and individual bowls.

Juliet tasted the salad, then looked up in surprise. "Is this dressing homemade?"

Cara nodded.

"Oh, I want the recipe." Juliet put a small amount of salad on each of her boy's plates before helping them with the beef and potatoes.

"I love roast beast," Casey said, to much laughter.

"Me too." Ethan tasted the salad. "But I think I like salad, too. Try it, Casey."

The younger one was about to protest, until he saw his mother's slight shake of her head.

He tasted, then began eating the lettuce, the tomatoes, the strips of red and yellow and orange peppers. "These are good."

"See what a little magic dressing can do?" Whit called to Cara.

Casey's eyes went wide. "You put magic in this, Cara?"

Before she could reply, Whit said, "Casey, listen to your old uncle Whit. Women have a way of putting magic in the darndest things."

That had everyone grinning and had Mad looking at his grandson a bit more sharply before muttering, "I wonder what other magic Cara is capable of?"

Cara merely ducked her head, while around her the conversation grew louder and more animated.

"New jeans and shirt, I see." Willow glanced across the table at Cara. "What did you think of Belle's?"

"I loved it. She has everything I could possibly need. And things I couldn't even think of."

Ash winked at his wife before asking, "Did my brother go in with you and help you pick out all those frilly feminine doodads that every woman craves?"

"Not on your life." Whit helped himself to more mashed potatoes. "Although I did offer. But Cara was having none of it."

"Belle's is no place for a cowboy," Cara said in defense. "I wanted a little privacy while I shopped."

"I don't blame you." Willow sipped her tea. "But next time you go to town, I may go with you. I haven't been to Belle's in months. I think I'm running low on"—she stared pointedly at Ash—"my feminine doodads."

They all laughed while Ash's face flamed and Brenna patted his hand. "It's all right, honey. Next time I need...my feminine doodads, I'll take you along to carry my bags."

After a long, leisurely dinner, the family settled into the great room. It was as big and informal as the family that lived there, with windows looking out at a breathtaking view of rolling meadows and a sun setting behind hills dotted with cattle.

Casey and Ethan, who had enjoyed a ride to the room

on Mad's scooter, were now sprawled on the floor in front of a blazing fire on the great stone hearth. Happily lying between them was Sammy, exhausted from play.

While the others settled on comfortable sofas and soft easy chairs, Cara and Myrna passed around a trolley of coffee and desserts, along with longneck beer and a bottle of Mad's favorite scotch whiskey, which he splashed liberally into his coffee.

"We have brownies and ice cream," Cara announced. "And fudge sauce for anyone who has room."

The two little boys were up and accepting bowls of brownies topped with ice cream and drizzled with warm chocolate fudge sauce.

Watching them dig into their desserts, Juliet gave a quick shake of her head. "I don't know where they're putting that. I ate so much I may not eat again for a week."

Griff brought her hand to his lips. "You say that every day. And every morning you find room to start again." He glanced at the boys. "As for them, I know where they put it. No matter how much I ate as a kid, I always had room for dessert."

Mad patted his stomach. "I might have room for a wee taste."

Whit winked at Cara. "That means only a double dessert, and not a triple."

She handed the old man a heaping bowl and he dug into the sweet treat with relish.

When she'd finished serving, she eased Myrna down into a chair and handed her a cup of coffee and a bowl of dessert.

"What about you?" the old woman asked.

"I'll just take these things into the kitchen." As Cara loaded plates and cups onto the trolley, Whit surprised her by taking hold of it and pushing it toward the other room.

Cara followed him. "You don't need to do this, Whit. You should be in there with your family. You've been working all day."

"You've been working, too."

"But I've been warm and dry. You've been freezing in that icy rain and mud."

He leaned close. "Know what kept me warm all day?"

"What?" She looked up just as he bent his lips to her cheek.

"This." He nibbled his way to the corner of her mouth. "Just thinking about the fact that you'd be here when I finished for the day."

"Whit..."

They stepped apart quickly as the door opened and Brady walked into the kitchen.

"Ah. Here it is." He reached for the bottle of scotch. "Mad wants one more before going to bed."

As Brady walked away, Whit turned to Cara, who was already pushing the trolley toward the sink.

He stepped up beside her and leaned close. "Now, where were we?" He pressed his mouth to her temple, while his hands moved slowly along her back. "Mmm, you taste so damned good." He ran soft, moist kisses along her cheek to the corner of her lips, nibbling, tasting, until she turned her head just enough to offer her mouth fully to him.

"Oh yeah." He took the kiss deep. "Now this is what I want."

The door opened again and they stepped apart quickly. Both wore matching looks of guilt.

Little Casey looked from one to the other. "Mama said I could have one more scoop of ice cream."

Whit managed a smile. "Are you sure your mom approved?"

"Uh-huh."

"Okay." He glanced at Cara, looking slightly dazed. "I'll bring you some in a minute."

With a yelp of joy, the little boy turned away.

Whit gave a shake of his head. "That's the trouble with having all this family. No privacy. But there's always later, when they go to bed." He lifted a hand to her hair. "I'll walk you upstairs when you're ready."

Picking up the carton of ice cream, he sauntered out of the kitchen.

Cara stared after him.

This man's kisses, and even the mere touch of his hand on her hair, had little fires igniting all through her system. A system so highly charged, she wondered that she didn't simply burst into spontaneous combustion.

Chapter Thirteen

In the early morning dawn, Cara moved effortlessly about the kitchen, stirring something on the stove, checking the oven, squeezing oranges for juice, and all with an efficiency that belied her inner storm.

She'd managed to slip away to her room the previous night while Whit and Mad were having a noisy discussion about the best way to shore up the eroding soil during the heavy spring rains.

Later, while lying in the dark in her bed, she'd heard his footsteps pause outside her room and knew that he was checking to see if her light was still on. She'd heard him move on and had exhaled slowly.

It wasn't that she didn't want Whit's attention. What really disturbed her was that she found herself yearning for it. For him. And she knew she wasn't ready. Before she allowed this to go any further, she needed to be certain in her mind just what she wanted.

There had been so many mistakes in her young life. Her mother had always considered the simple act of giving birth to her a mistake. And that was a heavy burden in Cara's heart. For years she'd believed that if only she could become a successful writer-illustrator, she would have the respect she craved. If she achieved her goal, she reasoned, she would no longer be just a silly dreamer. She would be somebody her mother wouldn't resent.

And then there was the dream she never allowed herself to admit to. The dream of being part of a loving family. That was an even more impossible dream than getting her children's book published.

She knew that was the reason she'd been so quick to jump at the chance to stay here. From the moment Whit had told her about his large, noisy, fascinating family, she'd wanted to see them for herself. Being an only child, with no living relatives, they sounded too good to be true.

She knew, too, that she was allowing her own fantasy to color reality. What she ought to be doing was finding a job somewhere and working toward financial independence. But at least for now, the lure of a paycheck wasn't as strong as the lure of earning the right to spend a little more time here, safe and snug, in the bosom of the rowdy MacKenzie family.

Safe and snug.

Was that a fantasy, too?

The texts had been coming with more frequency. Ugly, threatening texts. But though Jared knew her cell phone number, he couldn't possibly know where she was. Could he? Would a rich man spend money on expensive detectives to have her traced through her cell phone? Would he have her hunted and humiliated, just for the sake of settling a grudge?

"Good morning."

At the cheerful sound of Willow's voice, Cara looked over. "Good morning. There's juice and coffee on that tray."

"Thank you." Willow helped herself to a tall glass of orange juice and carried it to the table just as Whit and Brady walked in.

Cara paused to watch as Whit rolled his sleeves and washed at the big mudroom sink. He looked so wonderfully sweaty and dirty from his early morning chores. His hair mussed and falling over his forehead in the most appealing way. His plaid shirt sticking to his skin, displaying all those corded muscles.

Seeing the way Willow was staring at her, she forced herself to look away.

When Whit stepped into the kitchen, he greeted Willow with a quick kiss on the cheek before stepping up beside Cara.

"You went upstairs early last night without saying good night."

"Yes. I didn't want to interrupt your conversation with your grandfather."

"You know I would have welcomed the interruption."

He stepped back a pace when he saw Willow watching and listening.

Brady stepped into the kitchen and turned to Willow. "Mad said when he flew over Stone Canyon yesterday, most of the snow had melted in the higher elevations. So I'll be taking a group of wranglers up to the hills today. Time to move that herd from the canyon to the highlands, and then I'll backtrack and drive the trailer and flatbed down to the barn."

Willow thought a moment. "I could go along. I don't have anything pressing here today. That way you can stay in the hills with the herd, and I'll take the flatbed home."

Brady poured himself a mug of coffee. "Suit yourself. That's a big rig to handle."

"I can manage. I've driven it before."

He turned to Whit. "Think you can manage the rest of the roadwork without me?"

Whit nodded. "If I get stuck, I'll call on Ash or Griff."

"Griff will be flying to Hope Ranch with Mad."

That had Whit grinning. "Mad wasn't kidding when he said that scooter changed his life. Now he thinks he's the same young guy who tamed this wilderness fifty years ago."

Willow shook her head. "It isn't the scooter. It's Juliet, and the motivation she's given Mad to change his life."

"Did I hear someone mention my name?" The object of their discussion rolled his scooter into the kitchen with ease and helped himself to a mug of coffee.

"I was telling them that you're a changed man," Willow said with a smile. "Thanks to Juliet and her therapy."

"She gave me back my life, lass." He rolled closer and pressed a kiss on his daughter-in-law's cheek.

"I'd say she's given you wings."

"That she has." He wore a bright smile. "I think I'll be able to pilot the Cessna in another week or two, when I have some modifications made to the instruments."

"Wings indeed." Willow sighed. "Isn't it amazing how much one person can change another forever?"

That had Whit turning to study Cara as she finished the breakfast preparations.

When Myrna entered the kitchen with an armload of laundry, Cara began setting platters of ham and eggs and toast on the table.

Seeing it, Myrna halted. "You don't have to wait for me in order to eat."

Cara took the laundry from her arms. "Yes, I do. Now sit and eat. You put in more hours than anyone I know."

The old woman's eyes softened as she took her place at the table and accepted a cup of coffee from Cara's hands.

Around the table, Willow shot a look at her father-in-law, who was studying Cara with interest, and then at Myrna, who was helping herself to toast.

Cara set a little pot of jam in front of the housekeeper. "I noticed this was your favorite."

The old woman was humming as she spread jam on her toast.

Cara was unaware of the family watching her as she returned her attention to something on the stove.

The sun was already high in the sky as Willow sat astride her chestnut mare and watched the wranglers begin herding the cattle out of the box canyon where they'd been for the past week. Since they were restless for the lush grass of the highlands, it would be an easy task to get them to the hills that ringed the ranch. The toughest part of the job was getting them started on their long trek.

After their enforced imprisonment in the canyon, the herd was tense and edgy. There was much cursing and shouting as strays broke ranks and had to be lassoed and forced back to join the herd. As always, Brady was in the thick of the action, chasing down a stray, using his rope to subdue, cooing softly or sometimes swearing at an errant cow determined to break free.

Willow found herself laughing aloud at the antics of a particularly stubborn cow that refused to follow the herd. After its third attempt at freedom, Brady lassoed the animal, tied the rope to his saddle horn, and led it into the middle of the herd, where it would be hemmed in by too many animals to bolt.

He was still muttering a few well-chosen oaths when he rode up beside Willow's mount and came to a halt.

"I swear that ornery cow has a woman's mind. She's just not willing to go with the flow."

Willow's low rumble of laughter had him turning to look at her. "Spoken like a man. Can't you see she's heavy with calf and wants a little privacy for the delivery?"

"The plan is to have her deliver it, not here in this arid place, but cushioned in lush grass in the highlands, with a wrangler nearby to assist if she gets into trouble."

"That's your plan." Willow was still grinning. "That cow knows that time and babies wait for no man. Her plan is to make a break for it and have some time away from the noisy herd."

Her smile was infectious, and Brady found himself laughing. "So I should make plans to track her again and again until that calf is born?"

"You might want to think about it. Despite all the wranglers, and all the cattle, my money's on the cow to make a break to freedom."

He gave a slow shake of his head. "I'll tell young Carter to keep an eye on her."

He nudged his mount into a gallop until he caught up with one of the wranglers.

A short time later he returned to Willow's side.

She seemed surprised. "I thought you were heading upland with the herd."

"That was my intention. But looking at all this mud churned up by the herd, I'd like to be sure you can get this flatbed moving before I join the wranglers."

"Men," she muttered as she turned her mare toward the entrance to the canyon, where the tractor and flatbed trailer were parked. "You're beginning to sound just like Bear."

Brady chuckled. "Just looking out for your welfare." Over his shoulder he added, "And, yes, I know you can look out for yourself. But humor me."

She paused and turned in the saddle. Her voice softened. "Really, I don't mind. It's nice to know you have my back."

Brady trailed behind Willow, fighting to suppress the grin that tugged at the corners of his mouth.

If there was ever a woman who didn't need a man's help, it was Willow MacKenzie. In all the years he'd known her, he'd never heard her ask for assistance from Bear, her sons, or from any of the wranglers.

Still, he'd seen the way the tractor tires were mired. It had been parked here for over a week, after all, buried first in snow and now in all this mud and slush.

He promised himself he would simply remain here until that old tractor was safely along the trail, pulling the flatbed in its wake.

He couldn't help himself. He just had to know that Willow was safe.

* * *

The sun had long ago moved behind the hills, leaving the land in a rosy glow. The man and woman shoveling dirt beneath the tires of the flatbed failed to appreciate the beauty.

Willow climbed up to the seat of the tractor and put it in gear. It inched forward before grinding once more to a halt.

Brady shoveled more earth and stones beneath the tires of the flatbed and urged her to try again. Again the tractor balked.

She climbed down and walked over to join him.

"Looks like this thing is stuck until the sun can dry up all this muck."

"Yeah. And that's not going to happen now."

At Brady's words, she noticed for the first time that darkness was beginning to cover the land.

"Oh, Brady. I'm sorry. I've made you miss an entire day here, when you'd planned on being with the herd."

"Hey." He laid a hand on her arm. "You know there's no such thing as making plans on a working ranch. Plans were made to be broken." He looked around. "The real problem is, we're stuck here until daylight. There are too many miles, and too many pitfalls along the trails, to take the horses back to the ranch until morning."

Willow nodded. "It won't be the first time I've had to spend a night under the stars." She glanced around. "Let's find a good spot to make camp."

"We could set our bedrolls under the flatbed."

"Too muddy." She shook her head. "I'd settle for that if it were raining. But it's a clear night, and I want to see the stars."

"Let's take a look up there." Brady indicated a stand of Ponderosa pines on a hill overlooking the canyon.

They led their horses up the incline.

"There's plenty of grass, and we're sheltered from the elements on three sides by these pines." Brady tethered his horse and removed the saddle and saddlebags. "Best of all, it'll give you a perfect view of that sky." He turned away. "I'll get a fire started."

Willow unsaddled her mare and tethered her nearby before tossing the saddle and saddle blanket on the ground.

She turned to Brady. "How I wish I'd thought to bring along some supplies. But I thought I'd be home long before this."

He held up a blackened pot, a tin of coffee, and an assortment of wrapped packages. "Maybe you planned on being home, but I figured I'd be up in the hills for some time. I had Myrna fix me my usual care package."

A short time later, she and Brady were seated alongside a cozy fire, using their saddles as backrests as they reclined side by side, sipping strong, hot coffee splashed with some of Mad's scotch and nibbling hard-boiled eggs and beef jerky.

"Bless Myrna," Willow sighed.

"Yeah. I say that every time I'm in the hills. That woman does know how to pamper a cowboy."

Willow stared up at the night sky, ablaze with millions of stars that looked close enough to reach out and touch. "I've missed this. I've always loved sleeping up in the hills." She turned. "How about you, Brady?"

"It's good when it's a perfect night like this. But I've been stuck in rain, snow, and wind that nearly blows me off the side of a mountain. Then it's not so great."

He stretched out his long legs toward the fire. "But this... Now this is the best."

"Where did you grow up, Brady?"

He was silent for so long, Willow wondered if he'd heard her question. When she turned to him, he was frowning and staring off into the distance.

"I was born on a hard patch of land in the middle of Montana wilderness. Our nearest neighbor was more than a hundred miles away."

"Did you have brothers and sisters?"

He shook his head. "Just me and my mother and father."

"Were you close?"

"I looked out for my mother. My father was a drunk. I don't remember ever seeing him completely sober. He drank in the morning, in the afternoon, and at night until he passed out."

She turned to study Brady's stern profile. "Was he... abusive?"

He nodded. "It's the nature of drunks, I guess. They hate themselves for their weakness and take out their anger on whoever happens to be handy. At first it was my mother, until I got big enough to stop him. When he managed to drink himself to death, it was too late for my mother. She followed my father in death just a year later."

"And then you left?"

He shook his head. "By then I'd married, and I thought I could make a life there for my wife and our son."

"You had a wife and child?"

He met her look of surprise. "With them, I knew I'd finally found heaven. My wife's name was Maria. Our son was Daniel."

Was. That single word had all her breath backing up in her throat.

Willow waited, afraid to breathe. "What happened to them?"

Brady's tone was low, controlled, holding back any emotion he might be feeling. "Daniel got the fever first. Maria never left his side. She was such a good, loving mother. When I'd tend the cows in the morning, she'd be holding him. When I'd come in from the fields, he'd still be in her arms. On the very day that we buried him on a hillside beside my parents' graves, Maria came down with the fever. Within two days she was gone."

Willow reached a hand to his, squeezing gently. "Oh, Brady. That's just horrid. I'm so sorry."

His tone lowered. "I buried her beside our son, and then I packed up whatever I could carry before driving the herd to my nearest neighbor, almost a hundred miles from me. I told him they were his. He could have them free. And then I rode away." He paused. "I thought I'd leave Montana for good. I never wanted to stay anywhere near my memories."

"What changed your mind?"

"I made the mistake of stopping at Copper Creek. I walked into Wylie's. Not for a drink," he said with a wry smile. "The last thing I wanted to do was become my father. But I needed food. And while I was eating, I ran into Bear."

"You met Bear at Wylie's? He never told me."

"I'm sure he wasn't proud of himself. He was so drunk he could barely stand. I wanted to get as far away from him as I could. But when I saw him leave, I noticed two shifty cowboys follow him outside. I knew what they were up to. I found him in the dark, trying to fight off two gun-wielding tough guys. After I knocked them unconscious, I drove Bear home. I was about to walk away when he insisted I stay the night. He promised to drive me back to town in the morning to pick up my truck. In the morning, when he was sober, Bear told me why he'd been so drunk. He said that the great love of his life had left him to take a job modeling, and he knew he'd never see her again. He was so despondent, he begged me to stay on and help with the ranch chores. I told him about my father, and Bear vowed that if I stayed, he'd never drink too much again. We shook hands on it."

Willow was too stunned to say a word.

Brady smiled then. "When you came back to him, I understood why a strong man like Bear MacKenzie would be so crazy in love. He was a different man, a better man, with you. So I stayed on, as I'd promised, because Bear deserved to spend time with you. And then the years just blended one into the next, with Ash coming along, and then Whit, and I knew I'd found my place in this world. They were like my own sons. And you and Bear and your boys became the family I'd always dreamed of. You see, I owe everything I have here—the home I've enjoyed, the hard, satisfying work, the family—to that chance encounter with Bear."

With tears brimming, Willow leaned close to wrap her arms around his neck, her words muttered against his throat. "Thank you for telling me all this, Brady. I want you to know that you made Bear's life so much easier. He trusted you completely and knew that you would see to it that everything was done to perfection." She looked up into his eyes. "He used to tell me that meeting you was the second best thing that ever happened to him, after meeting me."

Instead of the grin she'd expected, he frowned and removed her arms from around his neck before pulling away, putting some distance between them.

His words were unexpectedly gruff. "It's not something I ever wanted to tell you. For Bear's sake, I thought it best to keep it a secret. I guess you…caught me in a weak moment."

He tossed aside the last of his coffee, causing the flames to sputter and flare. "Now, I think we'd better get some sleep."

Without another word, he rolled to his side and pulled his wide-brimmed hat low over his face.

Beside him, Willow lay listening to the night sounds around her, while the things Brady had told her played through her mind.

He'd once comforted her by saying that he understood her grief.

Only now was she beginning to realize just how much he understood pain and sorrow. It broke her heart to know that he'd been forced to grieve alone, without the comfort of family or friends.

It soothed her somewhat to know that her family had offered him a measure of love through the years. Brady had always been infinitely kind and patient with both Ash and Whit, treating them as his own. But could another man's family be enough for a man who'd suffered the painful loss of a much-loved wife and child?

Her heart continued to ache for the man who lay beside her, until sleep gradually stole her thoughts and brought her a measure of peace.

CHAPTER FOURTEEN

Brady and Whit shoveled sand while Willow eased the tractor out of the ruts and onto a dry, flat stretch of soil.

Brady turned to Whit with a wide smile. "I'm glad you were able to ride up here this morning and lend a hand, son."

"Hey. Any time." Whit laughed. "It beats mucking stalls." He looked over at his mother. "Okay. Who drives the rig, and who rides behind on the horses?"

Willow climbed down from the tractor. "I'll leave the driving to one of you. I prefer riding Dancer."

Whit hauled himself up to the seat of the tractor and put it in gear.

Behind him, Willow pulled herself into the mare's saddle before catching the reins of Whit's gelding.

Beside her, Brady shot her a smile. "Smart move. Driving that beast down the side of this mountain will rattle a body's bones."

Willow nodded. "We've all done it a time or two. I figure Whit has younger bones to rattle."

With a laugh they followed the flatbed at a leisurely pace, enjoying the warm spring sunshine and the beauty of the countryside.

Brady turned in the saddle. "You were a good sport last night when everything went south. I'm sure you'd have preferred your own comfortable bed to a bedroll in the grass."

She shook her head. "I wasn't kidding when I said I've missed this. There are a lot of chores I'd prefer to skip on this ranch, but I consider sleeping under the stars a bonus for all the hard work." She reached over to lay a hand on his arm. "It was a real treat for me, Brady. And I'm grateful you were there to share it."

Several hours later, as they approached the barns, a sleek plane circled before coming in for a smooth landing on the asphalt strip behind the barn that housed the family's Cessna.

Brady glanced at Willow. "Did you know young McMillan was coming today?"

She shook her head. "I wasn't expecting him." She sighed. "I'm sure he's bringing me more documents to sign. Since Bear's passing, I feel like I'm being buried in paperwork."

As they led their horses into the barn, she turned to Brady. "I want you with me when I meet with Lance."

He frowned. "I'm not Bear, Willow. I don't know any more about those legal documents than you do."

"But having you with me will keep me from feeling overpowered by Lance. When he starts talking about dour rights and estate taxes and trusts, I feel totally inadequate.

He always manages to gloss over my protests and get his way every time."

"You're a smart woman. You'll figure it out. Besides, that's why you have a lawyer."

She looked so unhappy he put a hand on hers. "Hey. If it means that much to you, of course I'll stay with you."

She brightened. "Thank you, Brady. I know you have a million things you'd rather be doing, but I want you there watching my back."

He sighed just as Lance McMillan paused in the doorway of the barn, walking carefully so he wouldn't step in anything that might ruin his expensive shoes.

"Willow." Lance remained where he was. "I guess you didn't get my e-mail."

"I've been in the hills." She stuck out her hand.

Instead of a handshake, he leaned in to kiss her cheek.

She took a step back. "Do I have time for a shower?"

"I have less than an hour. I have another appointment scheduled out this way before I fly to Canada to take my father fishing."

"How is your father?"

"Getting older. But I think he's enjoying retirement."

"I miss him. Please give him my love."

As Lance turned toward the house, Willow waited for Brady to join her.

Seeing him, Lance raised a brow. "Morning, Storm." He turned back to Willow. "Is he thinking of joining us?"

"Yes." She kept her tone even. "Do you mind?"

"Of course not." Lance made a point of holding the back door and allowing them to enter ahead of him. "As I said, this won't take long."

The kitchen was empty, and Willow could hear laughter in the great room and the deep voice of Whit, probably telling Myrna and Cara about coming to the rescue of his mother and Brady.

As she led the way to the office, she said, "I intend to hold you to that time limit, Lance. Because after the night I put in, as soon as this meeting is over, I intend to take a very long, very hot shower."

In the big, masculine office, with its towering fireplace, rough wood shelves filled with Bear's books and memorabilia, Lance pulled his chair next to Willow's at the massive desk, while Brady chose to stand. Restless, he moved to the window, where he stood with arms crossed over his chest to stare at the hills beyond, listening to Lance as he removed half a dozen documents from his custom-tooled briefcase.

"These just require your signature, Willow."

"What are they?"

"Documents required by law, since you're now assuming the assets of Bear's trust." He pointed. "Sign here and date. And since your foreman is handy, he can be a witness."

At his words, Brady crossed the room to stand slightly behind Willow.

As she accepted Lance's pen, Brady said, "You'll want to read those before signing."

She glanced up. "Yes. I suppose I should."

Lance set a second document on top of the first, and then a third on top of that. "If you intend to read every one of these, you'd better ask Myrna to bring your lunch on a tray. You'll be here for hours."

"That's all right." Willow smiled at him. "I have time to at least give these a quick scan before I sign them."

"I don't." Lance looked at his watch. "As I said, I have another stop to make before heading up to Canada." He pressed a finger on the line that required her signature.

Brady's tone was patient. "Why not read these at your convenience and then mail them?" He turned to Lance. "We wouldn't want to make you late for your next appointment."

Before Willow could say a word, Lance sat back and swiveled his chair to fix Brady with a look of surprise. "We?"

He turned to Willow with a look that changed to amusement. "Do you allow your foreman to overstep his bounds? Or has he been appointed your partner since the last time I was here?"

Willow ignored the documents. "Brady is here at my invitation. He was Bear's most trusted friend."

"I see. I wasn't aware of your...relationship. Like my father before me, Willow, I'm entrusted with your future, and the future of your family for, hopefully, generations to come. I can't imagine that Bear, who spent a lifetime amassing all this land and fortune, would be happy seeing you ask someone other than your life-long family counselor to make legal decisions."

"I'm certainly not disregarding your advice, Lance." Willow pushed back her chair and got to her feet. "But I think Brady's suggestion that I take the time to actually read these documents before signing them is a good idea. I'll mail them to you in a day or two."

"That's a fine idea." The lawyer scooped up all the documents and stuffed them back into his briefcase. "I'll have my assistant draft documents that you can read at your leisure."

"After studying them carefully, you'll need to take them to town to have them witnessed and dated, something we could have done here without all that trouble, since I'm authorized to witness the signature on documents." He started toward the door. "I should warn you, Willow. My father will not be pleased by the careless way you're dealing with Bear's estate."

"It's my estate, Lance. And please tell your father that I would welcome a visit from him."

The young lawyer strode out of the office.

When the door closed behind him, Willow turned to Brady. "Lance certainly didn't inherit his father's patience. His shabby treatment of you was inexcusable."

"Don't worry about my feelings, Willow." The foreman glanced out the window at the figure striding toward the waiting plane. "He's just doing his job, which is to look out for you. But he seemed hell-bent on having you sign a lot of papers without reading them. And I'm glad you held off signing until you have time to read everything. After years of working with Bear, I've never known him to sign anything without taking the time to read every word. Bear MacKenzie was a stickler for dotting every *I* and crossing every *T*. And I know for a fact that it's something he'd want you to do in his absence."

Willow gave a long, deep sigh. "I have to agree with you." She caught his hand. "Thanks for being here. I think, if I'd been alone, I would have just signed the papers and trusted Lance to see that they were delivered to the proper officials. Not that I don't trust him. We've known his father for a lifetime, and Mason has never been anything but helpful. But I doubt that Mason would have argued if I'd asked for time to read the papers before signing them."

She turned away with a thoughtful look. "I guess for now I'll just wait for Lance's assistant to send me the documents. In the meantime"—she started toward the door—"I'm going to take that long, hot shower."

Dinner was a boisterous affair, since the entire family was there.

Ash and Brenna's puppy, Sammy, lay happily under the feet of little Casey and Ethan, ready to devour any scrap of juicy steak that happened to drop from their plates.

Mad was in a rare jovial mood after spending a day at Hope Ranch with Griff and Juliet.

"Three hours in the saddle today, and not even a twinge of pain," he boasted.

"That's amazing." Willow smiled at her father-in-law across the table. "Before you know it, you'll be riding with the wranglers at roundup time."

"That's my goal." The old man winked at his grandson's wife, who had made such a radical change in his life. "Now that Juliet is a licensed therapist, she's busier than ever. I'm just glad I was able to have her all to myself when I could. Now that the word is out that she's a miracle worker, her schedule will be so crowded, she'll have no time for me."

"I'll always have time for you. And don't put this all on me. You worked your own miracles, Mad." Juliet glanced around at the others. "It isn't easy to force dormant muscles to learn to work again. It takes a person with real discipline and determination. The kind of physical transformation Mad has made requires a will of steel."

"We're not surprised," Ash deadpanned. "Everyone here knows that Mad's real name is Clark Kent."

That had everyone laughing.

Whit added to their laughter by saying, "Did all of you hear about Mom's night? She planned on driving the flatbed back to the ranch yesterday, but after all that snow melted, and the herd churned Stone Canyon into a muddy mess, the trailer was buried up to its wheels in muck. So she had to spend the night up in the hills until Brady and I could dig her out this morning."

"You're lucky it didn't rain," Cara said with a mock shiver.

"You're right." Willow turned to her. "But if it had rained, I was prepared to sleep under the flatbed to stay dry. As it turned out, it was the perfect night. I love falling asleep watching the stars. Bear and I used to make a point of bunking up in the hills whenever we could."

"You weren't afraid?" Cara asked.

"Of what?"

Cara shrugged. "I don't know. Bears. Wolves."

"They're more afraid of us than we are of them. But I had a rifle. And Brady had one, too."

Cara blinked. "Oh. I didn't realize both of you were there."

Brady grinned. "I'd planned on going up higher with the herd, but now I'm glad I decided to wait and see if Willow could drive that tractor out of the mud before I left with the wranglers."

"Not that I needed a man to protect me," Willow said in protest. "But it was nice having someone along who actually had some supplies." She turned to Myrna. "That care package you made for Brady came in handy. With coffee and biscuits, hard-boiled eggs and beef jerky, we had all the comforts of home."

The old woman looked from Willow to the foreman before saying, "Remind me to pack some fresh supplies tomorrow."

Brady shook his head. "No need. I talked with Carter today. The herd is settled. The wranglers will let me know if they need more help during calving, and I'll work here unless I hear from them."

Myrna stood. "Want to have coffee and dessert here or in the great room?"

Willow motioned to the doorway. "The great room."

Before Myrna could begin loading things onto the trolley, Cara nudged her aside. "You've done enough. Join the others and I'll bring this in."

The old woman looked absolutely delighted to do as she was asked before she walked away.

When the others were gone, Whit walked to the trolley and brushed a quick kiss over Cara's cheek.

She looked up in surprise. "What was that for?"

"Just thanking you for a great supper."

"You're welcome." She backed up when he bent close as though ready to kiss her again. "But you don't need to thank me every time. It's my job."

His smile grew. "We both know you do way more than your job. You keep spoiling Myrna like that, she'll start thinking you're after her job, too."

"Nobody could ever do all the things she does."

"You come in a close second." He brought his hands to her shoulders and felt her tremble slightly. "Cold?"

"No. I..."

"Say yes. That way I won't feel guilty about offering to warm you."

She couldn't help laughing. "You? Guilty?"

"Okay. So I won't feel guilty. But I get the feeling you're avoiding me. Why?"

"I'm not—"

"Just tell me what I've done wrong."

She shook her head. "It's not you, Whit. It's me."

"Oh no." He stepped back and lifted his hands as if to shield himself. "Whenever a woman says 'it's not you; it's me,' it means she's about to break a guy's heart." Though he spoke the words with a grin, he was watching her intently.

Cara couldn't help laughing. "I mean it. This time it's really me. I need to sort some things out. And whenever you get too close, my mind gets all muddled and I can't think."

"Whew. That's good." He wiggled his brows like a villain. "I like women who don't think."

"I think way too much. Gram used to say I overthink everything."

"I have the solution for that." He dipped his head and kissed her full on the mouth.

For a moment she stiffened, before he dragged her close and kissed her again, deeply, with great care.

Oh, why did her heart have to behave this way whenever Whit touched her? And now that he was kissing her, she wanted so much more.

She sighed and returned his kiss, pouring herself into it.

When they stepped apart, he said, "Now what are you thinking?"

"That I wouldn't mind doing that again." When he started to reach for her, she stepped back. "But not now. Your family is waiting for their dessert."

"Can we finish this later?"

She laughed. "I'll have to think about it."

"That's what I'm afraid of. It's that thinking thing again." He took hold of the trolley's handle. "I'll push this. You just hold on to a happy thought."

CHAPTER FIFTEEN

In the great room, everyone was lounging around the cozy fire. Everyone except Ethan and Casey, who were chasing little Sammy around the big sofa where Ash and Brenna were so close together they barely took up the space of one person.

Cara passed around slices of apple pie and ice cream.

Casey stopped running long enough to eye the dessert. "What's that, Cara?"

"Apple pie."

"Pie? The little boy made a face.

"Oh. You don't like pie?" Cara produced a bowl of warm cinnamon-spiced apple slices topped with a mound of whipped cream. "Would you like to taste this instead?"

Though he looked doubtful, he took a small taste before making a little hum of surprise. "Wow. That's good." He turned to his brother. "Efan, you gotta taste this."

The six-year-old looked about as happy as someone

being punished, but knowing everyone was watching, he followed suit and gave a quick taste. And then another. And another.

Both boys stopped running and settled down next to the hearth to empty their bowls, giving little Sammy time to jump up on Brenna's lap and promptly fall asleep.

When Casey and Ethan had finished their desserts, they looked over at the sleeping puppy.

Casey crossed the room and tapped a chubby finger on the pup's head. "Can Sammy wake up and play some more?"

Brenna gave him a gentle smile. "I think you and Ethan have worn him out. Look at that. He's sound asleep."

Casey looked so unhappy, everyone started grinning.

"Maybe you ought to take your cue from Sammy and think about sleeping, too," Juliet called.

"Oh, Mama. Not yet. Please," came the plaintive cry.

Whit shot a glance at Cara. "Maybe this would be a good time to try out your story on some kids who look like they need to settle down."

At his suggestion, Cara climbed the stairs to her room, returning minutes later holding her notebook.

She turned to Ethan and Casey. "How would you two like to hear the story I wrote?"

"Oh boy." Casey clapped his hands while his brother merely smiled.

Cara settled herself in a big easy chair next to the fireplace. The two boys needed no coaxing as Casey settled himself on her lap, and Ethan climbed up beside her.

She opened the notebook and pointed to the first picture. "This is a story about a girl named Arac, who lives with her grandmother on an isolated ranch in Montana, and her adventures with her magic horse, Peg."

As she turned each page, Cara read them the tale of a timid, shy little girl afraid of everything. Thunder. Lightning. Strangers. Talking in the front of a classroom. But whenever she became afraid of something, especially something she thought was dangerous, she and her magic horse would put aside their fear to fly into the thick of things, saving a boy trapped on a train track just as a train roars toward him, snatching a small child from the jaws of a mountain lion, and even dipping into a mountain stream swollen from spring runoff to save a brother and sister who had fallen in and were about to drown.

By the time she'd read the last page, Casey and Ethan had gone very quiet.

She closed the book and turned to Ethan. "Well? Did you like my story?"

He nodded. "I hope there's more. I want to be Arac and ride on the back of a flying horse."

"So did I when I was your age."

"Is that why you wrote it?"

She smiled. "I guess that's why. I used to think that if only I had a magic horse, I could do anything. And, like Arac, I was afraid of everything."

"So was Efan," Casey said. "Until a bad man stole him away from us. Then he was so brave. Weren't you, Efan?"

The six-year-old shook his head. "I was still scared. But my dad told me it's all right to be scared, as long as we do the right thing. Isn't that right, Mom?"

Juliet felt tears fill her eyes. "That's right, Ethan. And I'm glad you can finally talk about it. I've been waiting a long time for this to happen." She turned her gaze on Cara. "I think your book may give a lot of children ideas about facing their fears."

"I hope so." Cara turned to Ethan. "Now you realize that we're all afraid of something. But we all have some magic. It isn't a flying horse. It's the courage that lies inside us."

Seeing the way little Casey was fighting to stay awake, Juliet crossed the room and lifted him from Cara's lap. Over his head she said, "If you can hold the interest of these two for an entire book, I'd say you've written something wonderful. I hope you'll try to find a publisher, Cara."

And then her smile bloomed. "Cara. Arac is Cara backward, isn't it?"

Cara chuckled. "I wondered when someone would figure that out. Don't forget, I started writing this when I was just a kid. And since Arac was really me, I figured I'd just use my name, only backward."

Willow clapped her hands together. "What a clever little girl you were. Where did the horse's name come from?"

"Gram used to love it when I'd read her stories from Greek mythology. Pegasus was a winged horse. So my own flying horse became Peg."

"You should really try to get it published," Willow said emphatically.

Cara hung her head. "That was my idea. But now I think I need to face some hard truths. Dreams don't always have to come true."

"What nonsense." Mad gave a quick shake of his head. "I enjoyed your story every bit as much as the lads. And I agree with Willow. You should at least try to get it published."

Cara gave him a sad little smile. "Thank you, Mad.

Even if it never happens, just hearing you say that has made my day."

"I'm glad, lass. And now I'm heading off to my bed." The old man turned his scooter while calling over his shoulder, "If anyone can spare the time, I'd like to fly over to Hope Ranch again tomorrow. I have a lot to catch up on."

Ash stood and caught Ethan's hand. "I'll be here bright and early to fly over with you, Mad."

"Bless you, lad." The old man gave a wave of his hand as he scooted through the doorway.

The others followed, calling out their good nights. While Juliet carried Casey and Brenna carried the sleeping Sammy, Ash and Griff had their heads together, discussing how soon they thought Mad might be able to pass his test and reclaim his pilot's license.

Willow got to her feet. "I think my own bed will feel very welcome tonight."

She climbed the stairs, while Brady bid good night and made his way in the opposite direction.

Myrna stifled a yawn as she padded off to her room, leaving Whit and Cara alone.

When Cara began loading the trolley with dishes, Whit stopped her. "You've done enough."

As he began pushing the cart toward the kitchen, she trailed behind. "And you haven't?"

"I'm used to hard work. I'm afraid this is all going to catch up with you."

"Whit." She put a hand over his, stilling his movements.

When he paused to look at her, she said, "You're not obligated to help me. This is your home. I'm just working here."

"What if I wanted more than that for you?"

She took a step back. "What's that supposed to mean?"

He kept his gaze steady on hers. "I know you have dreams. And I don't want to step on them. But what if..." He chose his words carefully. "What if you had the chance to stay here? Would you?"

"Stay here? As the ranch cook?"

"Maybe more than the cook." Seeing the confusion in her eyes, he shoved the trolley roughly into the kitchen and waited for her to follow.

When she did, he turned to her. "Look, I know that you were hurt by your shabby treatment at the hands of Jared Billing—"

She lifted a hand to his mouth to halt his words. "I don't want to talk about him again. Not ever. He's a mean, cruel, selfish jerk, and I've given him way too much power over my thoughts."

"All right." He caught her hand and pressed a kiss to her palm. "Then let's talk about us."

"Us? There is no us, Whit."

"What if I want there to be?"

"You don't know me. You don't know anything about me."

"I want to. I want to know that scared little girl, and that talented artist, and the gifted chef who came along just at the right time in our lives, when we were about to lose our ranch cook. I want to know the compassionate woman who puts a glow on Myrna's face with every generous act. And most of all, I want to know the first woman ever to have me waking early every morning just so I can see her gorgeous face."

She opened her mouth, then closed it.

He gave her one of those heart-stopping smiles. "What's this? Is Cara Walton actually speechless?"

"I..." She blinked furiously to hide the tears that had sprung to her eyes. "I wasn't expecting that."

"Obviously. I'd better take advantage of the moment while I can." He reached out and gathered her close.

Against her mouth he whispered, "More than anything else, Cara Walton, I want to kiss you. I have to. Right this minute."

His lips moved over hers with a hunger that caught them both by surprise.

He lifted his head and stared down at her, all the while framing her face with his big hands and skimming his mouth over her eyes, her cheeks, the corners of her mouth, before kissing her again until they were both struggling for breath.

"Cara Walton." He whispered her name like a prayer. "What am I going to do about you?"

She stared up at him with eyes that had gone all soft with wonder. "You might try kissing me again."

"I will." His mouth roamed her face before dipping lower, to the little hollow of her throat, where her pulse was beating furiously. "But I'm not sure kissing you will be enough."

"Whit." She could barely get the words out over the feelings that were clogging her throat, making her voice a hoarse whisper.

"Shhh." He pressed a kiss to her pursed lips. "Let's not waste our time talking when we could be doing things that are much more fun."

He reached for the buttons of her shirt and opened the first, and then the second, all the while keeping his gaze fastened on her.

"Do you know that you have the most expressive

eyes?" He undid the last button of her shirt and began sliding it from her. "And, I might add, the most gorgeous body."

His lips burned a trail of fire down the long, smooth column of her throat, and then lower, across her collarbone, before dipping lower.

His voice was warm with humor. "What's this? Why, Goldilocks, you're just full of surprises, aren't you? Who would have believed that beneath that very modest shirt you wear lace?"

He reached up to unfasten the little wisp of nude lace that barely covered her breasts, freeing them for his touch.

For a moment he merely stared at her. Then, with a sigh of pure pleasure, his hands were on her, touching, tasting, until she leaned her head back, giving him easier access.

In a haze of passion, they were nearly crawling inside one another, wanting more.

Her arms were wrapped around his waist, as though to keep from sliding helplessly to the floor. He gathered her close, his mouth on hers, his big, work-worn hands moving along her back, igniting fires wherever they touched. And they touched her everywhere.

They were so lost in their own pleasure they barely heard the sound of Mad's scooter heading directly toward the kitchen.

At the last moment Whit lifted his head.

Dazed, Cara looked confused as Whit bent and scooped up her shirt.

Without a word, he eased her arms into the plaid shirt and managed two buttons before the door opened.

Both of them turned toward the sound.

Mad was smiling. "Thought I'd have the place to myself." He touched a control and rolled across the floor, reaching into a cabinet and removing the bottle of scotch.

He turned to the two, who were gaping at him in complete silence. "Going to enjoy a nightcap. Care to join me?"

Whit regained his composure first. "Thanks, Mad. I think I'll just go on up to bed now."

"Cara?" Mad held up a tumbler. "A nightcap before bed?"

She swallowed. "No, thank you, Mad. I'll just clean up here and then get out of your way."

"You're not in my way, lass. If I can't talk either of you into joining me, I'll just take this to my room."

Whit caught Cara's hand. "There's no need to clean these dishes now. Why not leave all this until morning?"

"I... suppose I could."

Whit turned to his grandfather. "Good night, Mad."

He waited until Cara followed and then closed the door behind both of them.

In the kitchen, the old man poured himself a tumbler of whiskey and took a small sip, and then another, before allowing the laughter to bubble up and spill over in a warm growl.

Oh, the sight of the two of them had told such a story. Guilt. Frustration. Humiliation.

And on the face of his grandson, a teeth-gritting determination to make the fastest getaway in history so he could continue what had been so thoroughly interrupted by a meddling old man.

He thought he'd detected a bit too much embarrassment on the face of young Cara. The lass would no doubt take a great deal of persuasion to pick up where she'd left off. His poor grandson might just have to bide his time and look for another opportunity.

And then he caught sight of a bit of lace lying on the floor where only minutes ago Whit and Cara had been standing.

He rolled closer and picked it up before setting it on the table, where Cara would be sure to find it before the others were awake in the morning. There was no point in having anyone else spot it before the lass could claim it.

His laughter rumbled up again, just thinking about what he'd interrupted.

Oh, to be that young and that caught up in the whirlwind, the chaos, the wonder and the misery of the first throes of love.

CHAPTER SIXTEEN

Long before dawn, Whit was up and dressed for chores. After the long night he'd put in, there was no point in trying to stay in bed. He needed the release of hard work.

He couldn't blame Cara for his frustration. No amount of charm could persuade her to continue what they'd begun in the kitchen. Poor Goldilocks was mortified to have been caught by Mad in such an awkward position.

Whit grimaced as he stepped into the kitchen. Though he wasn't happy about last night's intrusion, he'd been caught by Mad in embarrassing situations before and was still standing. He'd long ago learned that his grandfather's bark was worse than his bite. Besides, there had been a look in the old man's eyes. As though he knew exactly what he'd interrupted and wasn't a bit sorry for the intrusion.

Whit spied something out of place on the table and walked closer.

He stared at the lace bra, seeing in his mind the scene from the previous night. He'd barely managed to get Cara's shirt around her before the door had opened. At the time, he'd thought how clever he'd been to cover their tracks. Apparently not nearly clever enough.

He tucked the bra into his shirt pocket, to spare Cara any more embarrassment. If she knew that Mad had left this here for her, she'd be too humiliated to face him. Now, of course, he'd have to find a way to return this to her room. The perfect excuse to get her alone.

This couldn't have turned out any better if he'd planned it himself.

Whistling a little tune, he sauntered out the back door toward the barn.

As he began his chores, he found himself grinning. Last night he'd gone to bed thinking how clever he'd been to look cool and collected in front of his grandfather, and all along, Mad had known exactly what he'd interrupted.

That sly old fox. There wasn't much that got by the old man.

Cara heard the door shut and sat up in alarm.

She'd hoped to be up ahead of everyone, but after a night of tossing and turning, she'd finally fallen asleep, only to wake later than usual.

After a quick shower, she dressed and hurried down the stairs to start breakfast.

She set thick slabs of ham on the grill, along with sourdough bread, before slicing mushrooms, onions, tomatoes, and cheddar cheese for the omelets she was planning.

Along with the freshly squeezed orange juice, she set out tall, frothy glasses of milk and a carafe of coffee.

By the time the others began gathering around the big harvest table, the room was perfumed with the wonderful fragrance of a hearty breakfast.

"Well. Good morning, lass." Mad steered his scooter through the doorway and reached for a mug of steaming coffee.

"Morning, Mad." Cara slipped her hands into oven mitts to remove fresh cinnamon rolls.

"This place smells heavenly," Willow called as she helped herself to a glass of orange juice.

"It's the cinnamon." Cara drizzled a sweet glaze over the rolls before setting them on a plate.

"It's everything." Willow put a hand on Cara's shoulder as she moved to her place at the table. "You certainly know your way around a kitchen."

"Thanks." For the first time, Cara looked up and caught Mad watching her.

Taking a deep breath, she smiled and walked closer. "What can I get you, Mad?"

"Nothing, lass." He paused a beat, about to say more, when Whit stepped into the mudroom and began washing at the big sink.

Cara turned, fascinated, as always, by the sight of all those muscles straining the sleeves of his shirt. She was reminded of last night and the way those arms had felt holding her close. What a temptation he was turning out to be.

It wasn't just that toned body. It was the whole package, she thought. The hair, in need of a trim, curled over the collar of his shirt, with an errant lock that spilled over his forehead as he bent his head. It was those long, lanky legs in faded denims. That hard, flat stomach under the plaid shirt that was never quite tucked in. And the quirky humor always there in his eyes.

Whit strolled into the kitchen. Though he called out a greeting to all, his gaze never left Cara, causing her cheeks to burn. When Myrna started to pass through the room with an armload of laundry, Cara stopped her in midstride and relieved her of her burden, grateful for the distraction of Whit's knowing look.

When Myrna was seated at the table, Cara began passing around platters of food.

"Did I hear you up early, lad?" Mad helped himself to an omelet and a thick slab of ham.

"Yeah. Figured I'd get an early start before lending a hand to Brady with that equipment."

Brady held the platter for Willow before filling his own plate. "No need, Whit. I thought the motor of the backhoe had seized up, but I just tried it and it started up without a problem. So I guess it was just a temporary thing."

"Good. Are we heading up to the herd today?"

"I'd like to wait a day or so. For once, the calving is going smoothly without our help."

"Great. That's all good news." Whit devoured an omelet, two slices of ham, and three pieces of sourdough toast before sitting back and sipping coffee.

He turned to Cara, seated beside him. "I think you're spoiling us, Goldilocks."

Myrna looked over with an arched brow. "Why do you call her that?"

Whit grinned. "When I found her in the range shack, she was sleeping in the lower bunk and using the upper bunk as a clothesline. I told her she was sleeping in my bed, and claimed the bottom bunk."

"Not a very friendly introduction," Willow remarked.

"Not at all friendly." Cara sipped her orange juice. "Especially since he came in like a wounded bear, all bearded like some kind of mountain man and bristling with temper after a long, hard day on the trail."

"Weren't you afraid?" Myrna asked.

"Yes. But I certainly didn't want him to know that."

"Which is why she told me she was armed. Only her weapon turned out to be a broom handle stuck against my back."

That had everyone's attention.

Mad was grinning. "Sounds like you two are evenly matched."

Whit returned his grandfather's wicked smile. "I let her think so."

"Oh. Right. Don't act all soft and weak on my account." Cara slapped his arm before getting up and retrieving the coffee.

While she circled the table filling their cups, Ash walked in.

"I hope I'm not too late for breakfast."

"There's plenty." Cara hurried over to fetch a place setting before handing him a cup of coffee.

Willow seemed disappointed. "Brenna isn't with you?"

"Not today. She's out in her studio working on her latest project."

"Studio?" Intrigued, Cara's head came up.

"She's a sculptor. Does beautiful work." Ash's tone was filled with pride as he stabbed at a slab of ham.

Willow pointed to the sculpture of Bear astride a horse, waving his hat with one hand, holding the reins with the other. "That's some of Brenna's work."

"Oh. That's just gorgeous." Cara shook her head. "I've noticed it there, but I never dreamed Brenna made that."

Mad sat back, enjoying the last of his cinnamon roll and coffee. "The MacKenzie men pride themselves on marrying strong, talented women."

"And why not?" Willow smiled at her father-in-law. "You set the bar pretty high with your Maddie. She was unique."

"That she was, lass. One of a kind. And I was the lucky man to win her heart."

Ash dug into his breakfast. "You told me once, Mad, that her father made the two of you wait an entire year without seeing one another, hoping to discourage you from pursuing his daughter."

"He did. And then the old codger tried to add another year, but Madeline was having none of it. She told him he could either approve her choice of husband or miss watching his grandchildren grow up. In our day, it took real courage for a lass to stand up to her father like that."

Caught up in the tale, Cara rested her chin on her hands and regarded him across the table. "What did her father choose?"

"He sent us away without his blessing. Months later he packed up all he could in a wagon and showed up at our cabin, where he promptly built his own place next door so he could be part of our lives."

"Did he ever fully accept you?"

The old man gave a roar of laughter. "Not only accepted me, but also became a lifelong friend."

Ash polished off the last of his meal. "If we're going to fly to Griff's place, we'd better get moving, Mad. I promised Brenna I'd be back by supper time."

"I'm ready, lad." The old man fixed Cara with a look. "Another fine meal, lass. But I'm not surprised. You do everything well."

He turned his scooter. As he passed Whit, he muttered, "You might want to check your pocket."

Whit looked down to see a wispy lace strap poking out of his shirt pocket. He quickly pushed it down and out of sight.

With a wink, his grandfather turned his scooter and followed Ash out the door and along the wooden walkway that had been built to accommodate his infirmity.

Whit strolled into the kitchen, pleased to find Cara alone, polishing the counters and tabletop.

He glanced around. "Where's Myrna?"

"Upstairs. She said since I have everything covered down here, she'll catch up on some of the household chores."

"Do you have a lot to do?"

"Not that much. Why?"

"I'm planning on riding up in the hills. Not all the way to the highlands, but just around the northern perimeter, checking fences. Do you ride?"

"I'm a Montana girl, remember? I didn't grow up on a ranch, but all my friends had horses, so I had plenty of chances to ride."

"Good. Want to keep me company?"

She couldn't hide her surprise and delight at the chance to get away from the kitchen for a few hours. "I'd love it. But I don't want some frisky mount that thinks it's fun to toss his rider."

Whit chuckled. "I think I can come up with a horse

that's rider-friendly. Meet me in the barn." He looked her up and down. "And you might want to exchange those sneakers for some leather boots."

She looked down at her feet. "I don't have anything else."

"Check the mudroom. There are plenty of cowboy boots out there. Maybe something of Mom's will fit you."

"She won't mind?"

He grinned. "Now that she has two daughters-in-law, she's used to having her stuff borrowed. I'd say, from her reaction, she loves having some females around after a lifetime of all guys."

"Yeah. That would be a trial for any woman to bear."

"Hey. Watch it, Goldilocks." He was grinning as he started out the door.

Minutes later, Cara put away her cleaning supplies and made her way to the mudroom, where, just as Whit had predicted, there were shelves filled with all sizes of leather boots.

After trying on a couple, she found a pair that fit her comfortably. As she was leaving, she spied a row of denim and leather jackets hanging on pegs. With a glance at the sunshine streaming in the windows, she helped herself to a denim jacket, in case the weather turned, before hurrying toward the barn.

Whit was leading two horses into the sunlight.

"This is Dumpling. Mom named her because she was so fat when she was born, and so pale, she said she looked like one of Myrna's dumplings."

"Hello, Dumpling." Cara ran a hand over the mare's forelock. "You're not going to toss me out of the saddle, are you, girl?"

As if in reply, the mare gave a quick shake of her head, causing both Whit and Cara to laugh out loud.

"See?" Whit held the bridle and gave Cara a boost into the saddle. "She outgrew her baby fat, and Dumpling is a perfect lady."

"I'll hold you to that." Cara watched as he climbed easily into the saddle and turned his mount toward the hills in the distance.

Dumpling followed, without any direction from Cara, allowing her to release any tension she'd been feeling as she enjoyed the ride.

CHAPTER SEVENTEEN

It was one of those clear, cloudless spring days. With the snow gone, Cara found herself admiring the deep blue of the sky and the soft green of the grass beginning to sprout all around them.

There was no trail, so the horses could walk comfortably abreast as they began their trek up the hill.

Whit pointed to a bird in the distance, circling overhead. "See that eagle? I'm betting he's already spotted his lunch. Watch."

Just as he said that, the bird skyrocketed to earth with such speed, it looked as though it would crash headfirst into the ground. Instead it lifted high, holding a squealing little animal in its talons.

Cara shuddered and looked away in horror. "That poor thing."

"That poor thing will probably feed two or three babies in Mama's nest."

"I know. Still, it's terrible to see."

"Nature isn't always gentle breezes and pretty flowers."

She turned to him. "I suppose ranchers are more in tune with nature than most people."

"Everything we do is at the mercy of nature. Helpless calves are born just when hungry wolves are fighting to feed their own young. A baby eagle has lunch, at the expense of a mother rabbit's newborn. But somehow, it all evens out. Sometimes we just have to step back and let Mother Nature have her way. An extended bitter winter could decimate a wolf pack, allowing more time for our calves to survive those first hours after birth. A long, wet summer can grow lush grass that will fatten our herds and our profits at the end of a season."

As they came over a ridge, he pointed to the creek, its banks filled to overflowing with rushing water. "There's Copper Creek."

"So that's how the town got its name."

He nodded. "In spring, the runoff from the surrounding mountains causes it to overflow. By late summer, unless we get more than an average rainfall, it will be little more than a muddy creek."

As they neared the banks, Whit dismounted and Cara followed suit.

She caught a glimpse of his face and was startled by the change in him. His sunny smile had been replaced by a dark, tormented look.

His tone became hushed, almost reverent. "This is where a cowardly gunman killed my father."

"Oh, Whit." Stunned, Cara laid a hand on his arm. "I'm so sorry. I didn't realize it had happened right here."

There was a bleak look in his eyes as he led his horse along the grassy banks.

Cara fell back, keeping her silence, allowing him his space. The reverence she sensed in Whit had her feeling as though she were in a great cathedral.

"This is the spot." Whit dropped to one knee to study the crude, weathered cross he and his brothers had made just weeks after the funeral.

Beside him, Cara tethered her horse in the shade of a giant oak, allowing him to grieve in private.

He buried his face in his hands and for long minutes his shoulders shook, revealing the depth of his pain.

It was a shock seeing a strong man like Whit reduced to tears. Tears that were torn from his throat as he gave a low moan of pain.

The sight of him, torn and broken, and the sound of his torment, pulled at Cara's tender heart.

The longer he remained on his knees, flattened by his grief, the more desperate she became to comfort him.

She understood the grief of loss. And knew what it was to have no one to turn to.

When she could no longer stand by, feeling helpless, she dropped down beside him. His eyes, when he looked at her, were filled with such sorrow, all she could do was wrap her arms around his neck.

"We shouldn't have come here, Whit. I had no idea how deeply you're still grieving."

"I'm not sure it will ever end." He took a deep, shuddering breath, taking comfort from the feel of her arms around him. "What hurts the most is not knowing who killed Pop. I want the cowardly bastard who did this to pay for the pain he caused our family."

She drew him closer. "The authorities will find him, Whit. You have to trust that good always wins out over evil."

He got slowly to his feet before helping Cara to stand beside him.

A single tear shimmered at the corner of his eye.

With great tenderness, she stood on tiptoe and touched her mouth to the spot. "Oh, Whit. I hate that you and your family have to suffer like this."

He went very still.

Misreading his silence, she wrapped her arms around his waist and rested her head on his shoulder to offer him comfort. "I know how devastated I was when Gram passed away." Her words were spoken against the tender flesh of his throat. "But at least she died peacefully, of old age. But to be forced to deal with not only the loss of your father, but also to have him taken so violently, just breaks my heart for you."

"Cara..." He took a step back and put his hands on her shoulders as though to hold her at arm's length. "I know you mean well, but my feelings are too raw. I think..." He tried again, his tone gruff with emotion. "I think you'd better move away from me. You don't want to be around me when I'm in a mood like this."

She looked up, meeting his smoldering gaze. "You're wrong, Whit. Don't send me away. I sense your pain. I want to share it." She lifted both hands to his frame his face and took in a breath for courage. "Let me comfort you."

"You don't understand." Now his words were low with temper. He lifted her chin, forcing her to meet his hot, fierce look. "My mood is all tangled right now. I'm sad and I'm furious. And yes, maybe I'm hungry for comfort, and I'm grateful for your offer. But you need to get away from me. Now. My mood is too dark. There would be no giving on my part. Only taking. Right now, I'm not capable of tenderness. And once I start down this road, there won't be time for second thoughts. And afterward, with all you've been through, you could hate yourself and hate me as well."

All her senses were heightened as she continued staring into those stormy eyes. "I understand, Whit. I know I've made wrong choices in the past. But I've learned from them. I'm not afraid. Please let me comfort you. It's all I can give."

He swore. "Don't you see? I have no tenderness in my heart right now. In this temper, there's no going back when you have a change of heart. And believe me, you will change your mind when you see me in this kind of mood."

Instead of drawing away, she pressed her mouth to his. "I'm not going anywhere, Whit."

It was her goodness, her simple, generous spirit that was his undoing.

"Oh God, Cara."

And then, without another word, he covered her mouth with his in a kiss that was all heat and flash and fury. A kiss so all-consuming, it rocked her back on her heels.

His arms came around her, holding her when she would have surely swayed. And then his mouth was moving over hers with such hunger, she could feel herself wanting to give and give until they were both sated.

It never occurred to her to resist or to ask for time to think through what she was doing. At this moment it all seemed so right. So good. It was all she could give him.

And she wanted desperately to give him the comfort he craved.

And then all thought was wiped from her mind as his hands, those wonderful, clever, work-roughened hands, were holding her with a possessiveness that stole her will. Hands that moved over her, while his mouth continued working its magic.

She couldn't seem to catch her breath. With the urgency of each kiss, her fingers curled into the front of his shirt, pulling him closer. And then all she could do was cling.

His hands were almost bruising as he dragged her against him and plundered her mouth.

She absorbed the rush of heat, the quick, jittery charge to her system as his mouth moved almost savagely over hers, taking each kiss deeper, taking them both higher.

She could feel the heat building with each kiss, each touch. For so long now she'd thought about this. Just this. The rush of pure adrenaline. The feel of his hard, muscled body teasing her. It was unbearably arousing. And yet, she'd resisted the very thing she'd wanted for so long.

She moaned as he changed the angle of the kiss. Her blood heated and pulsed through her veins as his hands moved over her, touching her at will.

She offered her lips, her body, even as she took from him. Her fingers tangled in his hair as she struggled to crawl inside his skin. His wildly beating heart had her own keeping time, while she fought for breath.

"I warned you. I can't be gentle." The words were ground out inside her mouth.

"I don't need gentle, Whit. I just want to give. Take all

you can from me, until your pain is gone. It's what I want. What you need."

For the space of a heartbeat, he went very still, as though too touched by her admission to act on it. Then, very slowly, he framed her face with his hands and kissed her.

This kiss was different from all the others. A kiss that conveyed, on the deepest level, a need like no other. She felt a sense of strength, a surge of power that had her pouring everything into her response. She drank in the dark, purely masculine taste of him. On his lips she could taste his sorrow, his passion, and more, his reckless abandon. It was his recklessness that excited her. It gave her a sense of freedom to release whatever last vestige of fear she'd been harboring. She had but one thought. She would give this man everything that was in her power to give and hope it was enough to fill the hole in his heart.

With the passion unleashed, all she could do now was hold on as he took her on the ride of her life.

"I remember that first night." His words were a low growl as he reached for the buttons of her shirt, keeping his gaze steady on hers as he nearly ripped it aside in his haste.

Beneath it she wore a pale pink silk bra that revealed more than it covered.

He gave a dangerous smile as he unfastened her denim jeans and slid them down her thighs to reveal a matching pink thong. "I remember this even more, Goldilocks. Are you wearing this just to make things harder?" His smile widened. "Not that anything could make me harder than I am right now."

He gathered her against him and brushed slow, nibbling kisses down her neck, across her shoulder, before burrowing his mouth in the sensitive hollow of her throat.

Before she could respond, he lowered his mouth to her breast. At his touch, her nipple beneath the silk hardened instantly.

Annoyed with even that small barrier between them, he unhooked her bra and let it drift to the ground before he allowed his gaze to travel the length of her and back before lowering his head to her breast.

With a moan of pleasure, she let her head fall back, giving him easier access as he suckled first one breast and then the other, pleasuring them both.

"Cara."

At the sound of her name, she nearly shredded his shirt while struggling to remove it. He helped her, tossing it aside before the rest of his clothes joined hers in a heap at their feet.

Oh, how she'd longed to see this fabulous body. To run her hands over his chest, to feel the muscles of his arms as they wrapped around her.

She felt a ripple of excitement as she slid her palms down his torso, to the flat planes of his stomach, then lower, to touch him as he was touching her.

In his eyes was a fierce, hungry look that had her breath backing up in her throat.

"Whit." His name was torn from her mouth.

No one had ever touched her like this before. With lips and tongue and fingertips. One moment so gently she wanted to weep, and the next creating a frantic rush of desperate need that had her pulse speeding up. Taking her higher than she'd ever been without release. Faster, farther, until she wanted to beg him to never stop.

She followed his lead, feasting on his mouth, that warm, wonderful mouth that was giving her such pleasure. Her fingers were tangled in his hair when he gave a guttural moan.

They took each other on a wild, fast ride.

"I've lost all control, Goldilocks. There's no stopping now. I have to have you. Now. Now."

"Yes." Her heart was thundering. She couldn't bear another minute without release from this madness.

He lifted her off her feet and wrapped her legs around him as he thrust her backward against the trunk of a tree.

She took no notice of the way the rough bark scraped her flesh as she offered herself completely.

For a moment they both went very still.

"Open your eyes, Cara." His words were a harsh, ragged whisper.

Her lids flickered and she struggled to focus on him through a glaze of white-hot passion.

"Whit."

"I love hearing you say my name, Cara. Cara. My beautiful Cara."

"Whit. Whit."

He thrust himself into her with a fierceness that had their hearts pumping, their breathing harsh and ragged.

And then they began to move, to climb, to cling. With incredible strength they moved higher, then higher still, lungs straining as they climbed to the very top of a high, sheer cliff.

They were beyond words now. Beyond thought. Beyond anything of this world as they felt themselves slipping over the edge and soaring until they touched the very center of the sun.

Their shattering climax had them breaking into millions of tiny flaming pieces before drifting back to earth.

They stood, locked together, their bodies slick, their hearts thundering.

Whit's face was buried against her throat. He found himself wondering what had just happened. He couldn't remember a time when he'd been so out of control that he'd lost all direction.

He'd wanted this. Thought of nothing but this since he'd first seen Cara that night at the range shack. But he'd never expected to feel this. As though he'd been run over by a truck, and yet couldn't wait to be run over again.

And there was more. He was feeling...crazy happy. Here in this sad, haunted place, he wanted to shout to the world that he'd found something wonderful. Someone special.

She was...incredible. Amazing. Magic.

That was it. This woman was magic. She'd bewitched him. And instead of being afraid of her power, he was enchanted by it. Sucked in. Addicted. Intrigued.

In love.

Never.

Hadn't he vowed he would never get all sappy and stupid like his brothers?

All right. Not in love. It was just...lust. That thought seemed to steady him. He was in lust. And he wanted more of it.

It gave him little comfort, but it would have to do for now, until he could find his brain.

He eased her gently to her feet, then lowered both of

them to the cool, damp grass. It wasn't enough to cool their fevered flesh.

Leaning up on one elbow, he touched her face. "You all right?"

"Mmm-hmm."

He grinned. "I guess that's yes."

"Mmm."

"Sorry. Really sorry." His tone was a low growl of guilt. "I didn't mean to be so rough."

"We both were."

"But I'm bigger. I shouldn't have been so rough. I could've hurt—"

"You were fine."

"Really?" He looked down at the dazed smile on her lips. "You look the way I feel."

"Is that good?"

"Very good." He paused a moment before saying, "You know you're too tenderhearted for your own good. If you hadn't gone all soft and mushy about my grief, we might have made it home without…this."

"Are you sorry?"

"Hell no." He gave her one of those sexy grins. "You just made my day, Goldilocks."

"You didn't call me that a few minutes ago."

"I didn't? What did I call you?"

"My beautiful Cara." Her voice sounded all soft and dreamy.

"I must have lost my mind for a moment."

"Yeah. Just for a moment."

He brushed his lips over hers. "I wouldn't mind losing it again."

"Are you saying…now?"

"Well, yeah." He kissed the tip of her nose. "If you're not too exhausted."

"Don't you know that women are always ready? It's men who sometimes need time before they can…go for seconds."

"Not this man."

"Are you sure you're not just bragging, Cowboy?"

"I never make a claim I can't back up."

Before she could say more, he rolled her on top of him. Her hair fell forward, tickling his chest.

As she wiggled around, she suddenly went very still. "Oh."

He was laughing. "Told you."

He touched a finger to her mouth, still swollen from his kisses. "I never meant to be so rough. I was in a strange mood."

"I know." She brushed a lock of hair from his forehead. "You were so sad. And I needed to comfort you."

"Needed. That's a pretty strong word, Goldilocks."

"It's what I felt."

He brushed a kiss over her lips. "Know what I'm feeling right now?"

"Tell me."

"Better yet, let me show you."

And then there was no need for words as they took each other again.

This time, instead of a heated rush, it was a slow, easy, lazy and oh-so-tender dance of love, filling them with quiet whispers of tenderness and healing their wounded hearts.

Chapter Eighteen

"I like your family."

Whit and Cara lay in the grass along the banks of Copper Creek, pleasantly sated. Whit had pulled on his faded denims, though he was still shirtless and barefoot. Cara wore his shirt, which fell below her knees.

"I can tell that they like you, too."

"Who's older? Ash or Griff?"

"Griff by a year or more."

"When I saw the portrait of your father, I thought at first it was Griff."

He gave a dry laugh. "The first time I saw Griff, I thought I was seeing a ghost."

At her raised brow, he filled her in on the family history.

"But your mother seems so…comfortable around Griff. It never dawned on me that he wasn't her son."

"I guess that's just about the best compliment you

could give her. Believe me, she was stunned when she learned that Pop had a son. According to Mason McMillan, so was Pop."

"Who is Mason McMillan?"

"An old friend of my father's who has been our family lawyer for a lifetime. He recently retired, and his son, Lance, has taken over his law firm." Whit stroked Cara's arm as he looked out over the waters of the creek. "I was so mad when I first heard the news about Griff. It was like a sucker punch. And then, when Mason told us that Pop had included this stranger in the will, I was blindsided."

"How did your mother react to the news?"

"Like Mom always does. Whatever emotions she was feeling, she kept them to herself. And then we met Griff, and everything changed." He smiled down at Cara. "Not overnight. But gradually. Griff is so damned decent, it's hard not to like him. And with that face, every time one of us looks at him, we see our dad. It was impossible not to accept him as family."

She sat up, shaking her head. "That's so... amazing. But I'm not surprised. The more I know about your family, the more I admire them."

He lifted both hands to her face, his fingers tangling through her hair. "And, Goldilocks, the more I know about you, the more I want to know." He brushed kisses over her upturned face. "Want to go for thirds?"

She gave a playful smack of his hands. "Glutton."

But she was grinning and practically purring as she said it.

It was late afternoon by the time Whit and Cara arrived back at the barn.

As he led their horses toward their stalls, Cara touched his shoulder. "I'd better get inside and start supper or your family will starve."

He was grinning. "I'd much rather be back at Copper Creek, living on love."

"You won't say that when you taste the meal I'm planning." She hurried away.

A short time later, she heard the sound of the Cessna circling overhead before it came in for a landing.

She watched through the window as the little airplane taxied to the big barn that served as a hangar. Minutes later she saw Ash, Juliet, and Griff striding alongside Mad's scooter, while the two little boys sat happily on the old man's lap.

Ash followed the others inside and poked his head through the doorway to call a greeting to Cara. "Hey, I thought I'd warn you that Brenna's on her way to join us for supper. You're going to have the whole family here tonight."

"Great." She lifted a sack of potatoes from the pantry. "Dinner in less than an hour."

"Is Auntie Brenna bringing Sammy?" little Casey called.

"You bet." Ash ruffled the boy's hair. "He'd be lonely if we left him behind."

The family crowded around inside the big room, enjoying the fire on the hearth and helping themselves to the appetizers Cara set out.

Whit strolled in from the barn, followed by Willow and Brady.

Whit helped himself to a longneck before pausing beside their foreman. "You'll be glad to hear that the fences are in good shape after so much snow this winter."

"That's good news." Brady winked at Willow. "Did you check the south pasture?"

Whit shook his head. "I didn't get that far. Figured I'd save that for another day."

"Too busy down by the creek?"

Something in his tone had Whit looking at him a little more closely. "Yeah. I was down by the creek."

"I thought I saw a pair of horses there."

Whit avoided looking at Cara, though he could see, out of the corner of his eye, the way she paused to turn toward Brady and the others. "I invited Cara to join me for a ride."

"A good day for a ride." The foreman's voice was tinged with humor. "Actually, it's a good day for just about anything."

Whit drank his beer, aware that his grandfather had turned to study him. As casually as he could manage, he turned away. "Guess I'll grab a shower before supper."

As he passed Cara, he squeezed her arm. Then squared his shoulders and ambled away.

Across the room, Brady winked at Mad, and the two men shared a smile.

Dinner was a noisy affair.

Sammy lay under the table, panting from having chased a ball tossed by two busy little boys for the past hour. He lifted his head only when scraps of roast beef managed to land nearby.

Juliet was singing the praises of Mad, who had not only ridden across the fields for hours, but had also passed his latest pilot's test with flying colors.

"Do you realize you'll be the first patient treated at

Hope Ranch to resume both your ranch chores and your pilot skills?"

Mad sat back, beaming with pride. "If someone had told me a year ago that my life would be so drastically changed, I'd have called it a lie."

"Mama says lying is bad," Casey said solemnly.

Everyone around the table smiled.

"That it is, lad. But I'd have never believed I could do the things I'm now able to do." Mad turned to Brenna. "What are you working on in your studio, lass?"

"A statue of Dr. Mullin. He's celebrating twenty-five years here in Copper Creek, and his assistant Kate asked me to do something special."

"I'm sure it will be, lass." Mad turned to Cara. "And since we're giving out compliments, you deserve one for this roast beef. It's so tender, it falls off the bone."

"I'm glad you like it, Mad."

"Tell me about your day, lass."

Cara felt her cheeks flush. "I rode along with Whit while he checked the fences."

"I hope you weren't too bored," Willow remarked as she sipped her coffee.

"Oh no. Not at all." Aware that her cheeks were growing hotter by the minute, Cara ducked her head. But not before she saw Whit grinning beside her. That only made her flush more.

"Well, next time you go riding, let me know." Willow glanced over. "Nothing makes me happier than riding across these hills."

"I'll... Yes." At a loss for words, Cara got to her feet. "Is anyone ready for dessert?"

"Let's take it in the great room." Willow stood and led the way, with the others trailing behind.

At the kitchen counter, Cara let out a long, deep sigh of relief.

"You handled that pretty well."

At Whit's voice, she looked over in alarm. "Do you think Brady saw us?"

Whit shrugged. "It doesn't matter."

"Doesn't matter?" She looked outraged. "There we were, rolling around in the grass in our birthday suits, and someone may have been watching."

Whit couldn't help laughing at her choice of words. "You can't bring yourself to say naked, can you?"

Before she could protest more, he walked toward her. "Goldilocks, Brady's not just someone. He's a good guy. Whatever he saw or didn't see, it will be his secret."

"I don't want to be anyone's secret."

He caught her hand. "I just mean that Brady's a very old-fashioned cowboy. If he happened to come upon something he shouldn't be seeing, he's the type of man who would turn away without investigating further."

Cara lowered her head. "Am I making too much of this?"

Whit gathered her into his arms. "My family can be overwhelming. We're loud and rough and we pretty much say what we're thinking." He lifted her chin, forcing her to meet his gaze. "But think of it this way. You've got a lot of people on your side, Goldilocks. If any big, bad bears come charging through the woods, we've all got your back."

She was laughing as he lowered his head and kissed her. She kissed him back. "Thanks. I needed that."

The two stepped apart when the door opened and Myrna walked into the kitchen. "Do you need any help?"

Cara's face flamed.

Whit shook his head. "Thanks, Myrna. Cara and I can manage."

The old woman merely smiled and turned away, calling over her back, "Of course you can."

Cara gave him a weak smile. "Caught again."

"Which just proves one thing."

She waited.

Whit was laughing as he began filling the trolley with cups and plates. "Our only hope for privacy is to head back to the range shack up in the hills."

"Where we'd find ourselves bunking with a dozen wranglers tending the herds."

"Yeah. There is that." He waited while she went to fetch the dessert and coffee.

Leading the way to the great room, he whispered, "There's always the hay loft. Back in our teen years, Ash and I managed to hide a few hot babes up there after dark."

She burst into laughter. "Why am I not surprised?"

"Neither was Brady. But I don't think he ever ratted us out to Pop."

They were still laughing like conspirators as they passed around cups of steaming coffee, liberally laced with whiskey for the men, and slices of fresh strawberry shortcake mounded with whipped cream.

Afterward, both Casey and Ethan begged Cara to read her story to them again. And when she'd finished reading it three times, they were still talking about the adventures of Arac and Peg and wishing they could join them in some of their wild rides through the countryside.

It was Juliet who spoke up first. "You really need to think about having a publisher read your story, Cara."

"That's my dream."

"Then do it, lass." Mad fixed her with a stern look. "No dream ever gets realized until you act on it."

Willow nodded. "If Mad hadn't come out to this wilderness, against the advice of everyone, none of this would be here."

"And I'd've never met my sweet Maddie. I'd be nothing more than a lonely old man now, dreaming of what might have been. So listen, lass, when I tell you to follow your dream. I know what I'm talking about."

Cara's smile bloomed. "My gram always told me to listen to my elders."

"Your grandmother sounds like a smart woman."

As the conversation resumed, Cara sat back, running her hand lovingly over the dog-eared notebook. If she'd learned anything from Jared and his spoiled, selfish attitude, it was that chasing dreams at any cost could cause a lot of pain and humiliation.

Still, old dreams died hard.

Maybe she'd give it one more try. But only because this family was so persistent.

Chapter Nineteen

Thank you for coming all this way, Miss Walton." Sheriff Todd Hack shook Cara's hand as he walked her to the outer office where Whit was waiting.

She paused. "I hope I was helpful."

The lawman nodded.

He'd been a state police officer for nearly fifteen years, before deciding to accept the offer to move his wife and family to the small town of Red Rock.

"This is our first murder case since I've been sheriff, and I'm not happy that it hasn't been neatly resolved. I was sure Abe's nephew was guilty as sin, but there are enough doubts about his guilt or innocence that the state's attorney general isn't ready to issue an arrest order. So any new leads are appreciated. I intend to look very carefully into everything you said."

"I wish I could have told you more."

"Believe me, Miss Walton, every bit of evidence, no matter how insignificant, will be taken seriously."

Whit caught Cara's hand as the two walked to his truck.

As he drove the hundred miles back to Copper Creek, he saw Cara checking her cell phone.

"Did you tell Sheriff Hack about those threatening texts?"

"Yes." She sighed. "I knew when I agreed to meet with him that I would have to be honest about everything, including that entire mess with Jared. Sheriff Hack asked my permission to forward all the threatening texts to the state police crime lab, and now Jared will be asked some very embarrassing questions."

"Why are you unhappy about that?"

"Because it points out even more clearly how many unwise decisions I've made. Someone like Jared Billingham won't be happy to be interviewed by the police. I'm sure he'll want to get revenge. It will be just one more reason for Jared to muddy my name if he chooses to."

Whit's eyes narrowed behind his sunglasses. "Don't be too sure of that. I'm thinking Billingham won't want his shabby treatment of you to become public knowledge."

"I left him in a huff, without a replacement as food manager."

"And he caused you a great deal of pain. Don't be sorry that he's now being dragged into an investigation. He brought it on himself by sending threatening texts." He reached for her hand. "Don't give that jerk another thought. He isn't worth it."

Cara stared out the window, taking comfort in Whit's hand holding hers. It was funny how everything seemed simple and safe when she was with him. Now, if only it were true and not just some foolish, romantic illusion.

Willow stepped out of the ranch truck and looked up at the sound of a plane's engine. Shading her eyes, she watched the sleek silver plane circling over the barn in preparation for landing.

She turned to Brady, who tossed a sack of grain over his shoulder as though it weighed no more than a feather pillow. "Lance is here. You'll join us?" At his slight hesitation, she added, "Please."

Brady nodded. "I'll come to your office in a few minutes."

As he strode away, she remained by the back porch, watching as Lance stepped from the plane and made his way to the house. In his hand was the ever-present briefcase.

He seemed impatient as he pressed a kiss to her cheek. "You got my e-mail?"

"Yes. How is your father?"

"He's fine. We had a good visit. Fished every day. He's becoming quite the retiree. He built a fish table at the end of the dock and can filet a fish like a gourmet chef. He's looking better than I've ever seen him."

"I'm so glad he's enjoying retirement." She tucked her arm through his and led him inside, where Myrna was sorting the never-ending laundry.

The old woman looked up with a smile. "Would you like coffee?"

"That would be grand." Willow turned to Lance. "How about you?"

He nodded.

Myrna began placing a creamer and sugar bowl on a round wooden tray. "You two go along, and I'll bring this in a minute."

"Thank you, Myrna." Willow led the way down the hallway toward her office.

Minutes later, Cara emerged from the pantry. "I found these lasagna noodles. Guess what I'm thinking of making tonight?"

"Lasagna sounds great." Myrna filled a carafe with coffee.

Cara looked over. "Where are you taking that?"

"Willow's office. She's in there with her lawyer." The old woman wrinkled her nose. "More documents. Poor thing. She's sick to death of having to sign things since Bear passed away."

Cara reached for the tray. "This is too heavy for you, Myrna. I'll take it."

Just then, Brady walked in. After washing at the sink in the mudroom, he took the tray from Cara's hands. "For Willow?"

She nodded.

"Since I'm going there anyway, there's no need for you to bother."

"Thanks, Brady." Cara found her cheeks flushed, even though the foreman had given her no reason to feel embarrassed. Every time she thought about how boldly she and Whit had behaved down by the creek, believing themselves alone in the universe, she found herself blushing all over again.

She was grateful when the foreman disappeared down the hall with the tray of coffee.

* * *

"Just need your signature here and here and—" Lance looked up as Brady stepped into the office.

"Afternoon, Lance." Brady set the tray down on a corner of the big desk. "Coffee?"

"You taking over the household duties as well as wrangling, Brady?" At his joke, Lance shot a quick smile at Willow.

"Just saving Myrna and Cara from having to carry this."

"Cara? I haven't heard that name before." Lance turned to Willow. "A new hire?"

"Cara Walton. A friend of Whit's. They met up in the hills."

"In the hills? Is her ranch nearby?"

"No. She was just...passing through. She's turning out to be a real gift to all of us. The girl can cook like a pro."

The lawyer poured himself a cup of coffee and inhaled the fragrance before taking a sip. "Hey, that's good. Freshly ground beans. A hint of vanilla."

"Now you're the one sounding like a pro. A professional barista," Willow said with a laugh.

"I know my coffee. I couldn't function all day without it. Especially after the day I put in today."

"I thought you were coming from a relaxing visit with your father."

"That ended early." His eyes narrowed. "I had another appointment before coming here."

"And not a pleasant one, from your tone." Willow watched as the young lawyer took another long drink before returning his attention to the documents spread out in front of them on the desktop.

"As I was saying, Willow, sign here and here and on this one as well."

At Brady's arched brow, Willow took a seat behind the desk and began to read each document.

She looked up. "Are these the same ones you brought last week?"

Lance nodded. "I had my assistant fax them to me up at Dad's cottage. I asked him to go through them for any errors before I brought them along." He studied her as she read the last page. "Are they to your satisfaction?"

"They seem fine. And knowing that your father approved them makes it all the better."

He watched as she signed and dated each one before placing them in his briefcase. Before he could close it, he reached in and removed several more. "Oh, I almost forgot. Dad said you'll need to sign these, too."

He poured himself a second cup of coffee.

She started to do as he asked when Brady stepped up beside her.

He looked over at Lance. "Are these new?"

Lance couldn't hide his impatience. "I'm on a tight schedule, Willow."

Willow glanced at Brady before repeating his question. "Then tell me. Are these new documents, Lance?"

"Just copies of the ones you've already signed. You know how the law is. Everything in duplicate or triplicate."

Before Willow could reach for her pen, Brady gave a slight shake of his head.

Willow picked up the first page.

Lance made a point of checking his watch. "I really don't have time for this, Willow."

"There's always time for an important client to read documents." Brady's tone was dangerously soft.

Lance put down his cup with a clatter. "You know something, Storm? I need to be in Helena before dark." He swept up the documents and stuffed them in his briefcase before snapping it closed. "All I need are the single documents for now. Once the bank records are in order, I'll have my assistant send the rest."

He didn't bother kissing Willow's cheek this time before turning away. "You'll be hearing from me soon."

He made his way down the hallway and through the kitchen.

Hearing the sound of booted feet entering the kitchen, Cara, busy in the pantry, lifted her head to call out, "Did you forget something, Brady?"

For a moment there was only silence. It seemed to stretch out forever, before the footsteps continued through the mudroom.

Cara poked her head around the pantry doors in time to see a tall, well-dressed man striding across the porch and down the steps.

Minutes later the plane was airborne, a silver streak reflecting the rays of the late afternoon sunlight off its wings.

Brady shoved his cell phone into his shirt pocket before turning to Willow. "Carter tells me they're having a record number of calves. He and the wranglers are also spotting a record number of wolves prowling the perimeter of the herd. I'm going to head up to the highlands and give them a hand."

She pushed away from her desk. "I'll go with you."

"There's no need." Brady shook his head. "I could be up there for days."

"Good. I need as much time as possible away from this." She waved a hand at the paperwork littering her desktop.

The foreman grinned. "You'd risk crazy spring weather just to avoid doing what you know you'll have to do sooner or later anyway?"

"Later is much better than sooner." She snatched up a pair of weathered work gloves and followed him out the door.

In the kitchen they found Cara up to her elbows in bubbling marinara sauce and mounds of freshly shredded cheese.

"Brady and I won't be here for supper," Willow announced. "We're heading up to the herd."

"Oh." Cara gave them a glorious smile. "I'm fixing lasagna."

"It smells fabulous." Willow looked around. "Do you think you have time to fix us a handy carry-out? Maybe some sandwiches and a gallon or so of coffee?"

"You got it." Cara dimpled. "I'll bring it out to the barn."

"Thanks." Willow followed Brady out the door.

A short time later, Cara stepped into the cavernous barn with an armload of food and beverages.

"What's all this?" Brady asked in surprise.

"I thought, since I'm fixing something for the two of you, I ought to send along some goodies for the wranglers. I sliced roast beef and turkey, cheese, lettuce and veggies and wrapped them inside whole loaves of bread I baked earlier. And a couple dozen oatmeal raisin cookies."

"They're going to sing your praises," Brady said with a laugh. "Thank you."

Cara glanced around. "Where's Whit? I thought he was doing barn chores?"

"He is." Brady nodded toward the hayloft, where Whit was working feverishly with a pitchfork.

Whistling a tune, the foreman stashed the wrapped food in his saddlebags and led his horse outside, where Willow was already astride her mare.

Myrna stepped into the kitchen to announce, "Mad just phoned. He's decided to stay the night at Hope Ranch with Griff and Juliet and the boys. He said there's a storm brewing, and Ash isn't comfortable flying in it, so Brenna agreed to drive over to join him and the others for supper at their place." She was wearing a radiant smile. "That means that we have the place to ourselves for the whole night."

Cara looked at the sauce simmering, the shredded cheese, and the spinach she was about to steam before cooking the lasagna noodles. "But I have all this food ready to cook. I swear there's enough here to feed an entire team of wranglers."

"It'll keep." Myrna eyed it. "I'm not much for fancy food anyway. I think I'll just have a sandwich in my room and watch some game shows."

"But..." Cara let the words trail off as the old woman walked away.

Deflated, she turned off the stove and began searching for storage bowls. She would just have to make her fancy lasagna another day.

When the door opened, she looked up to see Whit

heading toward the big sink, rolling his sleeves before washing up.

He strolled into the kitchen and breathed deeply. "Do I smell pizza?"

"Tomato sauce. I was going to make lasagna. But I guess you and I are the only ones eating tonight."

His look sharpened. "I know Mom and Brady are up in the hills. What about the others?"

She shrugged. "Mad is spending the night at Griff and Juliet's because of a storm coming in, and Ash and Brenna are joining them there. When Myrna got the word, she went off to watch game shows in her room."

He stepped closer, wearing a wolfish grin. "Can you turn those fixings into a pizza?"

She shot him a puzzled look. "I don't understand..."

"Can you do that?"

"I guess. But..."

"Do it." He looked around. "I'll be back in a flash."

Alone in the kitchen, Cara took a package of dough out of the refrigerator and began dusting the cutting board with flour before rolling it into a huge circle. A short time later, she'd covered the dough with spinach, ham, sausage, onions, and the bubbling tomato sauce before topping it with the grated cheese and placing it in the oven.

When Whit returned, he was grinning from ear to ear. "Now I know I smell pizza."

She checked the oven. "You do. And it's ready."

As she set it on the counter and removed her oven mitts, he located a thick towel and used it to pick up the pizza.

"Where are you taking it? I thought we were eating."

"We are. But not here." With a mysterious grin he said, "Follow me."

"Where? Whit MacKenzie, tell me what's going on."

He turned with a wink. "Trust me, Goldilocks. You and I just won the lottery."

Chapter Twenty

Dusk was just beginning to settle as they stepped out the back door.

Cara looked expectantly toward the ranch truck, parked nearby. She was surprised when Whit took her hand and led her in the opposite direction, toward the barn.

"Is that truck broken?"

"Truck?" He looked over his shoulder and laughed. "We won't need it where we're going."

"Where…?"

He merely shook his head. "Did anybody ever tell you you ask too many questions?"

"All right." A picnic up in the hills? "I guess we're going by horseback."

She paused in the doorway to the barn, expecting to see Dumpling saddled. Instead, the stalls were empty. The occasional whinny of a horse could be heard in the corral out back.

More confused than ever, she followed Whit until he paused beside a tall ladder.

A wide, sexy grin split his lips. "Come on up, Goldilocks. We're going to be testing beds in the big house tonight."

She climbed the ladder, with Whit trailing behind, carrying the towel-wrapped pizza.

When she reached the hayloft, she stared in surprise.

Whit had spread his bedroll in the hay. Alongside it was a bucket of ice and several longnecks chilling. He placed the pizza on a small stool.

Laughter lurked in his eyes as he dropped down on his knees beside her. "Goldilocks, just seeing you here makes me so hungry."

"Then I'll cut you a slice..."

He caught her hand. "Not for food. There will be plenty of time for that later. First, I just want to take a big bite of you."

He gathered her into his arms and covered her mouth with his in a kiss that was so hot with need, all she could do was clutch his waist and hold on.

He lifted his head. "Not good enough, Goldilocks. This is no place to be passive. I expect you to get in the game."

"The...game?" She lifted a hand to his face and he caught her wrist, holding her hand as he sucked each finger slowly into his mouth, his gaze never leaving hers.

The hungry look in his eyes said more than words.

"Oh." The smile in her eyes matched the smile in her voice as she dug her hands into his hair and dove into a kiss in a way she never had before. All open and giving. All hunger and need. No barriers. Nothing held back.

"Mmm. Now that's better. Just remember, there's nobody around to hear us or see us. For tonight, we're free."

Free. The thought of it washed over her, and she found herself laughing.

"Oh, Whit. What fun. I've never been in a hayloft before."

"Then I'll try to make your first time memorable, Goldilocks."

He kept his eyes on hers as he reached for the buttons of her shirt. "Speaking of first times...I want to make it up to you for the rough way I took you at the creek."

"You didn't take me, Whit. You forget, I was the one who offered."

"A very generous offer. But I took you like an animal, and ever since, I've wanted to find a way to make it up to you."

He slid her shirt from her shoulders. As it drifted to the hay, he unhooked the tiny bit of lace that covered her breasts.

Without a word, he filled his palms with her and nuzzled her heated flesh.

She absorbed a jolt of sexual energy that coursed along her spine.

He reached for the fasteners of her denims. "You're so beautiful, you take my breath away."

Though she hadn't planned it, she blurted, "So are you, Whit."

His head came up and for a moment all he could do was stare at her. "Now this is a first for me. I've never been called beautiful."

Her laughter was warm on his face. "But you are. Look at you." She shimmied out of her jeans and the tiny lace thong before reaching a hand to his waist, helping him slide free of his clothes. Free and naked and splendid. "You have the most amazing, beautiful body."

He brushed kisses over her upturned face. "I hope you'll say that when the night is over. This body is all yours tonight, Goldilocks, to do with as you please."

She shivered in anticipation as he laid her down on the bedroll and leaned close.

"But first..." He ran hot, wet kisses over her face, down her neck, around each breast, before taking one moist nipple into his mouth.

She made a purring sound in her throat and locked her arms around his neck as he moved from one breast to the other, while those wonderful, calloused hands began moving over her, adding another layer to her pleasure.

"Your skin is so soft."

"And your hands are so clever."

"I'm glad you approve."

"Oh, I do." She was desperate to touch him as he was touching her, but he gave her no time as he continued pleasuring her.

"This is your night, Goldilocks. Let me pamper you. Let me love you."

And then he showed her, in every way, just how much he meant those words. With slow kisses, and long, leisurely touches that had her body humming with need.

Finally, unable to hold back, she rose up on one elbow, leaning over him, her hair tickling his chest as she began running wet kisses down his throat, across the flat planes of his stomach.

He lay back with a moan of pure pleasure, only to stop her moments later, though it cost him. "Hold on. We're getting ahead of ourselves. This is getting way too intense."

He sat up and gathered her close, pressing his mouth to a tangle of hair at her temple.

Against her flesh he whispered, "I don't want hot and fast. I plan on enjoying a feast tonight. A slow, lazy, all-you-can-eat banquet." He lifted her face and kissed the corner of her lips. "Let's just start with some appetizers."

He ran slow, easy kisses over her upturned face, lingering over her raised brow, trailing ever so slowly to her ear, where he flicked his tongue before tugging lightly on her lobe.

She followed his lead, kissing the curve of his strong jaw before whispering kisses over his throat and across his shoulder.

He gave a low, throaty chuckle. "Goldilocks, when you do that, you get me all tingly."

"Good. I like tingly." She moved lower, across his chest, while her fingers trailed his mat of dark, springy hair.

"So do I. But now you've got me tingling in other places," he said with a growl as he dragged her on top of him. "I thought I could hold back, but there's just something about you. I'm afraid there's no stopping it now."

He plunged his hands into the tangles of her hair, dragging her head down while he kissed her with a depth of hunger that rocked her to her very core.

His hands moved over her, building a fire that was threatening to consume them both.

Caught up in the frenzy of need, she wriggled over him, taking him in and closing around him like a velvet fist.

He groaned from the exquisite pleasure of it before going very still. His eyes, dark with pulsing need, were fixed on hers.

"I see we're doomed, Goldilocks. Like I said, there's no stopping this out-of-control train. We just have to ride it."

And then they were moving together with a strength born of desperation. Climbing. Clinging. Clawing. Chests pounding, breathing shallow, hearts galloping, they raced toward the moon. And climaxed in a shower of glittering stars.

"Sorry." Whit's face was buried in the little hollow of Cara's neck. She smelled of hay and sex and the faint hint of wildflowers he'd noticed on that first night when he'd slept on her pillow.

It would always remind him of Cara and the way she'd looked in those first few minutes, all terrified and putting up a brave front, with that broomstick at his back like a weapon. And then the revelation when he'd tugged aside the blanket.

"You're sorry?" Her words were muffled against his temple.

"Not for this. This was good. Not just good. It was fantastic." With an effort, he lifted his head to brush her mouth with his. "But I'd planned this night to be a long, slow seduction, to make up for that hot, sweaty display down by the creek. I guess I just can't let myself get too close to you or I forget all my good intentions and just fall into the same hot, sweaty, fast sex all over again."

She lifted a hand to his cheek. "I'm not complaining."

"No. You're not. Have I told you that it's one of the things I really like about you? You never complain, no matter what situation you find yourself in."

She smiled up at him. "Thanks. But this wasn't so much a situation as a celebration." She paused. "What other things do you like about me?"

"You fishing for compliments, Goldilocks?"

Her smile turned sly. "Maybe I am."

"You don't need to worry. You've got it all." He rolled to one side and gathered her close. "I like the way you smell. Like a field of wildflowers in springtime. And I like the way your hair falls all long and loose, especially when it's falling over me." He touched a finger to her lips. "I like looking at your face. You're gorgeous, but not like those cover models, you know? More like you just stepped out of a shower and you're all clean and natural and pretty. And I like the way you look when you're cooking. Like you've got everything covered. No rush, no nerves, just very cool, as though you could find yourself in a giant stadium filled with starving strangers, and you'd just go on fixing food without a care in the world."

She leaned up on one elbow to stare at him. "I had no idea you were thinking all those things about me."

"It's the truth." He brushed a lock of hair from her face, allowing his hand to linger a moment. "And it's a hell of a lot more than I'd intended to admit to."

As if to cover his lapse, he sat up and turned toward the ice bucket. "How about a beer and some pizza?"

As he twisted the top off a bottle and handed it to her, he added with a sexy grin, "We can always try for slow and easy after a good meal."

"You know, considering that you weren't planning on making pizza, this is really good. A lot better than the cardboard at Wylie's." Whit reached for another slice.

"Thanks. But you were right. I had all the ingredients. Why not use them for something portable?"

"Yeah. Lasagna just wouldn't be the same up here in the hay loft."

A clap of thunder had Cara looking up in fear. "That sounded close."

"Close enough." Whit pointed out the small, open window that gave them a glimpse of the land for acres. "I'm betting this storm is what kept Mad at Griff and Juliet's ranch for the night."

Cara leaned her head out and breathed in the wonderful, fresh scent of spring rain. "Oh, it's beautiful and frightening, all at the same time. And it smells so clean."

"Yeah." Whit leaned back, one arm under his head. "Ever since I was a kid I've loved to lie up here and listen to the rain on the tin roof." He looked over. "I hope you're not afraid of storms?"

She shook her head and sat beside him, her arms encircling her folded legs, her chin on her knees. "It must have been a fun place to grow up."

He nodded. "Despite Pop's temper, I had a lot of freedom. I was riding by the time I could walk. And heading up to the hills with the wranglers as soon as Mom would allow. I guess I was six or seven the first time I begged to go along. Pop was having none of it, and Mom was worried until Brady promised to watch out for me."

"He seems like such a gentleman."

"Brady? Yeah. He's a good guy."

"He's soft on your mom."

Whit's hand holding the beer paused in midair. "You

don't mean like romantic soft? You mean like watching out for her. Right?"

"Are you blind? Every time he looks at her, he practically melts. If she sneezes, he's beside her with a handkerchief. If she even thinks about making a cup of tea, he's there with boiling water and a tea strainer."

Whit sat up, running a hand through his hair. "That's just because he's one of those old-fashioned cowboys who only knows one way to treat a lady. And that's with respect." Reassured by his own words, he nodded. "Yeah. He's just treating Mom the same way he'd treat any woman."

"Except that Willow isn't just any woman to him. Haven't you seen the way he looks out for her? The way he watches her whenever he thinks nobody is looking?"

He set aside his half-finished beer. "You think he's... got special feelings for my mother?"

"Does that bother you?"

Whit had to think about that. He frowned. "No. I mean, I could understand if he felt that way. She's a beautiful woman. And she's still young. And Brady has been in all our lives since before any of us were born. But still... it's hard for me to picture anyone but Pop having that kind of relationship with my mom." He looked over. "Do you think she feels the same way about Brady?"

"Your mom's a very private person. She's much harder to read. And from everything I've heard, she was crazy in love with your father. Still"—she rolled her eyes—"Brady Storm is one handsome cowboy."

His strong fingers curled around her wrist. "You think he's better looking than me?"

She looked down at his hand, then up into his eyes with a glint of teasing laughter. "My, my. If I didn't know better, I'd think Whit MacKenzie is displaying a bit of jealousy."

"My ass." But he drew her closer. "Do you? Think he's better-looking than me?"

"Not even close. Feeling better?"

"Much." He lay back, easing her down beside him. "Okay. I told you about my childhood. Now it's your turn. Tell me how you learned to draw like that."

"Drawing is the easy part. For me, it's as natural as breathing. And the stories I wrote were really all about me and my imaginary friend as we lived through those wonderful adventures." She looked over at Whit. "While living with my gram, I used to wonder about my mom. I'd convince myself that one day she'd be back. I'd kneel by the window waiting for her to return. My stories took me away from the harsh reality that I was never going to live like other kids. Gram gave me an anchor, and she did her best for me, and I'll always be grateful that I had her in my life. But those stories about Arac and Peg, the magic horse, became my escape." She sighed. "The dream of seeing my work published became a lifeline for me. It's only now that I'm beginning to realize the price I've paid for trying to attain that dream."

"Hey, it can happen, if you're willing to do the hard work."

She looked over at him with a warm smile. "Those are words, Whit. The reality is this—I need to put my childish dreams aside and make a life for myself."

Hearing the pain beneath her brave words, his heart

melted. “We’ve spent enough time talking, woman. Now for that slow, lazy seduction I promised you.”

As the storm raged overhead, they came together in a storm of their own. And later fell asleep to the sound of the steady, soothing rhythm of rain beating a tattoo on the tin roof.

CHAPTER TWENTY-ONE

Willow and Brady, astride their horses, were keeping an eye on the approaching storm.

They'd spent the day with the wranglers up on the east meadow and were heading toward the west, where a smaller herd was kept, when the sky turned dark as night.

"We need to find shelter." Brady shouted above the wind. "That storm's coming in fast and furious."

"A range shack?" Willow stared around.

"Over that rise." Brady pointed. "We can try. But I don't like our odds."

They were forced to keep a steady hand on the reins of their horses, who were spooking at the sudden claps of thunder, followed seconds later by jagged slices of lightning.

By the time they reached the deserted range shack, rain was falling in torrents and the wind was whipping trees around them in a frenzied dance. They were greeted by a loud flapping sound coming from a door hanging by one hinge and blowing open and shut. The roof had blown off and the shack had collapsed in on itself. The only thing standing was the rear wall and the lean-to behind it.

Leading their mounts inside the lean-to, they worked quickly to secure the door with a length of rope before Brady withdrew a battery-operated lantern from his saddlebags.

He glanced over at Willow, shaking rain from her wide-brimmed hat before tossing it aside. "It's not much, but at least we're dry in here."

She gave him a smile as she unsaddled her mount and tossed the saddle and blanket to the ground. "And that's more than we can say for the wranglers babysitting the herd."

"They're used to it." He followed suit, unsaddling his gelding and spreading the saddle and blanket beside hers.

He filled the horses' troughs with hay and oats and used a dipper in the rain barrel outside the door to fill a second trough with water.

He looked around at their tight quarters. "I'm afraid we won't be able to make a fire in here."

Willow sighed. "Coffee would have been nice, but we can live without it. I wish we hadn't been so quick to go through that entire Thermos Cara sent. As for the chill..." She drew her cowhide jacket around her. "I'll be warm enough with this."

"Good." Brady unrolled one of the packages from his saddlebag. "We have the last of the beef sandwiches Cara sent, and a cookie."

Willow sat down on the blanket-covered earthen floor and leaned her back against her saddle before accepting half a sandwich from his hand. "All the comforts of home."

Brady settled himself beside her, stretching out his long legs.

They ate in companionable silence, listening to the storm raging outside.

"From the sound of that wind, I'll be surprised if any of this shack is still standing by morning." Brady touched a hand to Willow's. "If that last wall goes, this will go with it."

"Just so it doesn't take us and the horses, too," she said with a laugh.

His eyes crinkled. "That's what I love about you. Even in a crisis, when most women would be terrified, you find the humor in it."

She shook her head. "Brady, in my years of living life on a ranch, I've come to expect the unexpected. This storm is just a little bump in the road."

"Yeah." He finished the last of his sandwich. "We can't have coffee, but we can have some whiskey, if you'd like."

She nodded. "Now that I've eaten, I think whiskey would be the perfect touch. Let's save that cookie for our breakfast, if the storm doesn't blow us away first."

He reached into his saddlebag and removed a bottle. Uncapping it, he poured some in the cap that also served as a cup and handed it to Willow, who drained it before handing it back.

Brady poured a second capful. "Another?"

"No thanks." She laughed. "That one's still burning a path of fire down my throat. The rest is all yours."

He drank, feeling the warmth snake through his veins.

Content, relaxed, he drank a second shot before capping the bottle. "You have to be tired. We've put in a full day."

"It's funny." She eased off her boots before crossing her ankles. "Ranch work, even really hard, physical ranch work, doesn't tire me nearly as much as spending a few hours on paperwork. Now that really leaves me feeling extremely cross and cranky."

"You?" He chuckled. "You don't even know what cranky is." He folded his hands beneath his head. "Do you remember the day Bear was bringing home your brand-new truck? He came up over a ridge and had to veer off the road to avoid a bull that escaped the fence?"

Willow nodded. "Bear ended up running into a tree and totaling that truck before I even had a chance to drive it."

Brady started laughing at the memory. "He was so mad. He called me to come and pick him up, and all the way home he never once seemed grateful that he'd walked away alive from such a terrible crash. Instead, he was steamed about the fact that you'd have his hide for ruining something you'd ordered and waited over a month for and never even got to drive before he smashed it to bits."

She joined in his laughter. "When he walked in, swearing a blue streak, I took one look at his left eye turning shades of blue and purple and the blood dripping from a terrible gash in his head and asked him who he'd been in a fight with and how badly he'd hurt the other guy."

Brady wiped tears of laughter from his eyes. "And then he admitted that he'd been in an accident with your new truck. And all you said was, 'Thank heaven you're all right. It's easier to order a new truck than a new husband. Now let's take a look at that wound in your head.' And I thought Bear, after getting himself all worked up over telling you, was going to keel over right there in the kitchen."

"His bark was always worse than his bite."

"Only with you, Willow. With mere mortals, he was hell on wheels."

"Yes, I know." She fell silent.

After a particularly loud clap of thunder, she shivered before turning to Brady. "Thank you for telling me about your wife and son the last time we were together. It helps to know . . . It helps me to know that it's possible to survive and go on."

He looked over. "There's no road map for life. We just have to follow its twists and turns and figure things out as we go along." He listened to the steady beat of the rain. "But I do believe there are no accidents in life, either. When I ran into Bear at Wylie's that night we met, he was too drunk to make it on his own. I thought I was saving him that night, but he was actually saving me. You see, I wasn't sure what I was going to do. But one strong, steady thought was that I might be better off just ending things than trying to live with the pain of my loss."

Willow caught his hand in hers, her eyes revealing her shock. "No, Brady. You wouldn't have..."

He placed a finger over her mouth to still her words. "It's no good denying the truth. At that time, I had nothing more to live for."

She knelt up, wrapping her arms around him. Against his temple she whispered fiercely, "I refuse to believe you would have gone through with it. You're too good, too strong willed, no matter how painful your life had become."

He went very still, then allowed himself to gather her close. With one hand he stroked her hair. "When I saw what was about to happen to Bear, I decided I'd do one last good deed before leaving this world. I never dreamed that decision would change everything." He looked at her, his eyes hot and fierce, even though his words were barely a husky whisper. "When I learned that Bear was so crazy in love with someone he'd just lost, I could understand that and sympathize. But with every day I stayed on at his ranch, I heard more and more about the amazing, lovely, talented Willow Martin." His eyes gentled. "I think I was half in love with that mystery woman, too. And then you came back to him and admitted that you wanted a life with him more than you wanted a glamorous career as a model, and I understood why any man would fall under your spell. I did. Instantly. After meeting you, I knew that no other woman would ever measure up to you. Not the Willow of my imagination, but the real Willow, who was everything I'd ever dreamed of and more."

She was so stunned, all she could do was stare wide-eyed at him. "Brady, what are you saying?"

"I'm saying that I completely understand why Bear loved you more than his own life. I feel the same way. And through all these years, the only reason I've been able to admire you from afar and keep a steady hand on my feelings is because of my loyalty to Bear. Everything I have—my life, my satisfying years here on this ranch—I owe to Bear MacKenzie. I would never do anything to dishonor his memory. But I have to admit, Willow, the temptation to act on my feelings right now is almost more than I can fight." He touched one rough finger to her lips. "I can see by the look in your eyes that I've completely blindsided you, and for that I'm truly sorry."

He lowered his hands and turned away from her, arranging his saddle as a pillow before folding over his bedroll.

"Brady..." She twisted her hands together, unable to form a simple sentence.

She hadn't seen this coming. Hadn't had a clue.

On the one hand, she couldn't help but be moved by his admission. What woman wouldn't relish being admired and loved from afar? On the other hand, she had no doubt that it would be impossible to behave with him as she had in the past. There had been a level of comfort in her ignorance. Now she would be aware of him in a whole new light. As a man. A man who...loved her. Who desired her.

Brady Storm was her dearest friend.

Could she possibly think of him as more? And even if she could, was she ready for such a step?

Beside her, the object of her thoughts rolled to his side without another word. And though she agonized over this latest change in her life, she knew she could no longer seek the comfort of her best friend's arms. Because to do so would invite a storm of another kind.

Whit stared down at Cara, curled up against him.

It had been an amazing night. They'd had the freedom to love loudly, lustily. And to talk. She had a way of listening, really listening, that caused him to open up to her as he rarely opened to anyone. He'd told her about his childhood here on the ranch and the hurt and anger he'd felt when his brother Ash had left in a blind rage after another fight with their father. And the pain when he'd learned of his father's murder. And then the shock of learning that their father had discovered he had a son by a woman he'd known before his marriage to Willow.

All that talk had left him feeling somehow cleansed. As though just sharing it with someone else had forced him to take a hard look at his family and realize that, despite all they'd gone through, they were doing fine. They were all surviving. And he loved them. All of them. Ash, who had once left him feeling abandoned. Griff, the stranger with his father's face and voice and mannerisms. Brady, who had always felt like his second father. Mad, who, despite suffering a crippling injury, refused to be held back. Willow, who continued to be the heart and soul of their family. And even old Myrna, the closest thing he'd ever had to a grandmother, who had fussed over him and made his favorite foods during his growing-up years, as though trying to make up for the loss of his brother.

Cara had opened up, too. About her painful childhood and about the dream she'd nurtured all these years. No wonder she'd carried all her old notes and drawings with her throughout the years. They weren't just childhood treasures. They were a lifeline from her past to her dreams of the future.

She not only opened up about herself and listened, but she made him laugh as well. He couldn't recall the last time he'd laughed so hard. And all because of that quirky, silly sense of humor that always caught him by surprise. How could someone with so many painful memories have such a wonderful sense of humor?

She was such a surprise. Everything about her was new and fresh and wonderful.

When he'd found her in that range shack, he'd considered her simply an annoyance in his life. When he'd brought her here, he'd expected her to last a few days at the most before she figured out where she wanted to go next.

And now?

He studied the curve of her eyebrow, barely visible beneath the veil of hair that spilled over half of her face.

He'd thought he could enjoy her company, indulge in some casual sex, and watch her ride off to her next adventure. But something had happened to him along the way. Something that wasn't at all planned.

He found himself worrying about her. Caring about her safety and more, about where she would go and what she would do with her life going forward.

He lov—

He resisted permitting the very word to form in his mind. As long as he didn't think it, it wasn't so.

Hadn't he ridiculed his brothers for getting all mushy and gooey over their women?

Their women.

His woman.

That simple phrase had him feeling a rush of tenderness.

He felt a band begin to tighten around his heart. He had never meant for this to happen. Though he didn't want it, wasn't ready for it, it had happened anyway.

God, he loved her.

She sighed in her sleep and he used that moment to roll aside and head toward the ladder.

He needed coffee.

He needed air.

He needed…Cara. Needed her desperately. And that realization terrified him.

"Do I smell coffee?" Cara opened her eyes to find Whit kneeling beside her, holding out a steaming mug.

She sat up and took a deep drink before handing it back to him. "Oh, that's heavenly. Have you been to the house?"

"I have." He settled in beside her and held out a bagel and cream cheese. "I thought you might like this, too."

"Thanks." She took a bite before passing it to him. "Was Myrna up?"

"Not yet. But soon, I suppose." He motioned toward the window. "The rain's gone. How did you like sleeping up here?"

"Not that we got much sleep," she said with a laugh. "But I see why you enjoy hearing the rain up here. It's really soothing. Everything about your life is soothing." She stretched and reached for her shirt. "I'd better get moving."

"Why? There's nobody here except you and me and Myrna. And she's used to getting her chores started before breakfast."

Cara gave a shake of her head. "I can't remember the last time I had nothing at all to do. I'm not sure I'll know what to do with all this time on my hands. I feel like I need to get up and get busy."

Whit set aside his coffee and bagel and reached for the buttons of her shirt. "Oh, I'm sure we'll think of something to do."

She was laughing. "I don't believe you. Didn't you get enough of this last night?"

"Goldilocks." He drew her close and covered her mouth with his. "I don't think I'll ever have enough of you."

CHAPTER TWENTY-TWO

By late morning, the entire MacKenzie family had returned to the house.

Mad was the first to arrive, with Griff and Juliet and their boys, who'd flown in with Mad at the controls. Though Griff was prepared in case his grandfather needed help, the old man brought the little Cessna in for a perfect landing.

Willow and Brady were in the barn, unsaddling their mounts and turning them into the corral before joining the others.

Willow seemed surprised to see them. "You're just coming home now?"

"Spent the night with Griff and Juliet." The old man kissed his daughter-in-law's cheek as she bent down to his scooter to greet him. "That was some storm," Mad muttered. "It was probably worse up in the hills."

Brady nodded. "It was a doozy."

Juliet studied Willow and Brady. "Since your hair's not wet, I'm guessing you two found some shelter before it hit."

"Just barely." Willow strode along beside Brady, averting her gaze. Their morning routine had been awkward, since neither of them knew quite how to broach the subject of the previous night.

She turned to Mad. "That range shack up on the middle ridge will have to be rebuilt. We managed to stay in the lean-to with the horses, but the rest of the building has been destroyed by the weather. If the wind had grown any stronger, I doubt even the last wall would have survived."

"I'm not surprised. That was one of my original shelters, built when Bear was a lad." With the two little boys on his lap along for the ride, Mad maneuvered his scooter along the wooden ramp that had been built for him. "I'm sure you'll take a crew and get on it in a few weeks, Griff—that is, if you can spare them, Brady?"

The foreman nodded. "As soon as calving season is over, I'll pull a few wranglers from the herd. With an experienced builder like Griff to guide them, they'll have it as good as new in no time."

Griff was all smiles. "I'm always happy to be working with my hands. Maybe you ought to check out the rest of the cabins once the weather clears, Brady. No sense wasting spring and summer without making necessary repairs."

"I'm with you on that, Griff." The foreman held the back door for the others.

They trooped into the house, pausing to remove wide-brimmed hats and mud-caked boots before washing at the sink.

Inside, Ash and Brenna were already drinking coffee and chatting with Whit and Cara and Myrna. The minute Casey and Ethan caught sight of Sammy, the chase was on and they raced into the great room looking for the pup's favorite ball to toss.

"There's lemonade," Cara called to their retreating backs, but the two little boys were beyond caring, as long as they had the puppy in their sights.

Willow and Brady hurried off to their separate suites for a quick shower.

By the time a very late breakfast was served, the entire family had gathered around the table. While they filled their plates with omelets and country potatoes, along with thick slabs of ham, the talk centered on the storm and the havoc it had wreaked before blowing over.

After hearing about the range shack, Griff reported on the line of trees he'd spotted from the air. "A mile or more just flattened like matchsticks."

Willow glanced at Cara. "I hope you weren't too frightened by it. The storms always seem so much worse out here, far from civilization."

Cara was busy passing around a basket of rolls she'd just retrieved from the oven. "I guess I was just so mesmerized by the sound of all that lovely rain on the tin roof..."

She stopped and felt the heat burning her cheeks as she realized what she'd just blurted.

The conversation came to a grinding halt as everyone turned to stare at Whit.

"Busted." He lifted his hands in a sign of surrender. "I figured the storm was the perfect opportunity for Cara to hear what rain sounds like under the roof of the barn."

"That was really thoughtful of you, bro."

At Ash's sarcastic comment, he was forced to duck when Whit tossed a hot roll at his head. Catching it one-handed, Ash tossed it back. It whizzed past Whit's shoulder and landed on the floor behind him.

Willow shot both her sons the famous hairy eyeball that every mother has mastered from the time her children are toddlers. "What a fine example you're setting for little Casey and Ethan."

"Can you teach me to throw Sammy a roll, too?" Casey asked in all innocence.

Everyone turned to see the puppy devouring the roll that had fallen to the floor.

"That'll be enough of that." Mad glowered at the two men as though they were children.

Then, turning to Cara with a deceptively innocent smile, he said, "Go on now, lass. You were saying that Whit took you up to the hayloft to hear the rain. How did you like it?"

Her face was flaming. "I loved it. It's something I could listen to forever." Then she busied herself at the stove while knowing looks were exchanged around the table.

The sound of an arriving text on Brady's cell phone broke the silence.

The foreman read the words before typing in his response.

He returned his phone to his shirt pocket and glanced around at the others. "Carter needs help with the calving. I'm heading up to the highlands. Anybody care to join me?" He turned to Willow. "Sorry I can't be here to lend a hand with your business meeting with Lance McMillan."

Willow plucked up her own phone and spoke in low tones. "Lance, this is Willow MacKenzie. I'm sorry to mess with your schedule, but I'm needed in the hills today. Call tomorrow and we'll schedule another meeting."

She was smiling. "I'd rather spend an afternoon with the herd any time than be stuck in my office with Lance going over more of those tedious documents. And since he didn't pick up his phone, I was able to avoid talking to him and left a voice mail instead."

"Okay, then." Brady turned back to Whit. "With that storm, we never made it to the west meadow. Want to join us?"

"Yeah. Sure." Whit glanced at the rigid line of Cara's back, hoping he could find a way to ease her embarrassment before he left.

Brady turned to Ash and Griff. "I could use your help, too. I'd guess, from Carter's text, those calves are being born in record numbers."

"I'm in," Ash said.

Whit nodded. "Count me in."

Mad turned to Juliet. "I'll fly you and the wee lads home."

"Thanks, Mad. But I promised the boys a little time at Brenna's studio."

"That's okay." Brenna winked at the two little boys. "Casey and Ethan can hang with me, and you can go home and do your thing. Then we'll meet back here for supper. Does that work?"

Juliet nodded. "Perfect. But I'd like to stay long enough to give Cara a hand with this cleanup."

Cara turned, relieved at the change of topic but unwilling to be the center of attention. "That's not necessary."

"It is." Brenna picked up Sammy to keep him from eating any more of the scraps being dropped by the two little boys. "Since you cooked this marvelous brunch, the least Juliet and I can do is pitch in to help with the dishes."

Myrna smiled at them. "That will free me to do some of my chores." She flushed. "The house was so quiet this morning, I overslept. Now I need to catch up."

Cara shot a quick glance at Whit and felt the heat creeping up her neck again.

He winked, and she turned away, afraid everyone could read her guilty feelings.

Within half an hour, Willow, Brady, Whit, Ash, and Griff were gathering their gear in preparation to head out.

Mad and the two little boys rode off toward the great room in Mad's scooter, with Sammy trailing behind.

During all the commotion, Whit managed to pause beside Cara, who was setting dirty dishes in the sink.

He tugged a lock of her hair. "Don't make too much of all that."

"Really? What should I do? Just make a joke of it, like you do? Is that what I am, Whit? A joke to you and your brothers?"

His tone was rough with impatience. "You can't believe that."

"And why not? I could feel what everyone around the table was thinking. You told me you and Ash used to sneak girls up to the hayloft. Why should I be any different than the others?"

"You are different, Cara. You're special. You're—"

"Come on, bro." Ash stood in the doorway, bulging saddlebags tossed over his shoulder. "Let's get a move on."

"I'll be right there." Whit struggled to keep the frustration from his voice as he turned back to Cara. "When I come back, we'll talk. I promise. Okay?"

She hissed out a breath. "Sure."

"I want to kiss you."

She turned to peer at all the activity around them, her face bright pink. "Don't you dare. I feel silly enough already."

He pressed two fingers to his mouth, then touched them to hers. "Okay. This will have to do until I get back. Then I'll give you a proper kiss. And we'll talk."

She stood perfectly still, absorbing the tiny thrill of his touch along her spine. Then, with her hands still filled with dirty dishes, she turned to watch him stride from the room.

Minutes later came the sound of a convoy of trucks, some hauling loaded horse trailers, and deep, masculine voices calling out orders.

Brenna carried a stack of dishes to the counter while Juliet wiped down the table. Cara opened the dishwasher and began filling it with dirty dishes.

"So, Cara." Brenna reached for plastic wrap before storing the remaining ham in the refrigerator. "What do you think about Whit?"

And there it was.

Cara swallowed. "He's been really nice to me. Considering the circumstances of our first meeting, he would have been justified in calling the police chief and filing a complaint about me."

"That's not the MacKenzies' style." Juliet crossed the room to join the discussion. "Since joining their family, I've been really impressed with their goodness and decency."

"I wasn't just talking about the circumstances that brought them together." Brenna cleared another plate and handed it to Cara to stash in the dishwasher. "Don't you think Whit is adorable?"

"A...dorable?" Her face went all red again.

Brenna laughed. "He's been my buddy for years. After Ash left town, Whit and his family took me under their wings. So Whit feels a little like my brother. And if you don't mind me saying this, I'm seeing something new in him since you arrived."

Cara couldn't quite meet her eyes.

"He's...softer. Sweeter lately." Brenna turned to Juliet. "Have you noticed it?"

Juliet nodded. "Remember how he used to tease all of us about being too lovey-dovey? He'd complain loudly that all the sugar made him gag. And now...I've been tempted to tease him about the change in his attitude, but I figured he'd just become defensive. I don't think he even realizes yet what's hit him."

"Hit him?" Now Cara was intrigued.

Juliet glanced at Brenna before saying, "I guess it's contagious."

"What is?" Cara closed the dishwasher door and began drying her hands on a dish towel.

"Love."

Juliet's single word was met with a stunned silence, before Cara began shaking her head in denial. "Whit?"

"Whit and you." Brenna's smile was gentle. "Honey, very often the last ones to know about it are the ones most affected."

"Or maybe you should say 'infected,'" Juliet added with a laugh. "I think the first stages of love sometimes feel more like the flu than the soft, fuzzy feelings the poets write about. At least that's the way it was for Griff and me."

As the other two burst into gales of laughter, Cara watched them, letting their words sink in.

She had very strong feelings for Whit. Yeah, probably lovey-dovey feelings. But love? And even if it was love on her part, was it possible that he felt the same way about her?

She'd seen the way the females in Copper Creek looked at him. From Nonie Claxton and the women of all ages who hung out at Wylie's to the women on the street who practically swooned when he smiled at them, it was obvious that Whit MacKenzie could have his pick of willing women.

"I don't know."

She was shaking her head when Brenna laid a hand on her arm. "I've known Whit the longest. And I'm telling you, the man's drowning in love. So, if you don't feel the same way about him, you'd better guard your heart. Because Whit MacKenzie is a man who always gets what he wants."

"And from the look on his face at lunch, that man wants you. You may not have noticed, but I certainly did. Every move you made, his eyes were following you. And devouring you," Juliet added emphatically.

Before Cara could respond, Myrna walked in.

A ping on Cara's phone announced an incoming e-mail.

When Cara spotted the address of the sender, she felt her face go all hot again and wished she were alone in her room.

"Something important?" Brenna asked.

"It's from a New York literary agency."

At their collective gasp, she felt obligated to explain. "I realized that what you'd all said to me was something I really needed to hear. So I e-mailed half a dozen agencies that I found online, asking if they would be willing to read my illustrated manuscript." She winced. "So far, this will make my third rejection."

"You don't know that until you read it," Myrna said as sternly as she could muster. "So go ahead, honey, and read what this one says."

With her heart racing, Cara scrolled through the e-mail. Reading quickly, she looked up. "Well, it isn't an outright rejection. He says he's willing to read my manuscript, and if he likes it, he will accept me as a client while he tries to find an interested publisher."

"You see?" Brenna hurried over to give her a hug. "You've taken that critical first step. And it didn't hurt a bit."

"Brenna's right." Juliet followed suit, hugging Cara. "Who knows where this will lead?"

Cara felt the sudden rush of tears and blinked furiously. "Thank you." She looked at the three women and felt her heart swelling with love. "Really. I need to thank all of you. I would never have tried this if you hadn't planted that seed."

"Let's just hope that little seed produces a garden of success." Brenna turned to Juliet. "Now we'd better find your boys."

The two young women hurried into the great room, returning minutes later with both boys and Sammy in tow.

Behind them Mad followed in his scooter, clearly eager to take control of the plane again.

At the door Brenna turned. "Are you boys ready to spend some time in my studio?"

"Oh boy." Casey clapped his hands. "Can we play with the clay again?"

"You can."

"I'm going to make a doggy."

"Like Sammy?" Brenna asked.

He nodded. "Me and Efan are hoping we can get Mommy and Daddy to get us a puppy."

Brenna glanced at Juliet.

"But Mama says she'd rather have a baby," Ethan said with a little scowl.

"Wouldn't you like having a baby?" Brenna asked him.

The little boy shrugged. "I guess. But I'd rather get a puppy first. One like Sammy."

"Play your cards right," Myrna remarked, "and maybe you can have both."

They were all laughing as Brenna led the way out the door, with the boys and Sammy trailing behind.

Mad turned to Juliet. "Ready for that aerial view of our little piece of heaven, lass?"

"I can't wait."

They called their good-byes to Cara and Myrna before heading out the door, with Mad in the lead in his scooter and Juliet moving along behind.

When they were alone, Myrna turned to Cara. "This is the perfect time for me to do some chores upstairs, while the house is empty. I think I'll strip all the beds and get some much-needed work done." She paused. "And now that we're finally alone, I want to tell you how happy I am that you've contacted those people in New York. I just know one of those publishers will fall in love with your stories."

"Thank you, Myrna. I hope you're right."

Myrna stepped close and caught Cara's hand. "I know I am. Remember this, honey. Don't let anyone tell you what's right or wrong for you. You're allowed to make mistakes in this life. But you'll never go wrong if you just follow your heart."

"Oh, Myrna." Cara felt hot tears scalding the backs of her eyes.

As the old woman hurried away, Cara leaned a hand on the kitchen counter and allowed the tears to fall.

Tears of joy, over the hopeful response from a literary agency, but more, tears of hope and anxiety that Brenna and Juliet were right about Whit's feelings for her. Though she'd been trying to deny what was in her heart, for fear of having it broken yet again, she couldn't stop the tiny flicker of hope that Whit was different from all the rest.

She would cling to the words of his friend and sister-in-law Brenna, who believed that Whit MacKenzie was one of the good ones in this world.

Chapter Twenty-Three

Cara was humming a little tune as she moved around the kitchen.

Earlier she'd heard the sounds of the washer and dryer and had caught a glimpse of Myrna, arms laden with freshly folded sheets and pillowcases, heading up the stairs to tackle all those bedrooms. Now the only sound was the vacuum cleaner.

The thought of the housekeeper, happily having the entire upper floor to herself, had Cara grinning. Though the MacKenzie family was a constant delight, their sheer numbers probably created a bit of a problem for the old woman. No wonder she was happy to turn the kitchen duties over to someone else, leaving her to concentrate all her energy on household chores.

As soon as she was alone, Cara phoned the New York agent to eagerly accept his offer to read her manuscript. Her next step was calling Willow, asking permission to use the computer in her office to scan and send the stories and drawings electronically. She experienced a wild sense of relief when Willow agreed without asking for a lengthy explanation. It touched her heart that Whit's mother trusted her enough to say a simple yes to her request.

Cara paused in her work as the realization dawned that even now, while she was working in a ranch kitchen in Montana, her pages and drawings were being read and critiqued by a professional in New York City.

A professional.

Who did she think she was? The daughter of a father she'd never met and a mother who had unceremoniously dumped her to escape. And here she was, dreaming an impossible dream and beginning to think it might come true.

Despite the odds, she couldn't deny the feeling of anticipation, of absolute joy in her heart.

To celebrate, she intended to make a special dinner tonight. After all, everyone would be in a festive mood. Calves were being born in the hills. Always a reason for ranchers to celebrate. Add to that the fact that Mad had gained a measure of freedom and Casey and Ethan were playing to their hearts' content in Brenna's studio.

After checking the freezer and giving some thought to the kind of meal everyone, even the youngest, would enjoy, she decided to stuff several chickens for roasting, along with mashed potatoes, fresh garden vegetables for a salad, and soft, buttery rolls hot from the oven.

For dessert she settled on a Black Forest cake her gram used to bake. Chocolate layer cake with cherries in a rich cream filling and topped with warm chocolate fudge drizzled over all.

While she worked, Cara couldn't keep from smiling. After so much hardship and trouble, she had a double reason to celebrate.

Not only was she one step closer to her dream of being published, but she was also beginning to hope that she'd found a place where she was truly accepted. And if Brenna and Juliet were to be believed, she might even be loved.

Love.

The mere thought of Whit MacKenzie loving her had her pausing to take in a long, deep breath.

After a lifetime of loneliness, she'd begun to believe that she simply wasn't loveable. Especially after that situation with Jared. But Whit wasn't like anyone else. She had this sense that he would always be there for her in times of trouble.

After chopping the onions and celery and bread crumbs and mixing them with seasonings and a pinch of parsley, she stuffed the chickens and set them in a large roasting pan in the refrigerator to bake in the oven later.

Then she got busy with the cake batter. Over the sound of the electric mixer, she thought she heard a door open. Seconds later she felt a quick rush of cool, damp air and turned.

A man stood in the doorway of the kitchen. Though she was aware of his perfectly tailored suit, starched shirt, and knotted tie, the only thing she could focus on were his eyes.

Eyes she'd seen before, at a ranch in Red Rock.

Evil eyes, fixed on her with a look of pure hatred.

His voice, when he spoke, was as cold as his eyes. A cultured voice that she'd heard once before, in that rancher's kitchen. "I've been watching through binoculars, waiting until they all left so we could be alone. Today's my lucky day."

"How..." Cara's heart was pounding so hard, she was certain it would leap clear out of her chest. She licked her dry lips. "How... did you find me?"

"Pure chance. I happened upon you, but you were too busy to see me. The minute I saw your profile, I knew you at once. I could tell you hadn't spotted me."

"Where did you see me? In town?" She thought of her visit to the sheriff in Red Rock and shivered at the very thought of being studied like a specimen without her knowledge.

He merely lifted a brow. "I decided, since you weren't even aware I'd spotted you, to take my time and make some very careful plans."

"Plans?" She looked around. This stranger was obviously some sort of madman. Since he was blocking the entrance to the back door, her only avenue of escape was the door leading to the stairway.

The stairway. God in heaven. Myrna. She was upstairs, unaware of anything going on below.

Seeing the direction of Cara's gaze, the stranger was across the room in the blink of an eye, catching her roughly by the arm and twisting both her arms behind her back before imprisoning her wrists in plastic restraints.

He leaned close to whisper in her ear, "Don't even think about trying to escape. I pride myself on being a man who is very good at making careful plans."

His words caused a trickle of ice along her spine.

"I like everything neat and tidy. Like this." From his

inside pocket, he produced a folded paper. Unfolding it, he set it on the kitchen counter.

From her vantage point, Cara could see that it consisted of words and letters cut from newspapers and magazines.

"What is that?"

"Your confession."

"My…confession?"

He gave her a chilling smile. "Admitting that you killed poor old Abe over in Red Rock and came up with an elaborate lie in order to cover your guilt. And that you've been hiding out here while you mulled over a way to enrich yourself."

"Enrich?"

"Oh, did I forget to mention the bank withdrawal from one of Willow MacKenzie's accounts bearing her forged signature?" He deliberately dropped it to the floor and stepped on it to make it appear to have slipped unnoticed from a pocket.

"No one will ever believe that."

"Won't they?" He gave a cruel laugh. "They can't trace the handwriting on this note. But when they look into your background, they'll learn that your life has been nothing but trouble. Your absent mother slept with so many men she couldn't even identify which of her partners was your father. According to court records, she abandoned you. Years later she died in a cheap motel, leaving the town to bear the cost of her burial."

Seeing tears well up in her eyes, he plowed ahead almost gleefully. "As for her daughter, the records show that you've drifted from job to job, town to town, and your latest fiasco had you hooking up with a wealthy businessman who will claim to authorities that you talked your way into his life and into his condo and then left in the night with as much money and jewelry as you could carry."

"That's a lie. I never took a thing from Jared Billingham and he knows it."

"It's a funny thing about men scorned. All the pundits talk about a woman scorned, but humiliate a man with an inflated ego, and you'll find he's willing to go to great lengths to see vengeance served. Especially if he's richly compensated for telling a little white lie."

"How did you find out about him?"

"As the lawyer for poor old Abe Parson's estate, I've been kept up to date on the case by the authorities. I was the first to be called after your visit to Sheriff Hack's office. Since then I've had the time, the money, and the resources to put your entire life under a microscope, hoping to find your weaknesses, Cara Walton. In your case, it was a piece of cake. So deny all you want. It won't win over the authorities." He grabbed a handful of her hair, tugging her head back with a jolt. "Truth isn't important now. What is important is what the record will show and who the authorities will choose to believe. A girl with a sorry past or a wealthy man with all the right connections."

He looked up when footsteps sounded on the stairs. "It's a good thing I'm a man who thinks ahead. I even made plans to eliminate anyone who...happened to intrude upon my carefully laid scheme."

Seeing him reach into his pocket and withdraw a small silver pistol, Cara's eyes widened. And though her throat was clogged with terror, she managed to shout, "Myrna, stay away! Run!"

Confused, the old woman stepped into the doorway, staring at Cara with a look of sheer bewilderment. "What in the world...?"

The stranger took aim and fired a single shot. Myrna crumpled to the floor.

Cara twisted free of his grasp and raced to the old woman's side, tears of horror streaming from her eyes as she dropped to her knees.

"Oh, Myrna. I'm so sorry. This was all my..."

She was shoved aside as the stranger touched a finger to Myrna's throat before grabbing Cara by the arm and hauling her to her feet.

"Time to move. The old fool's dead. But just to make sure..." He fired a second shot at close range.

Then he boldly reached into Cara's shirt pocket and grabbed her cell phone, tossing it to the floor beside Myrna's body. "Wouldn't want the authorities to be able to track you. Besides," he added with a sneer, "you won't be needing that where you're heading."

As Cara was dragged toward the door, she turned for a final look at Myrna, who lay as still as death in an ever-widening pool of blood.

One of the ranch trucks stood idling at the back steps. The stranger hauled Cara around to the driver's side and forced her inside before shoving her across to the passenger side.

"See." His voice was triumphant. "You've even stolen one of the MacKenzies' ranch trucks. The poor, trusting fools leave all their keys on hooks on the barn wall. Something a clever thief like you would have taken note of."

"You're despicable." The more she tried to free herself of the restraints, the more the cruel plastic dug into her wrists, drawing blood.

"And you're nothing but an annoying little fool." He put the vehicle in gear and turned away from the driveway, veering toward the barns and then across a high meadow before heading toward back country.

In those first few moments, Cara gave in to the feelings of horror and revulsion that had bile burning her throat, threatening to choke her. Tears streamed from her eyes, and she couldn't stop them, nor could she wipe them away. All she could do was huddle in a corner of the vehicle, steeped in misery and self-pity.

This evil man had killed sweet Myrna. And all because of her. And now, the entire family would read that note and blame her.

My fault.

My fault.

Why shouldn't they believe she was guilty? Hadn't she always known she deserved the life she'd been given? Oh, she'd tried to hold on to her dreams. But the truth was, her course had been set years ago when even her own mother didn't want her.

While she huddled in the corner of the truck and brooded, she thought about Whit, coming home to find Myrna dead, his family betrayed. How long before he was persuaded that he'd been tricked into allowing a thief and a monster into his life?

He'd said he wanted to talk when he came back.

She'd foolishly begun to think that this time her life would turn around. He would declare his love, and they would live happily ever after.

She felt fresh tears well up in her eyes and blinked them away.

Whether Whit believed in her or not, she knew in her heart that she hadn't done anything to deserve whatever cruel fate this stranger planned for her.

As the driver maneuvered the truck up steep hills and across streams swollen by melting snow, she forced herself to put aside her misery and pay attention.

Slowly, with great effort, she pulled herself back from the edge of a deep, dark cavern of self-pity and felt her courage return.

If she survived this, she would have to find her way back. To prove her innocence. And possibly, to win back Whit's trust.

Though none of this territory was familiar, she was determined to commit it to memory.

She turned to the stranger. "Who are you?"

Through gritted teeth he hissed, "Your worst nightmare."

"What have I done to you?"

He turned the wheel sharply, and they passed through a line of trees casting light and shadow on the trail ahead. "You madc a fatal mistake."

"I don't under—"

"You had to poke your nose in where it wasn't wanted."

"What was that old rancher to you?"

"Abe had something I needed."

"You wanted a derelict ranch?"

They came out the other side of the trees into sunlight and he shot her a quick glance. "Land. Valuable land."

"Why didn't you just buy it from him?"

"He wouldn't agree to sell."

"But what does that have to do with me?"

"You went to the law."

"It didn't matter. I didn't really see anything, and I couldn't identify you. Why come after me now?"

He gave a chilling smile. "Your evidence had them taking a second look."

"That doesn't make any sense—"

His hand swept out in an arc, connecting with her cheek with such force, her head snapped to one side and she had to close her eyes against the shower of painful stars.

"Shut up. I'm sick of the sound of your voice."

She leaned back, trying to clear her head and stay focused. So far, none of this made any sense. He wasn't even under suspicion in the murder of that old rancher. Why risk killing her now and calling attention to himself?

"You realize you'll have the law searching for me."

"You? You're nobody. And the daughter of nobody. After a while, when they never locate your body, they'll just forget all about a cold case against someone with a reputation like yours."

When she turned to stare at him, he laughed. "Oh, I made it a point to learn all about you when that police chief from Red Rock started sniffing around the old man's business." His tone deepened with importance. "You didn't think I'd just let it go, did you? I'm surprised a nobody like you would bother going to the law and thinking you could win against someone like me."

"I don't know you. I don't even know your name. All I did was report what I'd overheard."

"You had to know, just by looking at me, that you

didn't stand any more chance than old Abe did. Once someone crosses me, they're dead."

"I may be nobody, but now that you've killed Myrna, the MacKenzie family will never rest until you're caught."

He sneered. "Right. Just the way Bear MacKenzie's murderer was caught."

It was as much his words as his smug, knowing tone that had her going perfectly still as an icy chill shot along her spine.

"You?" She swallowed, trying to dislodge the sudden lump in her throat. "You killed Bear MacKenzie?"

"The bastard had it coming." He gunned the engine and their vehicle shot up a steep hill and started across a high, flat meadow.

To Cara, the sight of all that shiny spring grass and those tiny wildflowers just bursting into bloom was almost more than she could bear to look at. How could the weather be so perfect, and the countryside so lovely, when everything in her world had suddenly turned upside down? She was in the hands of a cold-blooded killer. Bear MacKenzie's killer. Abe Parson's killer. And Myrna. Sweet old Myrna dead. It wasn't possible. But she'd seen for herself that still body, the pool of dark, sticky blood.

Tears pricked her eyes once more and she blinked them away, determined to remain strong and watchful and ready, in case a chance to escape should come along.

And if it didn't, if she was truly trapped and doomed to face the same fate as Myrna, as Abe, as Bear MacKenzie, she reminded herself that she would face it with as much courage as she could muster.

Not for Myrna or the others. Not even for Whit.

She had to do this for herself. To prove that no matter what life had handed her, she wasn't a nobody.

She was Cara Walton. She had survived so many trials that had threatened to take all the joy out of her life. But she'd kept on trying. And now, whatever her final moments were, she would do whatever she could to make herself proud.

Chapter Twenty-Four

Hey, Brady." Spotting his ranch foreman, the young wrangler, Carter, separated himself from the others and strolled up to the line of trucks.

Brady rolled down the window. "So, you're swamped, are you?"

Carter looked puzzled. "Swamped?"

"Your text said there were so many calves being born, you needed help fast. I texted back that I'd bring the troops. And here we are." Brady was smiling as he swept a hand to include the trucks following behind.

When he saw the look in Carter's eyes, his smile faded. "What's wrong?"

"I never sent any text. And never got yours." Carter shrugged before staring at the toe of his boot. "Truth is, I lost my cell phone. I don't know where or when. Last time I used it, I stuck it in the pocket of my parka that was hanging in the barn alongside the keys. When I got up here with the herd, I couldn't find it. It's probably been smashed under the hooves of a couple hundred cows."

Seeing the scowl on the foreman's face, he lifted both hands. "Hey, boss, don't worry. If there's any trouble, I can always use Ben's phone. As soon as I get time, I'll head to town and buy a new one."

"I don't care about your phone, Carter." Brady turned to Willow with a look of growing anger. "What I do care about is getting a text from a stranger. Who would do such a thing? And why?"

Willow shook her head, as puzzled as he was. "I can't figure it out. It almost sounds like someone wanted all of us up here together."

When Brady's cell phone rang, he yanked it out of his shirt pocket. Spotting the caller's identification, he said, "Ira. What's up?"

He listened before saying roughly, "How long ago?"

He turned to Willow while speaking to the police chief. "None of us are there. We're up in the hills. We'll head back now. But, Ira, you get a copter out there now."

After ringing off, he stepped out of the truck and motioned for the others to do the same. As the family members gathered around, he said, "Ira Pettigrew just phoned me. He got a distress call from the ranch. Myrna could only get a few words out, but it sounds bad. She's been shot."

"Shot? What the hell?"

At Ash's words, Brady held up a hand to silence him. "We don't have time right now to vent our feelings. Ira's phoned for an airlift to get Myrna to a hospital as fast as possible. She told him it's real bad."

Willow let out a cry before covering her mouth with her hand.

Whit grabbed Brady's arm. "What about Cara?"

"I don't know. The chief only knows that, according to the ID, Myrna used Cara's cell phone to tell him she'd been shot."

"Then Cara could have been shot, too. Otherwise she'd have made the call herself."

At Whit's stunned reaction, Brady nodded toward the others. "We're heading home now. See that Whit doesn't take the wheel. He's in no condition to drive."

Ash steered Whit to their truck and forced him into the passenger seat before climbing behind the wheel.

Brady turned to Carter. "Keep only the wranglers you absolutely need. Send the rest down to the ranch house. We'll need all the cool heads we can get."

And then the convoy of trucks turned in a wide arc and began the tortuous trek down the trails that would lead them home.

Mad hadn't felt this lighthearted in years. Just taking control of the little plane had him feeling like a frisky youth again.

Now, as they skimmed over the treetops and stared down at the hills black with cattle, he pointed out places of interest to Juliet. She sat beside him in the copilot seat, enthralled by the glint of sunlight off the sparkling water of Copper Creek.

"Oh, look." She stared down at the line of trucks snaking along the side of a hill. "Are those MacKenzie trucks?"

Mad studied them. "That they are, lass. Looks like they're heading back to the ranch." He glanced at his watch. "Odd. Why would they turn around so soon after reaching the herd?"

As if in answer to his question, his cell phone rang. He snatched it up and, seeing Griff's name, pressed the speakerphone so he could keep both hands at the controls. "What's up, lad? Your wife and I are having a grand time surveying our kingdom."

"While you're up there, do you see anything out of the ordinary?"

"Such as?" he demanded.

"Someone on foot, running away from the ranch. Or maybe a vehicle that is somewhere it shouldn't be."

Mad shared a look of annoyance with Juliet. "Speak English, lad. What is it you're asking me to look for?"

"We're headed back home because Myrna has been shot."

"Shot? Myrna? What...?"

"We don't know anything yet. She managed to call Ira from Cara's phone, and the authorities are on their way to fly her to a hospital. We don't know if Cara's been shot, too. We just don't know anything."

"What in hell...?" The old man's hands tightened on the controls. "So am I looking for a lone shooter, or more than one?"

"I don't know that either, Mad. We're hoping to get some answers when we reach home. But since I heard your engines overhead, I figured you're in the perfect position to spot something, anything out of the ordinary. A car. A truck. Somebody on foot..."

"We'll start looking right away." He glanced over at Juliet, whose face had gone ashen. "And, lad, let us know the minute you hear anything."

"Will do, Mad."

Even before the phone went dead, Mad was turning

the plane in the direction of the ranch and then circling overhead, hoping to see anything that would lead to the answers they were seeking.

By the time the family arrived at the ranch house, Chief Ira Pettigrew was inside, moving somberly from room to room, weapon drawn.

Dr. Dan Mullin was kneeling beside Myrna, who was wrapped in blankets from head to toe.

"She's in shock," the doctor said when the family hurried over to form a circle around her. "She's lost a lot of blood, and I have her on an IV until the copter gets here."

"Can she speak?" Willow knelt beside the old woman and took one cold hand in hers.

"I wouldn't advise it." Dr. Mullin removed a sterile packet from his bag and peeled it open as he prepared to inject a sedative into Myrna's vein.

"Has she spoken at all?"

He shook his head. "Not to me." He nodded toward the police chief. "Ira was the first one on the scene."

Willow got to her feet and caught Ira's hand. "Has she been able to tell you who did this?"

He shook his head.

Whit was staring around as if in a daze. "Ira, where's Cara?"

"Gone."

Whit closed the distance between them. "What do you mean gone?"

"I've searched the house. There's no trace of her." Wearing gloves, he gingerly held up a cell phone and the note left on the table. "The phone is hers. And this appears to be a confession from Cara."

The family hastily gathered around him as he explained. "I'm hoping the state lab can find some prints."

"You said it's a confession." Brady put a steadying arm around Willow's shoulders. "Just what exactly is she confessing to? Attempted murder?"

"It's a jumble of words and letters pasted together to explain why she killed old Abe Parson over in Red Rock and stole from Willow's bank account, before making her escape. She thanked all of you for making it so easy."

Willow's head came up. "But no mention of Myrna?"

"Maybe the shooting happened so suddenly, she had no time to add Myrna to her confession."

Whit's face went deathly pale. "I don't believe it. I don't believe any of this."

When he reached out a hand to snatch the paper from Ira's hand, the lawman shoved him backward with as much force as he could muster. "Don't even think about it, Whit. I won't have you contaminating evidence."

"That isn't evidence. It's a damned lie."

"That could be. But then the question would be why? Why not just write a letter? This thing had to take time, finding the exact words, cutting them out, pasting them on this paper. This was totally premeditated. It could be a fake or the real thing. That's for the lab to determine, if they can lift any prints. As for the phone, we'll be able to trace every call she's made from it. But by leaving it behind, she knew her whereabouts couldn't be tracked by our state technicians. I'd say this was very carefully planned."

He dropped it into a plastic bag and sealed it before turning to Willow and holding up a bank receipt. "Willow, did you withdraw a hundred thousand dollars from the ranch fund?"

"A hundred thousand? Why would I want such a sum of money?"

Ira shrugged. "Someone withdrew a hundred thousand dollars from the ranch funds." He held up withdrawal slip. "Is this your signature?"

She examined the paper before shaking her head. "It's a good forgery, but it definitely isn't mine." Willow turned her face into Brady's shoulder and gave a shudder. "This is a nightmare."

"Did Cara Walton have access to your office and your bank ledgers?"

Willow went pale as the knowledge dawned. "She called me just after I left the house today, asking if she could use the computer in my office. Of course I told her she was welcome to it."

They all looked up at the sound of the helicopter circling overhead before landing on the runway behind the barn. Within minutes, a team of medics hurried into the kitchen, carrying a gurney.

As they prepared Myrna for the flight, under Dr. Mullin's direction, Willow hurried over to catch the old woman's hands in hers.

"Stay strong, Myrna. We love you and we're sending our prayers with you."

The housekeeper lay as still as death.

Willow leaned close to press a kiss to her cheek. "Oh, how I wish you could tell us what happened here, and where Cara has gone."

Though her eyes remained closed, Myrna's lids flickered. Her lips moved in a feeble whisper.

As the medics carried the gurney toward the door, Willow turned to the others. "She was obviously agitated and trying to tell me something, but I couldn't make out the words."

Whit caught his mother's hand. "Did you catch anything?"

"Just gibberish. It sounded like she said 'trance' or 'dance.' But that doesn't make any sense."

"Neither does that 'confession.'" Whit's voice was low with anger as he turned to Ira. "I don't care how all this looks—I know Cara isn't capable of doing any of this. She could no more harm Myrna than you could, Chief. She loves that old woman. As for stealing money from my mother's account, it just isn't something she would ever consider."

The police chief put a hand on Whit's shoulder. "She came here with nothing but the clothes on her back. She's been living on the hospitality of you and your family since you first met her. Met her, I should add, under questionable circumstances." When Whit looked as though he were about to raise his fist, the chief stopped him. "Look, son. I know you have feelings for this girl. But you know that old saying. Love is blind. And those feelings are blinding you to the truth."

"The truth?" Whit pulled away with a look of fury. "What truth do you see here, Ira?" He pointed to the mixer on the countertop. "Why would someone who intended to commit a crime calmly go about preparing to bake a cake and then stop halfway through the process to shoot Myrna and then run away?"

The chief looked perplexed. "I know it doesn't make sense. Attempted murder rarely does."

"But this is crazy and you know it."

Ira paused before saying quietly, "If Cara Walton isn't the one who put together this crazy confession, and isn't the one who shot Myrna, and I'm beginning to have my doubts about that, then she's in the hands of the one who did. And that means that little lady's in serious trouble."

Whit latched on to the only words that mattered. "So you don't believe this confession either?"

"I don't know what to believe, son. We have Myrna's words that she'd been shot. She didn't say Cara's name. And then there's all this." He waved a hand. "Like you said, would someone go to the trouble of preparing cake batter if she intended to confess to a crime, steal a fortune, and shoot anyone who stood in her way?"

Whit nodded. "Thank you, Chief." He turned to the others. "We can't wait for help on this. Cara's life is on the line. We need to fan out and search for her all across these hills."

Ira raised his voice to be heard above the words being shouted by the others. "Now, folks, I suggest you all settle down and let the state police do their jobs. They've got an aerial team on the way."

"There's no time for that, Ira." Whit turned to Brady for support. "Mad's already in the air. He and Juliet can circle the area. But there are too many places where people on foot or in a vehicle can hide from a plane's view."

Brady nodded. "I agree. We have enough manpower and enough vehicles that we can cover a lot of miles. I say we get on this before they get too far away, or darkness falls." He turned to the police chief. "I promise you, Ira, we won't get in the way of the authorities. But we all have cell phones. Once the state police get here, they can let us know what they see from the air and where we're needed. And we can do the same by contacting you if we spot anything."

Ira gave a reluctant nod. "I can see there's no stopping you. And I have to agree that the sooner we get on the trail, the better."

"Good." Brady pointed at Griff. "See that all our ranch trucks are gassed and ready to go."

"I'm on it." Griff started out the door.

"The rest of us should start in Bear's office," Willow called. "We have a locked cabinet of weapons and ammunition."

They trooped down the hall, and Willow was parceling out rifles and sacks of bullets when Griff came running into the office with a look of alarm.

"There's a truck missing."

Whit's eyes narrowed. "You sure of that?"

"I am." He turned to Brady. "We took four trucks up to the hills, leaving six in the barn. There are only five now. And while I was checking, I stepped on this." He held up a cell phone. "Didn't Carter say his phone was lost?"

"In the barn." Brady nodded. "It makes sense. If someone, whether it was Cara or someone else, was making plans and got in there overnight, it would have been an easy matter to slip Carter's phone out of his pocket." He gave a deep sigh of disgust. "I hope to heaven it isn't Cara. But whether she's guilty or not, we've been set up from the beginning."

At a sudden thought, his head came up sharply. "Do you think this could have been set into motion by that scum ex-boyfriend…" He looked toward Whit to supply a name.

"Jared Billingham." Whit spat the name from between clenched teeth.

"I guess we'll only know the truth when we find Cara. Finding her is the only way we'll have our answers."

Their faces were grim as they marched out of the office, weapons in hand, and headed toward the convoy of trucks idling outside.

Chapter Twenty-Five

Cara couldn't stop thinking about Myrna. Sweet Myrna, treating her with so much love. Opening her heart and her kitchen to someone she didn't know but trusted without reservation. And now that trust had been so cruelly betrayed.

She shuddered at the image playing through her mind. Myrna, innocently walking into a trap and now lying dead on the kitchen floor in a pool of blood. So much blood. Tears ran down Cara's cheeks and she knew she would never be able to erase that image.

Hadn't she known, the first time she saw this man's evil eyes, that he would stop at nothing to have what he wanted? But what did he want from her? She had nothing. And she knew nothing, except threatening words she'd overheard. How could she possibly be a threat to him?

She knew she had to brush aside any distractions and concentrate on the trail they were taking through this wild tangle of forest.

She forced herself to note landmarks. An odd-shaped boulder. A gnarled, twisted ponderosa pine. A cluster of trees in the middle of a high meadow forming a huge horseshoe shape.

She clenched her fists, desperate to free herself of the plastic restraints that cut into her flesh. She wouldn't let him take her without a fight. If she saw even the smallest window of escape, she would risk it. She knew, without a doubt, that this stranger intended to kill her and leave no trace of his evil deed to be discovered. She would be left in an unmarked grave in the wilderness, and no one would ever know the truth about how she had disappeared or what had become of her. She would be, as he'd promised, a cold case, never to be resolved.

Forgotten. A nobody.

"Check in with me every half hour," Chief Pettigrew said sternly as the MacKenzies started toward their trucks. "I have a direct line to the state boys. Since they've now updated their search for a ranch truck, they'll need to know where you are at every turn so they don't mistake any of you for the one they're chasing."

There were nods of agreement all around before they pulled open truck doors in preparation for their search.

Ash caught hold of Whit's arm. "I thought I'd ride along with you."

Whit gave a quick shake of his head. "It makes more sense if we take as many vehicles as possible and fan out in different directions."

"Look, bro. I know what you're going through. I don't think you should be driving."

Whit shot him a cool look. "I'm driving. And I'm going to find Cara."

He slammed the door shut and put the truck in gear.

With a shrug of his shoulders, Ash walked to a second truck. He hadn't just been mouthing platitudes. He knew all the emotions his brother was experiencing right now. Hadn't he been half mad with worry when Brenna's life was in danger?

Still, he hated the thought of Whit dealing with this alone. Sometimes just having someone to talk to could ease the fear gnawing a hole in his heart.

He watched the cloud of dust from Whit's truck and sighed. If Cara wasn't found, and soon, his little brother would be inconsolable, and true to MacKenzie tradition, would become a dangerous hothead.

While the other trucks fanned out, taking the back roads as well as the highway, Whit turned his vehicle toward the hills. He'd made up his mind to try his best to think like a cold-blooded killer. He knew in his heart that whoever pulled the trigger and shot Myrna was heartless and beyond cruel. That sort of person would avoid civilization and flee to the wilderness, where he could do his dirty work in secret.

From all that Cara had told him about Jared Billingham, the jerk fit the description of heartless. But could a millionaire living the good life in his fancy ski resort be depraved enough to kill a helpless old woman just for the sake of revenge? After all, Cara may have rejected Billingham, but such a thing didn't warrant this kind of cruelty.

But if not Jared Billingham, who?

He thought of the words Chief Pettigrew had spoken. Though they'd made his blood boil, he couldn't fault the chief for saying them. There were plenty of lovers who woke up one day to learn they'd been betrayed. That's what made prenuptial agreements so popular. Hell, even Cara had been betrayed by a guy she'd trusted.

But that didn't mean he had been persuaded to lose faith in her.

He knew her heart. Knew the goodness in her. A goodness that couldn't be faked. And knew, without a doubt, that someone had forced her to flee. Someone evil.

Evil eyes.

The words leapt into his mind, chilling his blood.

He pressed the speed dial that held the police chief's number.

At the sound of that deep, businesslike tone, his own voice was suddenly breathless. "Ira, do you remember when you followed up on Cara's story about the suit-and-tie guy and the old rancher?"

"Of course I do, Whit."

"Do you remember what she said about him?"

Ira didn't even hesitate. "She knew he was a villain because he had evil eyes."

"Exactly. She didn't think or wonder. She knew. Because she could see the evil in his eyes." Whit paused, feeling his throat go dry. "Did Sheriff Hack over in Red Rock ever identify Suit-and-Tie?"

"No."

"Is that case closed, then? The nephew is guilty?"

"I thought so. But Sheriff Hack met with the lawyer who inherited old Abe's ranch. He let him know that even though the nephew doesn't have an alibi for the night his uncle was shot, enough of his neighbors have come forward to vouch for his character that the authorities are having second thoughts. Sheriff Hack was hoping Abe's lawyer might have insight into what was going on in the old man's mind and might have some idea of anyone who would want old Abe dead."

"So this makes two unsolved murders in our territory within a year."

Ira uncharacteristically swore. "Don't remind me, son. Every morning, as soon as I'm awake, that fact lies heavy on my heart."

"Ira, what if Evil Eyes got some inside information that the nephew is no longer under suspicion and wants to make certain the only witness against him is eliminated?"

There was a long, silent pause before Ira let out a breath. "Weren't you the one who told me you couldn't be sure if Cara's story was true or just a figment of her wild imagination?"

"Yeah. But now..." Whit clamped his jaw tight as he considered the implications. "Now I think there are just too many coincidences."

"You listen to me, son. Just keep searching. Right now, I'm open to believing anything."

As Whit gunned the engine, it occurred to him that throughout his lifetime he'd almost never been afraid of anything. His friends and family had teased him about being not only foolish, but also fearless. He'd taken brutal spills from the saddle, once even falling under the thunderous hooves of a stampeding herd, and had emerged feeling a rush of adrenaline rather than the fear that was natural to most men. He'd once slit open his leg from ankle to thigh on razor-sharp barbed wire and had driven himself more than fifty miles to the clinic, wrapped in a dirty towel, without losing hope or losing consciousness.

But right now, thinking that Cara could be in the hands of a desperate killer, the cold, hard pit of fear clawed at his insides, leaving him shaken to the core.

Willow rode shotgun while Brady drove. They'd taken back roads in the belief that anyone on the run would prefer them to the highway, even though the trail would be slow and possibly fruitless.

Willow's voice was muted, as though feeling her way through too many conflicting feelings. "I know how it all looks. The confession, the bank withdrawal slip... Myrna." She shuddered before taking in a long, slow breath. "But I just can't bring myself to believe that Cara would do any of this."

She turned to study Brady's stern profile. "You're a good judge of character. What do you think?"

He gave her a quick glance before returning his attention to the bumpy dirt road. "I'm inclined to think she was set up. None of this fits the girl we know."

"Of course, we have to take into account what Ira said back there." Willow clasped and unclasped her hands. "Nobody ever really knows the deepest, darkest secrets of others. Even the people we've known the longest." She turned to stare out the side window. "It never occurred to me that Bear had a relationship with someone while I was out of the country."

Brady laid his big hand over hers, stilling her movements. "What's important is this. Bear was a good man.

So good, so true to his basic morals, he provided for a son he never even knew about, treating him as fairly in his last will and testament as the sons you and he share."

"I know that, Brady. And I agree that he was a good man. But it certainly proves that even the ones we know intimately can harbor secrets."

"That doesn't make Cara a killer."

Willow gave him a weak smile. "We've known her scant weeks."

"And she's been honest about her tough childhood and the mistakes she's made along the way."

Now it was Willow's turn to place a hand over his. "I'm sorry, Brady. I didn't realize what I was saying... This has to bring back so many memories of your own childhood."

He nodded. "Not all of us are lucky enough to grow up in a loving family like yours, Willow. We don't get a choice in the cards we're dealt. But we do get to say how we'll play those cards. I never told you, but Whit found an envelope in the range shack bearing Cara's signature and fifty-seven dollars and twenty-five cents. All the money she had left in the world. And she was leaving it to pay for her room and board, even though she could have walked away without anyone ever knowing she'd been there. You don't find that kind of integrity every day. Cara Walton strikes me as a wounded bird desperate for a second chance to fly."

Willow blinked back the tears that threatened. "Now you've done it."

He shot her a questioning look.

"When did my ranch foreman become a poet?"

His handsome face relaxed into a smile. "That's me.

The poet of Copper Creek, Montana. Though most of your wranglers would prefer to call me a badass."

"That's just a façade. Now that I've spent enough time with you, I know you're really a good, tenderhearted man who sees the goodness in everybody."

"Careful. Next thing you know, you'll be telling me you're starting to fall for me."

She turned away and watched the line of trees along the roadside. But though she pretended to be searching for the missing ranch truck and its occupants, the truth was, she could barely concentrate on the matter at hand.

...starting to fall for me.

Could Brady see? Was she so transparent, her entire family could see? Were they all tiptoeing around her, pretending not to notice the way she was drawn to him like a magnet?

Oh, sweet heaven. What was happening to her?

Bear had only been gone a year. His murderer was still walking free.

Her youngest son had gone off like a madman, chasing after a young woman who might easily break his heart this very day.

Her dear friend and housekeeper was fighting for her life.

And she was allowing herself to think about her foreman, and Bear's best friend, in a way that shamed her.

Maybe Brady was wrong. Maybe it was much more than "starting to fall for him." Maybe she'd gone way beyond that and was just too much of a coward to admit it, even to herself.

Chapter Twenty-Six

"Mad. Can you hear me?"

Chief Pettigrew's voice boomed over Mad's speaker-phone.

"Half of Montana can hear you," Mad shouted over the drone of the Cessna's engine.

"I'm notifying everyone involved in this search to change your frequency to the following."

After giving the state police frequency, Ira instructed each family member to identify themselves and their current locations.

Once Mad had changed the frequency of the Cessna, he and Juliet listened in silence as all members of the search party were brought on board and up to date.

For long minutes, Mad and Juliet remained silent, too shocked and stunned to process all the information that had been released.

Mad shook his head at the news. Sweet old Myrna

shot and fighting for her life at the hospital. A bank withdrawal slip for a huge sum of money, bearing an excellent forgery of Willow MacKenzie's signature. Carter's cell phone stolen and used to send a text urging help with the herd in the highlands, presumably to ensure that the household would be empty and vulnerable. One of the ranch trucks stolen from the vehicle barn. And finally a note composed of pasted words and letters, left behind and claiming to be a confession from Cara Walton.

"I'll not believe it," Mad muttered as he began a slow circle above the ranch. "Are ye listening down there?" He knew every word was being monitored by the police as well as his own family. In his agitated state, his Scottish burr thickened. "Until I hear the lass admit it in her own words, I'll not be persuaded that she had a hand in any of this."

Juliet studied the ground below them. "What about the confession?"

Mad's voice rose. "Any criminal can paste words on a paper. But if the criminal doesn't have access to her handwriting, there's no way to forge her signature." He softened his tone somewhat. "So you listen to me, Whit, wherever you are. Whoever this clever hoodlum is, he had to resort to words cut out from magazines, because it was the only way he could try to incriminate the lass."

Ira's voice came over the plane's intercom. "I wish I could afford your luxury of emotion right now, Mad. Willow saw the signature on the bank withdrawal slip and pronounced it a fine forgery."

"There you go, then." Mad's voice was a growl of anger. "Whoever did this deed has access to Willow's signature, but not Cara's."

Whit's voice came over the line and had all of them paying attention. "All right, then. At least some of us are in agreement that Cara simply isn't capable of committing the crimes she's accused of. Now let's find her. It's the only way she can clear her name. And the only way we can bring this monster to justice." He paused before adding, "Ira, I think this eliminates from the list of possible suspects Jared Billingham, even though he's been sending Cara threatening texts. There's no way he would be able to closely duplicate my mother's signature."

"I already have someone on it." Ira's voice was amplified as it crackled over all their cell phones. "The state police are interviewing Billingham as we speak."

"That's good." After another pause, Whit said, "Mom, you need to think about how many people have access to documents bearing your signature. Maybe someone at the bank has a grudge against our family. Whatever the reason, someone has gone to a lot of trouble to steal a small fortune and make Cara appear to be the guilty one."

While the conversation swirled around the cockpit, Mad turned to Juliet. "Keep a close eye, lass. Until the state police copters get here, we're their best chance of spotting that missing truck." He sighed. "Unless, of course, it's already been ditched somewhere in the wilderness."

Along the main highway, Ash was driving while Griff was using binoculars to scan the area beyond.

As they listened to the conversation on their cell phones' speaker systems, Ash drummed nervous fingers on the wheel. "I agree with Mad and Whit. I don't believe for a minute this was all orchestrated by Cara. I liked her the minute I met her. What's more, Brenna really liked her. And I trust my wife's instincts."

Griff nodded. "Juliet and Brenna had a bet going as to how long it would take before Whit realized he was in love. They were both thrilled with the prospect of having Cara for a sister-in-law." He turned to glance at Ash. "There's something to be said for a female's intuition. I just think our smart wives would have caught on if Cara was a phony."

Ash checked the truck's navigation map. "So where is she now?" He studied the various routes in and out of Copper Creek. "If I wanted to hide my crime and dispose of a body without anyone ever finding it, I'd head to the hills right up there"—he touched a spot on the dashboard map—"and find the most isolated spot I could."

His voice, carried over the entire network of family phones and police intercoms, declared, "Griff and I are leaving the highway and heading toward the hills. We think that's the most likely spot a kidnapper would go."

Whit's voice came on instantly. "I agree. In fact, I'm already heading toward the west range. It's got everything a criminal would want. Wilderness, almost impassible trails, and because of the heavy forestation, little chance of being spotted from the air."

He gave a sudden curse when he noted tire tracks in the soft earth where snow had melted. His heart started racing. A vehicle had gone this way, and recently. The tracks were fresh. "I've just come across fresh tire tracks in the damp ground. I'm no expert—they could have been made by any sort of vehicle—but I'm betting there weren't too many visitors to this barren stretch of landscape in the past few hours."

Mad's voice joined in. "Juliet and I are over that area now. We'll keep a close eye, lad."

Willow listened to the others before turning to Brady. "Do you agree with their choice of location?"

His eyes narrowed in concentration. "I do. But I'm not sure all of us should converge on a single location. If we're wrong, we could all be in one place while our crook is somewhere else, getting away with the perfect crime."

"Not perfect." Willow's voice was soft, to mask the pain. "If Myrna lives, we'll have a witness to what really happened."

"That won't do Cara any good if he succeeds in carrying out his plan for her."

"So you believe Cara has been kidnapped?"

He closed a hand over Willow's. "I do. Now more than ever."

She squeezed her eyes shut for a moment, as if to block out the fear. "I agree." Then she turned to him. "Whit spotted tire tracks. That's enough for me. Hurry, Brady. We need to get there."

The foreman turned the wheel and left the dirt road, heading across a flat stretch of MacKenzie land before starting up to the ridge of a high meadow.

Cara struggled to spot landmarks as the truck continued a slow, steady climb.

She turned to the surly driver. "Are we still on MacKenzie land?"

He shot her a dark look and held his silence, breaking it only to mutter a fierce oath as their vehicle jerked over a hidden boulder. For a moment the truck listed to one side, and Cara was unable to stop the momentum that had her sliding across the seat and slamming against him.

He gave her a rough shove that sent her crashing into the passenger door. Her head jolted against the side window hard enough to make her see stars.

She shook her head, struggling to clear her brain. Whit had said their ranch was big. But she couldn't imagine owning this much land. Maybe they'd already left the MacKenzie ranch. Maybe they'd already left the county, for all she knew. The only thing she knew for certain was that this wasn't the area where she'd met Whit.

Whit. Had he returned home yet? Had he read that phony confession? Was he cursing her and calling himself every kind of fool for having ever trusted her?

The thought of hurting Whit, of having him think the worst of her, sent a fresh stab of pain to her already breaking heart.

While Mad turned the Cessna in a slow circle, Juliet grabbed his arm. "I think I see something."

He eased back on the controls, allowing the small plane to slow.

"There." She pointed and he followed the direction to catch a beacon of light.

The old man frowned. "It could be sunlight reflecting off water. Except that there's no stream in this particular area. The creek and river are up ahead." He pointed to the binoculars. "I'll hold steady. You take a closer look."

She peered through the binoculars and gave a slow shake of her head. "It's gone."

"Then that could mean movement." He pointed. "Look ahead or behind and see if you catch something."

After several seconds of silence, Juliet grew excited. "There." She peered intently. "Yes. Sunlight. I think it's on a windshield. It's barely visible, but I believe that's a vehicle moving in an upward direction." She followed the movement before saying, "Up that hill. Directly into that forest ahead."

Mad gave their location and shouted into his speaker, "A vehicle moving up the west ridge. Barely visible through the canopy of trees. Unless I miss my guess, it's headed toward the high ridge where Copper River meets Copper Creek. Probably the most inhospitable piece of land we own. But a good place for a crime. Now get on it, lads."

Ira's voice crackled over the intercom. "I hope all of you got that."

After a jumble of voices, Ira took command. "I'm aboard one of the state police helicopters. We should arrive in six to eight minutes. Whit, where are you?"

Whit's tone was rough with emotion. "I'm practically there. Once the copters get close, there's no chance for surprises, so I'm going to try to slip around to the far side of the ridge and get there ahead of this slimeball."

The police chief's voice remained calm. "Remember this. We still don't know if Cara Walton is driving the vehicle or if she's been abducted. Either way, all of you need to be prepared for anything."

Whit gritted his teeth and floored the gas pedal as he veered off the trail he'd been following, determined to stop this madness. Ira could say what he wanted. Whit knew in his heart that Cara was being taken against her will. And he was willing to do whatever it took to save her.

* * *

Brady and Willow listened to the directions given by Chief Ira Pettigrew before changing course and heading toward the distant ridge. Ash and Griff did the same.

Mad and Juliet, from their vantage point in the air, were able to see the movement of ranch trucks converging on the lone truck up ahead.

Mad turned to Juliet, who was tracking every move through the binoculars. "If the driver gets even a hint that he's being followed, he could easily kill Cara to keep her quiet."

Juliet was trembling with agitation. "I feel so helpless."

"Aye, lass." The old man made a calculated decision. "I'm heading for the ridge, but I'll aim for the back side of it, to throw the driver off the track. With any luck, there may be enough of a clearing to allow me to land this bird."

Above the sound of the truck's engine, Cara thought she heard something. Sitting very still, she scanned the sky outside the window. Seeing nothing, she decided it was probably only the pounding of her heart. This man was going to a lot of trouble to get her as far from civilization as possible. He'd made no secret of his intention to kill her. What's more, he intended for his crime to never be discovered. She had to come up with a way to save herself. But her mind was such a jumble of worries, all she could think of was running, as soon as possible. With her wrists bound behind her, she wasn't even able to reach for the door handle; otherwise, her best bet would have been to leap out while they were moving. But, she vowed, as soon as he came to a stop and let her out, she would run, regardless of the absolute certainty that he would shoot her in the back rather than let her get away.

His foot hit the brake pedal. "What the hell?"

In the silence that followed, he lowered the window and the sound of a plane's engines could be heard.

As the minutes dragged on, it became obvious that the plane was drawing closer.

He put the truck in gear and moved deeper into the woods, where it would be impossible to be seen.

The plane continued on until the drone of the engines faded.

The stranger shot Cara a grim smile. "For a minute I was afraid someone might be looking for you. I guess it was just some hotshot rancher checking on his herd. Like I said, why would anybody care about a nobody like you?"

They rolled forward, deeper into the thick tangle of dark, gloomy woods.

Chapter Twenty-Seven

Whit reached the summit and parked his truck in the shelter of a thick cluster of ponderosa pines that completely hid the vehicle from view.

Keeping to the woods on foot, rifle in hand, he watched the trail below, hoping for a glimpse of the stolen ranch truck bearing Cara and whoever had abducted her.

Hearing the sound of an approaching vehicle, he took refuge behind the trunk of a giant pine.

As the truck came into view, his heart nearly stopped when he caught sight of Cara's pale face peering through the passenger window. In her eyes he could read all the pain, all the terror she was experiencing. Though she blocked his view of the driver, he felt an overwhelming sense of fury at the stranger who had inflicted such pain on the woman he loved.

The woman he loved.

That knowledge left him shaken to the core.

Hadn't he known ever since meeting Cara Walton that she was different from all the other women he'd known? That she'd touched some special place in his heart that he'd always believed was untouchable? Why had it taken something this dark and dangerous to make him accept the truth?

He felt a wild surge of emotions. Fear that he wouldn't be fast enough, or accurate enough, to keep her safe from this monster. Absolute fury at the madman threatening her life. And a fierce sense of protectiveness for this one small woman who had already been through so much pain in her life.

When the truck halted, Whit's finger tightened on the trigger. All he needed was one clear shot and this stranger would pay dearly for what he'd done.

When the truck came to a sudden halt, Cara's blood started throbbing in her temples. She stared around the vast wilderness and felt so alone.

Alone, but not helpless, she vowed.

This was the moment she'd prepared for, and dreaded. As soon as the driver opened her door, she would have to run, no matter what.

The stranger stepped out of the truck and circled around to the passenger side.

Cara braced, ready to make good her escape.

Instead, as he opened the door, he took a firm grasp on her arm, hauling her so roughly from the truck, she lost her balance and fell. He swore and yanked her to her feet, keeping an iron grip on her as he forced her to move along beside him. Though she tried to twist free, he wasn't about to let her go.

As they walked, she saw signs of small, freshly dug holes in the ground. They were too small to have been made by a shovel, but they appeared to be deep.

"What—"

"None of your business," he snarled.

He dragged her forward until they came to a fallen log. Before releasing her, he pressed her forcibly down on the log.

"Could you at least release my wrists?"

"Aw, are you feeling uncomfortable?" His tone grew dangerously quiet. "In a few more minutes you won't feel anything at all." Kneeling behind her, he reached into his pocket and produced a switchblade. With the press of his finger, it opened and he quickly cut through the plastic restraints.

As they fell away and Cara began rubbing her bloodied wrists, he leaned close to whisper in her ear, "I'm not doing this for any humane reason, but I need your hands free so you can kill yourself."

Her eyes went wide. "What do you—"

"If anyone ever happens across what remains of your carcass when the wild animals are through with you," he said with an evil smile, "an autopsy will prove that you actually took your own life. With this gun."

He used his handkerchief to wipe the pistol carefully before lifting it and pressing the muzzle to her temple.

She used that moment to push herself up, ramming the top of her head under his chin, snapping it so hard he could taste blood as a tooth broke after piercing his lip.

He gave a bellow of rage and fell backward. That was all the time Cara needed to start running.

Before she'd managed more than a couple of steps,

the stranger's hand tangled in her hair, pulling her back with such force she cried out in pain, her hope of freedom dashed.

Across the clearing, Whit stepped out of his place of concealment, his rifle aimed at the man. Until now, Cara had blocked his chance for a clear shot of her abductor. But now, as he took aim, the man spotted him and quickly wrapped an arm around Cara's throat, pressing his pistol to her temple.

"Now you have two choices," the figure behind Cara called. "Drop your weapon, or, if you decide to be a hero, you can take that one-in-a-million chance of shooting me before I manage to blow her away. You willing to gamble on her life?"

"Let her go." Whit dropped his rifle. "Kill me instead."

"I have a better idea. I'll just kill two for the price of one." The man laughed at his little joke as he pushed Cara ahead of him until he was close enough to kick the rifle aside.

Whit made an audible gasp when, for the first time, he was able to see the man's face.

"Lance? Lance McMillan? What the hell...?"

At Cara's blank look, Whit said, "This is the son of my father's trusted lawyer and one of his oldest friends. He's also our family lawyer since his father retired. What is this all about, Lance?"

The lawyer kept a firm grasp on Cara's neck, his arm wrapped around it so tightly he was cutting off her breath, while his pistol was pressed painfully against her temple.

Leaning close he said, "If you get any more clever ideas about running, it'll be the last idea you ever have." He looked over at Whit. "And if you're thinking about being a hero, just remember that you'll be the cause of the lady's sudden demise. I can pull this trigger faster than you can move."

"Why, Lance? What am I missing here? Why would a successful lawyer resort to criminal activity?" Whit demanded.

"I wouldn't expect a guy who shovels manure and tends fat, stupid cows for a living to understand. I realized years ago that there was a better way to live than to shuffle documents for rich old men who called themselves friends of my father. Hell, my father had no ambition beyond doing their bidding, driving clear across Montana to draw up wills and land purchase agreements and be invited along on their hunting and fishing trips as his reward. I'll choose my own rewards, thank you very much. And I prefer my private plane and pilot, my new car, my million-dollar house in Billings, and my own hunting lodge, where I'm the host, not the guest."

"And you got all this by stealing?"

"Let's just say I decided to forge my own path instead of following my father's advice to earn everything the old-fashioned way."

"Yeah." Whit took a step closer, watching for any opportunity to get close enough to attack. "Why work for it when you can steal what others worked so hard for?"

"Now you get it." Lance gave a chilling laugh. "Like old Abe."

Whit's head came up. "You killed him? For his land?"

"Not just land. I needed to be assured that he'd retained mineral rights to his land. I had some soil borings done. The old geezer was sitting on acres of gold-rich land."

Cara's eyes widened. "Is that the reason for those holes we just passed? Soil borings?"

Whit looked from Cara to Lance. "You've had soil borings done on MacKenzie land? Why?"

"When I took over my father's work, I learned that your father and grandfather retained all the mineral rights to their land. More than a year ago, I hired a private firm to do some work in secret. To see if I've... inherited more than just wilderness."

"Inherited?" Whit's blood started heating as the implications of what Lance was revealing began to register.

"I guess you haven't put it all together yet. Too much for a stupid cowboy to ponder, is it?"

"That's the second time you've called me stupid." Whit inched closer. "Since you seem fixated on your brilliance, why don't you fill in this stupid cowboy?"

Lance's head lifted. His chest expanded. It was obvious that Whit had tapped into his source of pride. "Since I was a kid, I've watched all these wealthy ranchers work like dogs, fighting the weather, the predators, determined to protect their precious cattle, when all along, the true value isn't what's being fed by the land, but what's beneath it. So I decided I'd use my brains to my advantage and get my hands on as much land as I could."

"Even if it meant killing a few hard-working ranchers along the way?" Whit's eyes narrowed. "So you needed to get rid of Cara, the only witness to your threat against old Abe. But if there were other victims, won't you have to eliminate any witnesses to those crimes as well?"

"I'm too smart to leave witnesses. That's why I had to shoot the old biddy at your place."

"Myrna. A sweet lady you've known for a lifetime. And you did it without an ounce of regret?"

"I'd do it again. All it takes is a brain and a steady hand. And I have both. I actually felt a rush of adrenaline, especially when I took out a legend like Bear. That rich, arrogant fool never even saw it coming."

His words hit Whit with all the force of a bullet to the heart.

"You...killed my father?"

"I killed the great Bear MacKenzie." Lance spoke the words almost gleefully. "He found out I'd forged his signature on some documents. After I begged his forgiveness and said I'd make good on any debts, he agreed to meet with me before telling my father what I'd done. So, of course, I had to work fast to see that my secret wasn't revealed."

All the color drained from Whit's face. His hands fisted at his sides. His eyes were blinded by a red mist of fury.

From the look on his face, it was obvious that he was so overcome with pain and rage he was beyond words or reason.

Lance turned from Cara and took aim at Whit with the pistol, intending to fire at point-blank range. In that same instant, Cara reacted instinctively, knocking his hand upward and causing the bullet to deflect to a nearby tree.

Before Lance could try again, Whit was on him like an enraged animal, driving him backward into the dirt.

As he fell, Lance managed to hold on to the pistol, and as Whit's hands closed around his throat, he squeezed off a shot.

Whit's body jerked backward and his right arm dropped uselessly to his side. Still, he managed to knock the pistol from Lance's hand before landing his left fist squarely into Lance's nose, causing a fountain of blood to spurt.

The two men rolled around on the ground, grunting with pain and exertion as they exchanged lethal punches.

Despite Whit's fury-driven frenzy, Cara could see his energy flagging with every blow. When Lance sensed victory, his fingers scrabbled around in the dirt until they encountered the gun.

He gave one of his most chilling laughs as he took aim. "All for nothing. You're going to die, MacKenzie. And I'll see to it that the only prints on the gun belong to the woman."

The sky above seemed to fill with helicopters, their blades whirring. The Cessna roared directly overhead before coming to a bumpy landing. Emerging from the woods, half a dozen trucks and police vehicles circled the two men on the ground.

Seeing all his chances of laying blame on Cara slipping away, Lance turned his full fury on Whit. Before he could fire, he gave a shocked scream at the red-hot pain emanating from his back. A quick glance behind him showed Cara standing over him. In her hands was the switchblade he'd left lying beside the log.

"You'll pay..." He struggled to aim the pistol, but before he could take a shot, his body betrayed him, and he fell forward.

"Don't kill him," Whit cried as the police sharpshooters surrounded them. "I want him to pay for a lifetime for what he..." His words trailed off as he lost consciousness.

"Whit." Cara scrambled to lift the heavy burden of Lance's body away before kneeling beside the still form of Whit, blood oozing through his shirt.

Had the bullet torn through his heart?

Cara was gripped by a feeling of absolute terror. "Oh no, Whit. Please don't die. This is all my fault. Please, Whit. Oh, please. I don't know what I'll do if you die."

While the police and the MacKenzies hurried forward to assist, Cara wrapped her arms around the unconscious Whit, rocking him while her tears spilled over him in a torrent.

She looked up at his mother, who joined Cara, pillowing Whit's head in her lap.

Seeing mother and son, Cara felt her poor heart break in two. "I'm so sorry, Willow. Myrna's dead, and now Whit. And it's all because of me."

After several moments of stunned silence, the air was suddenly filled with shouts as Ira and the police took charge.

"We need a medic," the chief called. "What's the holdup?"

Uniformed officers rushed forward. While several bent over Lance, proclaiming him alive and securing him to a gurney, more gathered around Whit.

One of the medics ordered Cara to move away, but she didn't seem to hear.

"Ma'am," the officer said gently, drawing first Cara and then Willow aside. "We need to examine the patient."

Juliet, who had been racing to keep up with Mad's scooter, dropped to her knees beside Cara and drew the young woman into her arms while Brady gathered Willow close and attempted to soothe her.

"He's dead," Cara whispered. "And it's all my fault."

"Shhh." Juliet smoothed her hair in an attempt to comfort. "Let the medics do their job."

As the others formed a close circle around the still form, they seemed to stop breathing until the medic lifted his head to declare, "There's a pulse. It's feeble, but he's alive. Get a gurney over here."

As they strapped Whit onto the gurney in preparation for the flight to the clinic, Mad clapped a big work-worn hand on his grandson's shoulder. "I hope you can hear me, lad. You stay strong. All of us will be fighting right along with you."

"Mad..." Whit's voice was little more than a croak. "Mom." He struggled to see through the hazy mist that clouded his vision. "Lance...killed...Pop."

For a moment Mad appeared too stunned to speak. He looked at the others. "Is the lad hallucinating?"

Cara turned from Juliet's arms. "No, Mad. Lance admitted it. In fact, he bragged about it."

"But why?" Willow's face was drained of color. Her voice was little more than a shocked whisper.

"He bragged that he killed Bear and that old man in Red Rock. He boasted that he killed others because he wanted what they'd worked a lifetime to obtain—their land and the mineral rights."

Around the clearing, there were muttered curses and passionate oaths as both the family and the authorities considered the implications.

When the crew lifted the gurney, Cara leapt to her feet to clutch Whit's hand between both of hers. With tears streaming down her face, she moved along by his side.

When they reached the copter, one of the officers

turned to her. “I’m sorry, miss. You’ll have to say your good-byes here. This is as far as you can go.”

She started to follow orders, but Whit’s hand tightened on hers.

Seeing it, the medic glanced at the others. “Looks like our patient has a mind of his own. Our job is to heal. And I’d say this young woman is probably the best medicine of all.” He smiled at her. “I think you’d better come with us, or our patient might refuse to go without you.”

With a shy wave to the others, Cara climbed inside the police chopper, all the while holding tightly to Whit’s cold hand.

As they rose into the air, creating a whirlwind of dirt and grass, those on the ground were left to comfort one another while trying to fully comprehend the enormity of what had just transpired.

After a year of questions and doubts and mistrust, Bear’s killer was finally revealed. He was motivated not because of a grudge, or the famous MacKenzie temper, or a debt that was owed, but because of greed. A coward who had coveted what Bear MacKenzie had spent a lifetime earning by the sweat of his brow, simply shot him in the back and left him to die by the banks of Copper Creek.

And now that same cowardly killer had left both Whit and Myrna fighting for their lives.

Chapter Twenty-Eight

Morning, Doc." Mad wheeled his scooter along the hall of the Copper Creek Clinic. "How are our patients doing today?"

"Fine. Day four now, and I'm amazed at how much both Myrna and Whit have improved." The doctor paused outside a closed door. "We got your grandson up and walking yesterday. He was as wobbly as a toddler, and not happy about his weakness. But he kept on pushing himself until he didn't need any help. As for Myrna, she must have a guardian angel on her side. Two bullets and she won't have any permanent injuries, except for some stiffness in one shoulder. I have a therapist working with her. She'll be good as new in no time."

"Poor thing." Willow, standing alongside her father-in-law, shook her head. "She's just itching to get home."

"She's not as bad as Whit." Dr. Mullin chuckled softly.

"I swear, if he could fly, he'd already be there. The only thing keeping him sane is having Cara at his side."

Willow's voice lowered. "I'm worried about that girl. I know she's glued to Whit's side, but she hasn't been herself since her abduction."

The doctor nodded. "I've noticed that, too. She's quiet and withdrawn. She seems to be carrying a heavy load of guilt."

"What does the lass have to be guilty of?" Mad demanded. "She did everything right. Kept her head, never lost her courage, and according to Whit, was the innocent victim in all this."

"She believes she brought all this trouble to your doorstep."

"Bear was shot long before she came along." Willow's lips quivered just speaking those words.

"But Evil Eyes, as she calls her abductor, shot both Myrna and Whit, and she blames herself because she believes that had she not been with your family, they would have been spared."

"And we'd have never known about his hideous crimes." Mad's burr thickened. "Have ye told the lass that?"

The doctor nodded. "I've tried. But she's not convinced."

At his words, the two fell silent for a moment before he gave the news he'd been withholding. "I do believe we may be able to send your patients home within the next day or two."

"That's the news we've been waiting for, Doc." Mad's frown of concern disappeared and his face was wreathed in smiles. "You've made a lot of people a whole lot happier today."

They shook hands before going their separate ways.

* * *

At dinner that night, the discussion, as usual, centered around those who were missing.

"Dr. Mullin agreed with us about Cara," Willow said as they gathered at the big kitchen table. "He thinks she somehow feels responsible for bringing all this trouble on our family."

"That's crazy." Ash dropped his fork with a clatter. "If anything, she's responsible for uncovering the mystery of Pop's death. If Lance hadn't come after her to keep her from identifying him as the stranger she'd seen at Abe's ranch, we would still be in the dark about who shot Pop and why."

Willow reached over to Brenna before glancing around the table at the others. "I think Brenna's assessment the other day was right on. Poor Cara seems to have drawn into some sort of protective shell while she helps Whit through his recovery. But I'm afraid that sooner or later she may snap if she doesn't let go of this wrongheaded belief that she is somehow responsible for luring Lance out of the shadows and into our lives."

"Speaking of guilt..." Mad shoved aside his plate, his dinner half eaten. "Mason McMillan left a message saying he was horrified by the news of his son's crimes and hoped we could find it in our hearts to someday forgive him for his ignorance."

"This wasn't Mason's fault." Willow got to her feet in agitation. "That poor old man must be reeling." She turned to Brady. "I need to phone him. Will you meet me in my office after you've finished eating?"

Brady shoved back his chair. "I don't seem to have much of an appetite lately."

When the two disappeared down the hallway, Juliet let out a deep sigh. "We should be thrilled that a murderer has been exposed and both Whit and Myrna are recovering nicely. But in truth, we're all more nervous and jumpy than ever."

Mad put a hand over hers. "These things take time, lass. I doubt we'll find any peace until we're all together again, whole and healthy, and ready to stand together as a family once more."

Griff managed a smile. "What amazes me is that I spent a lifetime alone, and in the short time I've been part of this family, I've begun to accept it as my right. After the last few days, I'll never again take it for granted." He drew his wife and two small sons into the circle of his arms before adding solemnly, "And, like Whit and Cara, I'd fight like a wounded bear if anyone tried to harm the people I love."

Whit watched as Cara dozed in the reclining chair pulled up alongside his bed. He was grateful that she'd finally fallen asleep. In the days and nights he'd been here, she had refused to leave. And whenever he awoke from a drug-induced sleep, she'd been hovering at his side, watching for any sign of pain or trouble.

Like an avenging angel.

The thought had him smiling. He'd been so proud of the way she'd handled her ordeal. Proud of the fact that, despite what must have been a terrifying situation, she'd remained cool and ready to fight her abductor.

He'd tried to tell her how he felt, but between the bone-jarring pain and the drugs Dr. Mullin kept forcing him to take, there'd been no time.

Today, for the first time since he'd been shot, he was feeling strong enough to resist any more drugs. He intended to force himself to walk the entire length of the corridor and back to convince the doctor that he was ready to get out of this place.

Myrna, too, was anxious to leave. The old woman had insisted on being wheeled into his room yesterday to see for herself that one of her "boys" was healing. She and Cara had fallen into one another's arms and wept a river of tears. Long after Myrna had returned to her room, Cara had been inconsolable, as though, Whit thought with a frown, she'd been the one to shoot that sweet old woman.

"You're awake." Cara's head came up sharply and she was on her feet instantly, touching a hand to Whit's forehead. "Oh, thank heaven. No more fever."

"That's odd." He closed a hand over hers. "If I don't have a fever, what's got me feeling so hot?" With a grin, he answered his own question. "I guess it must be the hot babe standing beside me."

Instead of the chuckle he'd expected, she looked almost sad. "Don't joke, Whit. You need to take this more seriously. You almost died up in those hills."

"But I didn't. Thanks to you."

Her head snapped up as though she'd been slapped. "Thanks to me, you got shot."

"As I recall, it was Lance who shot me, not you."

"But it was my fault you were there. It was my fault he came to the house and shot Myrna. And my fault that old Abe Crawford was killed."

"Hey. That's a whole lot of heavy guilt for one little woman." He reached out and grabbed her wrist, forcing her to lean toward him. "Thanks to you, I finally know who shot my father."

When she remained silent, he pulled her down until she was perched on the edge of his bed. "What's wrong, Cara? What's going on in that mind of yours? Talk to me, please."

She wouldn't meet his eyes. Instead she stared at his hands, gently holding her against her will. "Lance was right. He called me a nobody whose mother was a tramp with so many men in her life she couldn't even identify which one was my father. Even though he was a stranger, Lance knew everything about me. The fact that I was homeless, drifting from job to job. He knew about Jared Billingham and had even bribed him to say I'd stolen from him."

"Chief Pettigrew said the police detective who interviewed Billingham got him to admit the truth. He'd done everything he could to control your life and hadn't given a thought to what effect that might have on you and your future. And he's admitted to sending you those threatening texts. Now that his secret is out, he's feeling ashamed and sorry."

She shook her head. "It doesn't matter. Everything else that evil-eyed man said about me was the truth. I'm a loser. A nobody."

"You saved my life and exposed the coward who shot my father in the back. I'd say that's something to be proud of."

She looked away. "Really? I finally did something right. Are you suggesting that makes up for a lifetime of wrongs?"

Whit sat up and caught her chin in his hands, forcing her to look at him. "Cara, you're the finest person I've ever known. You're fun and sweet and good." His tone lightened. "And you're not bad-looking, either."

When she didn't respond with a laugh as he'd hoped, he gathered her close and covered her mouth with his.

He felt her shivering response and knew she wasn't as unmoved as she tried to appear.

"Mind if I try that again?" He drew her even closer and kissed her until they were both breathless.

He drew a little away. "Okay. Your turn. Is there anything nice you'd like to say to me before I kiss you again?"

She looked as though she might cry. "Whit MacKenzie, you're the finest man I've ever known. I can't even imagine finding anyone who could come close to you. You think I saved your life, but in truth, you saved mine. And I can never repay you or your family for what I've been given. Your entire family is so good and fine. They welcomed a stranger into their home and made me feel like I belonged. For someone who's never belonged anywhere, it's the greatest gift I've ever been given. I've never known anyone like them, or you. Especially you. Even with my crazy imagination, I could have never created a finer man than you."

"Thank you." He touched a thumb to her lower lip. "So why does that make you so sad?"

"Because I'll—"

They both looked up as the doctor walked in, followed by his assistant.

"Good news, Whit. I know you've been chomping at the bit, so today is your lucky day. You and Myrna are both being discharged. I've already phoned your family to pick you up."

"Thanks, Doc." Whit shook his hand.

"When you're dressed, Kate will wheel you to the door."

"I can walk."

Dr. Mullin shook his head. "Protocol. You'll ride, whether you like it or not." He beckoned to Cara. "Myrna's asking for you."

She nodded and started to follow him to the door.

Whit caught her hand and drew her back for a long, lingering kiss.

With a sexy grin he said, "I just needed that to hold me until I can get you alone."

She walked away without a word.

When the truck bearing Myrna, Whit, and Cara drew near the ranch house, they could see the entire family waiting on the back porch.

Brady and Willow, who'd come to fetch them home from the clinic, both started laughing.

"Prepare to be smothered in love," Willow said.

Once they stepped out of the truck, they were mobbed.

"About time." Ash slapped his younger brother on the back before pulling him close in a fierce bear hug. "I'm tired of handling your duties, bro. I hope you're feeling up to mucking stalls by morning."

"I can't wait."

Griff touched a hand to Whit's forehead. "You must be feverish. I can't imagine anybody eager to shovel manure."

That had everyone laughing.

"Oh, Myrna." Brenna wrapped her arms around the old woman's neck and burst into tears. "I'm so happy to have you home where you belong."

"Not nearly as happy as I am to be here." Myrna knelt down to welcome Casey and Ethan, who threw themselves into her outstretched arms.

Mad rolled his scooter close enough to grab his grandson's hand. "You've been missed, lad."

Whit swallowed. "Thanks, Mad. I've missed everyone here. You'll never know how much."

"I've made all your favorite foods to celebrate your return." Mad was grinning. "Steak, thick and rare. My garlic mashed potatoes. And for dessert, that gooey sponge cake topped with whipped cream and berries that you always used to beg me to bake you when you were a lad."

"Flan? You made me a flan?"

"That I did. I actually baked two of them, in case you wanted one all for yourself."

As the others turned to go inside, Mad reached out and caught Cara's arm, forcing her to pause.

"Welcome home, lass."

"Thank you, Mad."

"In all the excitement, there's not been time to thank you, lass. You kept your head when all around you were losing theirs."

She smiled. "I guess it pays to grow up in a lot of chaos."

"Is that what made you so strong?"

She seemed surprised. "I don't see myself as strong. Incompetent, maybe. Weak, definitely. But strong? Never."

"Then you're not looking at the young woman I'm looking at. What you did up in those hills was simply remarkable. And I'll never forget it. None of us will." He pressed the button, engaging the scooter, and she moved along woodenly by his side.

Once in the house, the noise level was deafening. Everyone was talking at once. Every minute or so there was a fresh round of laughter as they lifted frosty longnecks in a salute and finished one another's sentences.

In an effort to blend in, Cara picked up a pair of oven mitts and began lifting pans and trays from the oven, setting sizzling steaks on a platter, and breaking apart steaming rolls before filling a linen-lined basket.

As she was about to announce that dinner was ready, she spied her cell phone on the countertop. As she scrolled through it, she discovered a voice mail. Noting the name and number, she lifted it and touched the button to listen.

When the message was completed, Cara stepped out of the room to place a call.

Whit watched her leave before removing a small box from his pocket. Seeing it, a hush settled over the room.

Willow's eyes were bright. "Is that what I think it is?"

Whit nodded. "I bought a ring for Cara."

There were whoops from his brothers and sighs of pleasure from their wives.

Willow was smiling. "When did you find time to shop?"

"Online. Kate let me use her computer at the clinic." He tucked the silver box back into his pocket.

"When will you ask her, lad?" Mad rolled his scooter up beside his grandson.

Whit shrugged. "I guess I'll just see how the evening goes. But I thought maybe later tonight..."

They all looked up as Cara stepped into the room.

Her eyes were a little too bright. There were two spots of color high on her cheeks. Her voice, when she finally spoke, was strained, as though unsure of what she would say.

"I found a message on my phone from Fred Eberly, the agent who had asked to see my stories and illustrations. You remember, Willow. I asked to use your computer that day..." She cleared her throat. "Anyway, I just returned his call and he told me that he's been in contact with a publisher that is owned by a conglomerate that also produces animated films. They want to meet with me and discuss a deal that would include a series of children's books and a series of movies, and they want to talk about licensing a line of related toys and clothing."

For the space of several seconds, there was silence as the family members looked from Cara to Whit and back again.

Whit crossed the room and gathered her close for a powerful embrace. "That's outstanding news. It's what you've been dreaming of your whole life."

"Yes." Her single word lacked conviction.

Willow walked over to take her hands. "Oh, Cara. Are you as dazed as you look?"

Cara blinked and forced a smile. "Yes, I guess I am feeling a little overwhelmed at the moment. I can't quite wrap my mind around this."

The others gathered around to offer their congratulations.

It was Mad who finally asked what everyone was thinking. "You said they want to meet you. Will they be flying here to Montana?"

She shook her head, avoiding Whit's eyes. "They want me to...come to...New York."

"How exciting. When will you go?" Willow glanced

at her son, who was watching Cara with a look of such hunger it had her stomach clenching.

"Fred Eberly said if I agreed, they'll send a plane for me tomorrow."

"So soon? Isn't this all happening too fast?" Despite the look in Whit's eyes, his tone was deliberately cool and unemotional. "Not that it isn't wonderful for you. After all, it's what you've dreamed of. But you'll need some experts to advise you."

"That's what Mr. Eberly said. He wants me to meet with a law firm and an accounting firm. He said they could sit in on the meeting tomorrow."

"Tomorrow. What did you tell him?"

"I...told him yes."

"Well, then." It was Myrna who spoke when the others couldn't find any words. "It's a lucky thing we'd planned a special supper. Now we have one more reason to celebrate."

They all looked up at a loud knock on the door.

Ira Pettigrew paused in the doorway, hat in hand. "Am I in time for supper?"

"Just in time," Myrna said.

He hung his hat on a hook and carefully wiped his boots on a mat before stepping into the kitchen. "I figured you folks would be happy to hear all the details, now that we're managing to put all the facts together."

As the family gathered around the table and began passing platters of amazing food, they allowed the police chief to fill them in on all the information the state's attorney general had gathered from the various authorities.

"When the state police searched Lance's home, they found a stash of weapons. Among them was a Remington. The state lab tests prove it was the one used to kill Bear." After long moments of silence, Ira said, "It was greed, plain and simple. An arrogant, educated fool who really began to believe he was smarter than most ordinary mortals, and because he was familiar with the law, he figured he knew how to use it to his advantage."

"His poor father," Willow remarked.

Ira nodded. "A good man who can't imagine how things went so very wrong." He glanced at Cara, who had remained silent. "We have a signed statement from young Billingham about what he did and how he was coerced into giving false testimony against you. You'll be happy to know that your record is clear."

"Thank you." Cara ducked her head, ashamed to have Jared's name mentioned in this company.

Ira shook his head, still in disbelief over all he'd learned. "To think of the number of people who trusted that snake in the grass. As you folks can imagine, I'm relieved to have all of this resolved. It was weighing heavily on my mind, as it was on yours." He glanced around. "I know this doesn't make your loss any less painful, but I hope it gives you some peace of mind to know that Bear's killer will pay for the rest of his life for his hideous crimes."

Around the table, their voices were muted.

And though Whit remained outwardly composed, his family was aware that he answered Ira's questions in a monotone, and he moved his food around his plate without really tasting any of it.

Cara was equally careful to smile and nod at all the right times. Her lack of appetite could have been blamed on her amazing news. Or it could indicate that she had already turned her attention away from the MacKenzie family and toward the shining dream that had once seemed as distant, and as impossible to reach, as the stars.

Or it could mean that she was as torn about this news as Whit.

How was it possible that this one day, which they had all been yearning for, had become, in a matter of hours, both the best and the worst day of their lives?

Chapter Twenty-Nine

Whit had been up since before dawn, mucking stalls in the barn. He was grateful for the release of hard, physical labor and the pain inflicted with each and every movement. He muttered under his breath with every stab of his pitchfork, every muscle-straining lift of the filthy dung-filled straw into the wagon.

When he was finished, he leaned into the wagon until he'd managed to shove it out the doorway of the barn and around to the back. There it would remain until its contents could be spread later over the fields for fertilizer.

He looked up at the sound of Mad's scooter.

"You'd best get a move on, lad, if you're going to get Cara to town on time."

"I thought I'd let Mom and Brady drive her."

"They're heading up to the hills as soon as they say their good-byes."

He gritted his teeth. "Ash or Griff?"

"At their own places, lad. Don't you remember? They and their wives said good-bye to Cara last night."

He remembered. Every word, every sad look, every awkward hug. The entire family had been subdued, the women practically in tears.

Mad held out a set of truck keys. "You can do this, lad. Drive her to town. Say good-bye and wish her luck. And mean it."

"I can't, Mad."

"You will, lad." The old man's burr thickened. "You're a MacKenzie. It's what we do. Now get through this."

"Yeah." Whit flushed and looked away.

Feeling his grandfather watching him, he turned and headed toward the house.

Inside, he kicked off his dung-covered boots and hung his wide-brimmed hat before rolling his sleeves to wash at the big sink. While he slipped into fresh boots, he could hear voices in the kitchen as Myrna said a tearful good-bye to Cara.

"Remember what I told you, honey." Myrna gathered Cara close. "Always follow your heart. It will never steer you wrong."

Willow stepped close and gathered Cara into an embrace. "I hope you'll find time in your busy, successful new life to come back. You know you're always welcome here, Cara. We consider you one of the family."

"Thank you. For everything." Cara's voice was soft, breathless. "I love you all. And I'll"—she looked up to see Whit in the doorway—"I'll miss you all terribly."

Whit jingled the keys. "If you're ready, we'd better get started."

"Yes . . . I. Yes." She picked up the small bag that held

her meager belongings and followed him out the door and into the truck.

The drive to town was the longest Whit could ever remember. Except for the voices on the all-country radio station, there were awkward stretches of silence between him and his passenger.

Cara turned to stare out the side window. "Summer will be here soon. It's all so green and pretty."

His eyes narrowed behind the mirrored sunglasses. "I'm sure it can't compete with the bright lights of New York."

She turned to him. "I wish you were coming."

He shook his head. "Not my style."

"I understand. You have important things to do. I have no right to ask you to give up your work for me."

"It's not that. You don't need me. I'd just be a fish out of water."

"That's how I've always felt. Like I don't really belong anywhere."

"You fit in just fine with all of us."

She looked away. "I didn't give any of you a choice. There I was, a squatter in your range shack, and then I became the uninvited guest who never left."

"We never wanted you to leave." *Go ahead. Say it. I never wanted you to leave. And still don't. Please stay. I can't imagine my life without you.*

But to say it, he would rob her of her joy in seeing her dream come true. If he loved her, truly loved her, he had to let her go without adding to her burden.

As they drove along the main street, past the medical clinic, past the police chief's office and jail, and pulled into the fairgrounds where a sleek company jet was idling, Whit felt his heart hitch.

He couldn't do this. Couldn't calmly say good-bye and watch her walk out of his life. And yet, if he loved her, he had to. Didn't she have the right to chase her dreams?

As they drove closer, the door of the plane opened and a stairway was lowered to the tarmac. Two uniformed men descended the steps and waited until Whit brought the truck to a stop.

Before Whit could circle around to assist Cara, the pilot walked to the passenger door. "Miss Walton?"

"Yes."

"Captain Mike Phelps. I'm your pilot today." He held out a hand and she stepped out of the truck before turning to grab her small bag.

"I'll take that. We're ready to leave as soon as you're aboard. Copilot Will Swanson will assist."

The pilot walked away and entered the plane, while a second uniformed man remained standing at the foot of the stairs.

She turned to Whit, who had circled around the front of the truck and stood, his eyes hidden behind his sunglasses.

Ask me to stay, Whit.

Her heart was so heavy in her chest, she could barely breathe.

Just say the words, and I'll happily spend the rest of my life here with you.

"I guess..." She swallowed and stuck out her hand awkwardly. "Good-bye, Whit."

He ignored her outstretched hand and put both hands

on her shoulders, giving her a quick hug. "Bye, Cara. I want to..." He saw her eyes go wide and prayed he could get through this. "I want to wish you luck. Nobody deserves it more than you. And like my mom said, I hope you know you'll always have a home with us. We all love you. And I hope you never forget us."

"I love you...all of you, too."

The light seemed to go out of her eyes as she turned away and walked to the plane.

The copilot took her hand and guided her up the steps and inside. When she was settled in her seat, she peered out the window.

Whit was standing beside his truck.

As the plane made a slow arc before rushing along the runway and lifting into the air, Cara looked down below.

The man and the truck were still there.

She turned and buried her face in her hands, finally free to let the tears fall. Tears she'd been holding inside for so long, her throat burned with their bitter taste.

Mad's scooter was parked at the big kitchen table when Willow walked into the room. The sky outside the windows showed that it wasn't yet dawn.

"You're up early, lass."

"I could say the same to you, Mad. Can't sleep?"

He shook his head. "There's coffee."

"Thanks." She filled a mug and sat across from him. "Ira was right. It helps to know that Bear's killer has been found. But it doesn't ease the pain of losing him."

Mad nodded. "And to know that his killer was a young man we've known for a lifetime, and trusted like family.

Our only consolation is knowing Lance will pay for the rest of his life."

"My heart is so heavy." She sighed. "And think of poor Mason's heart, knowing his only son is a murderer. I hope somehow he finds healing."

"That's my hope, too. The heart is an amazing gift. It can swell with love, and you think you'll never love that much again. Take my Maddie. I'd have walked through fire for her. But when Bear was born, it was a different kind of love. And I thought my heart was too full. But then you and Bear gave me those wee lads, and my already full heart was bursting." He fixed her with a look. "If there's one thing I've learned, it's that there's always room for one more."

"I know that look, Mad. Is there something you want to say to me?"

"It's my way of telling you that I'll not be hurt if you find yourself ready to let someone else into your heart. I know Bear would want you to be happy, lass."

For the longest time she merely sipped her coffee. She finally spoke haltingly. "I want you to know I never planned this."

He smiled. "Love usually happens when we least expect it. Though I believe that for Brady it's been a long time coming."

"How did you guess? About Brady and me?"

"I've known before either of you knew."

She shook her head. "It's too soon. I've told Brady that."

"I didn't know there was a timetable for love."

"You know what I mean. Bear's only been gone a year."

He sighed. "It seems like a lifetime."

Willow nodded. “Some days. At other times it seems like just yesterday. I still expect to see him walk through the door.”

“I know the feeling.” He sipped in silence before closing a hand over hers. “Anyway, I want you to know I’m happy for you. For both of you.”

“Don’t worry. We’re going to take our time with this.”

Mad frowned. “It’s Whit I’m worried about.”

Her head came up. “What did he tell you?”

“Nothing. He doesn’t talk. But he works until he can’t work anymore. And then he falls into bed and hours later he’s up again, pushing himself to the limit.” He nodded toward the door. “He’s out in the barn right now. Been out there for an hour or more. He can’t keep this up, lass. Maybe you could talk to him.”

Willow sighed. “I can try.”

She topped off her coffee and filled a second mug before heading to the mudroom for a pair of sturdy boots and a frayed denim jacket.

Outside, a soft, misty rain was falling. She lifted her face, enjoying the feel of it on her skin.

Inside the barn, she breathed in the familiar scents of dung and earth and leather.

“Good morning.” She paused outside one of the stalls.

“Morning.” Whit didn’t stop working.

Willow watched as her youngest son spread fresh straw before filling the trough with water. Though she saw the ripple of muscle and the scraggly growth of beard, indicating that he was now a man, she could still see, in her mind’s eye, the chubby baby he’d once been, the gangly youth, the pride and joy of his father. The delight of his mother.

"You're up early."

He glanced away, trying not to make eye contact.

"Have you heard from Cara?"

At the mention of that name, she saw him flinch before he moved on to the next stall.

She trailed behind him. "Got time for some coffee?"

He turned. Seeing the mug, he set aside his pitchfork and led the way toward a long bench.

The two of them sat and Willow handed him a steaming mug.

"Thanks." He sipped his coffee.

She laid a hand on his arm. "I know how you feel, Whit."

He looked over. "Yeah. I guess you do. In a way, it's like a death."

"But not as permanent. She could decide to come back."

"Would you? Would you give up a dream to live like this?"

She smiled at the irony of his words. "I did."

That had his attention. "Yeah. Sorry. I guess I forgot about that fancy life as a model. But that was a lifetime ago. And it was different. You and Pop were already engaged. At least you knew how he felt. I…never got the chance to tell Cara."

"She'll figure it out."

He shook his head. "She's been chasing this dream since she was a scared, lonely little kid." He drained his coffee and handed her the empty mug. "I had my chance with her and I blew it. Now I just have to figure out how to live without her."

He picked up the pitchfork. "When I finish here, I

think I'll head up to the highlands. Along the way, I want to stop at Copper Creek."

She took in a breath. "Your dad will enjoy a visit."

"Yeah." He turned away.

Willow stood for long moments, watching him. He was solid like his father. And he felt things deeply. Like his father. And like his father, he was a one-woman man. After Cara Walton, no other woman would ever be good enough. He would wait, and suffer, and endure. Like his father.

The misty rain had blown away, leaving the land fresh and lush and green. Sunlight sparkled on the waters of Copper Creek. High in the branches of a dead pine a mother eagle returned to the nest to feed her pair of hungry fledglings.

Whit tethered his gelding and walked to the banks of the creek to study the faded wooden cross he and his brothers had fashioned shortly after their father had been killed. Maybe it was time for a more permanent marker. Something that would explain, to anyone who stopped here, the terrible, heart-wrenching loss of the man who had died here.

He knelt in the grass, feeling again the pain of that loss.

And then he was thrust back to the time he'd brought Cara here. Seeing his grief, that tenderhearted female, who had fought so hard to remain aloof, had done the only thing she could to ease his pain.

She'd been so loving. So generous. And in his misery he'd taken her like an animal.

He wanted her. Dear God, he wanted her with every

fiber of his being. He didn't think he could stand living this way for the rest of his life.

He lowered his head, trying to think of something else. Anything that would distract him from this never-ending pain.

He looked up at the sound of muted hoofbeats drumming against the soft earth.

Cara slid from the saddle and held the reins of a pale gray mare. She was wearing some sort of floaty, pale yellow sundress with cap sleeves that fluttered at her shoulders and a long skirt that billowed around her ankles. Not at all what a woman would wear to ride a horse.

The fact that he could conjure such a vision only reminded Whit how much of a fool he'd become. He blinked, thinking the vision would disappear. Instead, she tethered her horse next to his and walked closer.

His voice caught in his throat. "Are you real?"

She smiled shyly. "I am."

He shook his head. "If I'm dreaming, don't wake me."

"You're not dreaming, Whit." She touched a hand to his scratchy cheek. "You forgot to shave."

"No reason to." He waited a beat before asking, "Why? How? I thought you were in the big city, chasing your dream."

"I was."

"And?"

She shrugged. "When I signed the contracts, I waited."

"Waited? For what?"

"For the magic to happen. Aren't we supposed to feel the magic when we finally hold our dream in our hands?"

"Yeah. I guess so."

"There was no magic, Whit. Those people were offering me fame and fortune, and all I felt was…empty."

"You didn't take the deal?"

She laughed, a clear, lilting sound that drifted on the slight breeze. "Oh, I took the deal. I guess I'm rich now. And maybe one day I'll be famous. But I realized it wasn't enough."

"What'll it take? More books? More money?"

She shook her head, sending pale hair dancing at her shoulders. "I realized my dream was here." She clasped her hands behind her back and looked down at her toes, peeking from bright yellow sandals.

Whit placed a finger under her chin, forcing her to look at him. "That's a bad habit of yours. Don't look away. You've come all this way to tell me something. Whatever it is, however painful, look me in the eye and say it."

She took in a deep breath. "You're my dream, Whit. You. Your family. This life. And I was so blinded by my insecurities, I turned my back on the best thing I ever had. I thought if I was only rich enough, and successful enough, I could forget my childhood and feel a sense of accomplishment."

"What's different now?"

"I kept hearing your words. That I was brave when it counted. And Myrna's words. That I should always follow my heart. And that's when I realized that I didn't need money or the respect of strangers to be a success. All I need is to live the life I want, with the man who owns my heart."

"I love you, Whit MacKenzie. I didn't think I was worthy of you, and maybe all of this is too late, but I need you to know that I love—"

He cut off her words, dragging her into his arms and kissing her, pouring everything into it. All his needs, his desires, his heartbreak. His joy and relief that she'd come back to him.

His feelings, so long contained, just spilled over and drenched them both with an all-consuming passion.

He lifted his head, taking in a deep breath of air and feeling his heart begin to beat once more. "And I love you, Goldilocks."

Her smile bloomed. "You haven't called me that in such a long time."

"Haven't I?" He dragged her close and kissed her eyes, her cheeks, the tip of her nose. "Remind me to call you that at least once a day."

"Sounds as though you intend to keep me around."

"Only for a lifetime, Goldilocks." He reached into his pocket and withdrew the small gold box. "I happen to have something that belongs to you, if you'll accept it."

She opened the box and stared in surprise at the glittering diamond ring. "What are you doing with this?"

"I was planning on tossing it into the creek, along with all my dreams. But now I'll do what I was planning on doing when I bought it." He slipped it onto her finger. "Cara Walton, will you marry me and spend the rest of your life loving a man who smells like a barnyard?"

"I can't think of a better way to spend the rest of my life." She stood on tiptoe and brushed her mouth over his. "Oh, Whit. I was so afraid to come to you. Afraid it was all too little, too late and that you'd hate me and send me away forever. But now..." She kissed him again. "My heart is so full. Will we go and tell your family?"

As she started to turn away, he caught her by the shoulders and dragged her into his arms, kissing her with a thoroughness that had them both gasping for breath.

"We'll tell them. Eventually. First, I want to love you here, where you so generously loved me that first time. And this time I promise to go slow and easy."

Her eyes danced with laughter. "Don't make promises you can't keep, Whit MacKenzie."

And then, without a word, she leapt into his arms and wrapped her legs around his waist, forcing him to forget every word he'd just spoken. As they fell into the grass in a tangle of arms and legs, they showed each other just a hint of how delicious their future together would be.

EPILOGUE

The fields around the MacKenzie ranch had been washed clean by a week of early summer rains. But this day dawned clear and sunny, as though even Mother Nature was aware of the magnitude of this special occasion.

The MacKenzies were the closest thing to royalty to the folks in Copper Creek, and the wedding of Whit, the youngest grandson of Mad MacKenzie, was special indeed.

Talk around town was that Whit's bride-to-be was a shy little thing. That made the fact that she had generously agreed to invite everyone for miles around all the more appreciated.

There were none who refused the invitation.

As folks arrived, a wrangler directed them to the big flatbed wagons adorned with white bows and streamers and pulled by a team of horses to the spot where the vows would be spoken. The exact location hadn't been revealed, but the townies were enjoying the intrigue after being told that refreshments would be served while they awaited the arrival of the wedding party.

Brenna and Ash arrived just as Griff and Juliet and their boys were stepping from their plane. They glanced around at the beehive of activity in the yard, where wranglers were putting the finishing touches on rows of wooden picnic tables. Each was covered in a white cloth, with folding chairs decorated with matching white bows set in perfect symmetry.

Cara was in the kitchen, looking perfectly serene as she set a steaming tray on the countertop and placed another tray in the oven.

She turned to greet Griff and Juliet before hugging Casey and Ethan.

"Efan and me got new shirts. See?" Casey was happy to model, while his older brother merely smiled, showing a gap where a tooth had been.

"You look perfect," Cara said. "Ethan, you lost a tooth?"

"Uh-huh." He smiled wider.

"I hope the Tooth Fairy found it."

"She did. Mama said I had to leave it under my pillow, and this morning it was gone and there was a whole dollar in its place."

Casey's eyes were shining. "I can't wait to lose a toof so the Toof Fairy can visit me, too."

Juliet looked around at the array of hot and cold foods covering every inch of space. "You're not supposed to be working this hard on your wedding day."

"She's done," Myrna declared as she hustled into the room. "Cara, honey, you have to go upstairs now and dress. Most of your guests are already gone in the wagons." When it looked as though Cara might object, Myrna gave her a gentle shove. "Out with you. Mad and I want to decorate your cake now, and you can't peek."

Reluctantly Cara turned away. "Brenna and Juliet, will you give me a hand upstairs?"

The two young women trailed behind, while Ash and Griff took the two little boys in hand and led them away from all the tempting desserts.

Upstairs, Cara made a dash to the shower, then, clad in only a towel, allowed her new sisters-in-law to fuss over her hair and makeup.

At a knock on the door, Willow entered carrying a long white zippered bag on a hanger. "I know you wanted to keep things simple, Cara. Whit told me the two of you intended to wear denim, but I had this in my closet and wondered if you'd like to try it on."

She unzipped the bag and held up a shimmering white sundress with a round, scalloped neckline and a rope of pearls at the tiny nipped-in waist, which then flowed to a swirling, ankle-length skirt.

Cara's hand flew to her throat. "Oh, Willow. It's so beautiful. I think it's far too exotic for me. I don't deserve..."

Seeing the looks exchanged between the others, she laughed. "There I go again. You'd think I'd have learned my lesson by now." She took the dress from her soon-to-be mother-in-law's hands and slipped it over her head. When she turned toward the three women, there was a collective sigh of appreciation.

Willow directed her to the oval looking glass.

Seeing her reflection, Cara was amazed at the transformation. "I feel like a princess."

"You look like one, too." Brenna smoothed the skirt before stepping back. "It's perfect, Cara."

The bride-to-be nodded before turning to Willow. "I don't know how to thank you."

"The smile on your lips is all the thanks I ever need." Willow drew her close. "You've made my son so happy, darling."

"Not nearly as happy as he's made me."

The door opened and Myrna stepped inside, beaming her pleasure. "Oh, look at you. I told Willow it would fit you perfectly."

She handed Willow a pair of white strappy sandals. "You wanted these?"

Willow was laughing as she explained, "I wanted to be sure you liked the dress before I offered the rest. See if these fit, Cara."

Cara slipped her feet into the sandals and danced around the room.

"And there's this." Myrna reached into her pocket. "Since Willow gave you the 'something new,' I wanted to give you 'something old.' They belonged to my mother, and I wore them when I married my Harold."

She fastened a single strand of pearls around Cara's throat and added tiny pearl earrings before stepping back to admire.

"This is all so perfect. Thank you." Cara reached into a handled bag. "Since you're all here together, I'd like to return the favor." She handed each of them a tissue-wrapped parcel. "My publisher sent these mock-ups of the first book's cover and dedication page."

Brenna was the first to read hers aloud. "To Brenna and Ash..." She glanced at Juliet, who took up the narrative.

"And Juliet and Griff and their sons, Casey and Ethan. You are the brothers and sisters I always wanted."

Myrna's lips quivered as she read aloud, "And to Mad and Myrna, my newly acquired grandparents, whose words of wisdom are engraved on my heart."

Willow's eyes were shining as she finished the dedication. "And to Willow MacKenzie, who has taught me courage and trust and love of family. Lucky me. I get something not many get in this world—the chance to choose, not only my one true love, but my forever family as well."

The women circled around her, openly weeping as they embraced her.

In the kitchen, Casey and Ethan were seated at the table, enjoying frosty glasses of lemonade, while Ash, Griff, and Brady stood nearby, tipping up ice-cold longnecks.

When Whit strolled in wearing his best Western jacket and string tie over a starched white shirt and crisp denims, the teasing began.

"How long were you standing under that shower, bro?" Ash winked at Griff. "You smell like you used a whole bottle of some fancy shampoo."

Whit merely grinned. "Maybe I did."

"Just so you didn't pour on a whole bottle of Mad's favorite Old Spice before you got dressed."

"I'm saving that for tonight."

Casey looked over. "Will you and Aunt Cara read her new book to me until I fall asleep tonight, Uncle Whit?"

Whit ruffled his hair. "Not tonight, Casey. Your aunt Cara and I have plans."

"I know. You're getting married. But that's for today. I'm talking about tonight. I'm really looking forward to it."

Whit winked. "So am I, Casey."

Mad filled five tumblers with fine, aged scotch whiskey and passed them around. "I propose a toast to the lass who won the heart of my youngest grandson."

The five men solemnly touched glasses and drank.

"And here's to Bear," Brady said. "You know he's smiling on his sons today."

Again they touched glasses and drank.

Whit lifted his tumbler and grinned at his brothers. "Here's to family."

"To family." They drank again, and even the two little boys hurried over to touch their lemonade glasses to the others.

"And here's to the man who started it all." Ash nodded toward his grandfather, and the others touched glasses to Mad's.

The old man shook his head. "To tell the truth, I never dreamed I'd live long enough to see all my grandsons happily wed. It's a blessing, and one I'll never forget."

They looked up at the parade of women coming down the stairs, their eyes misty, noses red.

Whit shot a surprised glance at Mad, who gave a quick shake of his head. "Nothing to worry about, lad. There's nothing a woman likes better than a good cry on a friend's wedding day. The closer they are to the bride, the more tears shed."

Whit let out a long breath. "That's a relief. I was afraid for a minute there they were coming with bad news."

Willow paused and looked around at the men. "The bride is ready. Let's get to the wagon."

Ash grumbled, "I still don't know where we're going. Does anybody around here know what's going on?"

"Efan and me know. We're going to the barn."

Griff turned to look at his younger son. "Why would you think that?"

"'Cause mom said we're going to Uncle Whit's and Aunt Cara's favorite place. And Uncle Ash said that would be the hayloft."

With a roar of laughter, Griff and Juliet caught their boys' hands and led the way toward the waiting wagon.

Ash and Brenna followed, with Willow and Brady moving along beside Mad and Myrna.

As soon as they were gone, Whit turned and raced up the stairs. Without knocking, he opened the door to find Cara staring out the window. The sight of her in a white sundress, her long blond hair cascading down her back in a riot of soft tangles, had his heart nearly bursting out of his chest with emotion.

"Thinking of running back to New York?"

She turned, her eyes bright with tears.

Seeing them, he hurried across the room to gather her close. "Don't be sad."

She wiped at her eyes. "I'm not sad. These are happy tears."

He felt a wild rush of relief.

She caught his hand and led him to the window, where in the distance, they could make out the foundation that had already been set in place for the ranch house they were planning. It would guarantee them a bit of privacy but keep them close enough that they could always be near the family they both loved.

"Every time I look at what we're building together, I

feel so lucky. All my life I've been so alone, and feeling like I would never belong anywhere. And now..." She turned to him and felt the tears threaten again. "Now I have you and all your wonderful family. So many people to love, and who love me."

"Don't you ever forget how much you're loved."

When Whit bent to brush his mouth over hers, she felt the quick sexual tug deep inside.

"Come on, woman." In his best imitation of an old Western codger, he caught her hand and led her to the stairs. "It's time we got ourselves hitched."

In the kitchen, he paused to offer her a lovely nosegay of wildflowers he'd picked. "Every bride should have flowers."

She buried her face in them, fighting more tears.

"No more crying, woman." He led her outside toward the small fancy horse and carriage awaiting them.

With a flick of the reins, they headed across the meadow, up a hill and down the other side, where everyone was waiting.

As they walked toward the creek, they passed Willow and Brady standing close together, smiling into one another's eyes like lovers.

Griff and Juliet hugged them both, and Whit winked at their two little boys before whispering, "Sorry this isn't the hayloft. But this is probably better for all these people, don't you think?"

Casey nodded in agreement, feeling very important.

As Whit and Cara passed Ash and Brenna, Ash gave them a thumbs-up.

And then they were at the banks of Copper Creek, standing beside a tall, marble cross the family had commissioned to honor Bear.

Reverend Hamilton, who had officiated at the weddings of Willow and Bear, Ash and Brenna, and Griff and Juliet, and at the funeral of Bear MacKenzie just a year ago, beamed his approval as they spoke their vows.

It occurred to Cara that, for a girl who'd only dreamed of success, she had found it, not in the way she'd expected, but rather in the simplest of all things. Roots. Family. Tradition.

"You may kiss your bride."

At the minister's words, Whit turned and gathered Cara close, to the applause of everyone.

"Welcome to my world, Goldilocks." Against her mouth he whispered, "As soon as the celebration winds up, you and I are heading to a very special honeymoon."

"Did you already send up the supplies?"

He thought about the wagonload of goodies already in place at the newly renovated range shack, including a generator so they could take warm showers. "And for the next week, it'll be just you and me. And the only chore will be opening a bottle of champagne or a longneck and grilling an occasional steak."

"Think anybody will find us?"

"If they even come close, they'll face the end of my rifle. It's just you and me and the wildlife, Goldilocks. Just the way it all started."

And then they were surrounded by well-wishers, hugging and kissing and shaking hands.

Cara looked over to see Whit exchanging high fives with his brothers.

Not just his brothers. Her brothers, too.

From this day on, she would never again be alone.

Ever since she was a little girl, she'd nurtured a very

special dream. Soon, children the world over would be reading her stories, watching them in movies, and even playing with her characters and wearing clothes bearing their likeness. It was much more than she'd ever hoped for. And yet, of all her fantasies, this one had always seemed the most unreachable. Maybe that was why she'd refused to let herself believe.

Until now.

Family. Friends. And one very special man to love her just for herself, with all her flaws, all her fears, all her weaknesses. Somehow, with Whit MacKenzie beside her, she truly believed she could do anything she wanted.

Dreams really did come true.

R. C. Ryan presents a thrilling
new series featuring the Malloy family.

Please see the next page
for a special preview.

In the hills above the Malloy ranch, Matt unsaddled his horse and filled the troughs with feed and water before stepping out of the lean-to behind the range shack that served as a storage shed and stall.

He'd had a great time riding across snow-covered pastures, drinking in the sights and sounds that nourished his soul. He'd charted the path of a pair of eagles soaring on currents of air and had paused to watch a pure white mustang stallion leading his herd toward a box canyon that offered shelter and food. He intended to relate the location to Maggie, since she'd been hunting that stallion for a year or more.

Hearing the sound of an engine, Matt ran a hand through his beard and rounded the cabin in time to see Burke just stepping down from the driver's side.

The old man was grinning like a fool as he circled the truck and opened the passenger door.

Matt stopped in midstride at the sight that greeted him.

The passenger was tall, blond, and gorgeous. She was wearing a charcoal suit jacket over a skinny little skirt that barely skimmed her thighs. When she stepped into the snow, her high-heeled shoes sank ankle-deep, causing her to hiss out a breath before she gamely forged ahead, extending her hand.

"Matthew Malloy? Vanessa Kettering." Her smile may have been forced, but the handshake was firm.

"Vanessa." Matt's hand closed around hers while he looked beyond her to where old Burke was clearly enjoying his little joke as he retrieved a laptop case. "Do you prefer Vanessa or Miss Kettering?"

"My friends call me Nessa."

"Okay." He glanced down. "Sorry about the snow. This is springtime in Montana."

"I'm sure it wasn't something you could control." She managed a smile as she removed her sunglasses and looked around. "Though, if I'd known our meeting would be in the hills, I'd have dressed more appropriately."

"I'm sorry about that as well. I agreed at the last minute to stand in for my grandmother." Matt led the way to the door and held it while she entered.

He shot the old cowboy a killing look before following her inside.

Burke set the leather bag on the table before walking to the door. "I'll just get those supplies you asked for, boss, and I'll be on my way up to the herd."

"Make yourself comfortable, Vanessa." Matt turned to Burke. "I'll give you a hand with those supplies."

He trailed Burke out to the truck.

"Very funny. You could have called and told me to expect a woman."

"Yeah. I could have." Burke chuckled. "I even packed some of your grandpa's whiskey, just in case she drinks like all the other Eastern lawyers."

"You're enjoying this, aren't you, old man?"

Burke chuckled. "More than I should. I wish you could've seen your face. It was priceless."

Matt burst into laughter. "Okay. You got me. But you have to know I'll find a way to get even with you for this."

"Oh, don't I know it." The old cowboy was whistling as he hauled a box of supplies to the cabin. He was still whistling as he walked back to the truck and drove away.

Matt glanced at the young woman, who bent to remove first one shoe, then the other, all the while wiping away the snow with a tissue. As she did, Matt found himself admiring her backside in the trim skirt that fit her like a second skin.

When she turned and caught him staring, he tried to cover himself by indicating a rocker in front of the fireplace. "Why don't you sit here and I'll crank up the heat?"

While Vanessa settled into the rocker, he added a fresh log and kindling to the embers and soon had a fire blazing.

She gave a sigh of appreciation. "Oh, that feels good." She glanced around the tiny cabin. "Is there someplace I can freshen up?"

"Bathroom's over there." Matt pointed and she slipped into her shoes before crossing the room.

Minutes later she emerged and took her time looking around the room. "This is a lot more comfortable than it looks from the outside. When we first got here, I really thought Burke was having fun with me. Especially since he was grinning from ear to ear."

"Yeah. That's Burke." Matt clenched his jaw, wishing he could have a do-over for the day. If he'd known he would be stuck entertaining some prissy female lawyer, he'd have sent her packing without the benefit of a meeting. "That old cowboy's always the joker."

Matt nodded toward the kitchen counter, where he'd unpacked the supplies he'd requested. "Would you like to warm up with coffee, beer, wine, or whiskey?"

She laughed. "I think I'd better keep a clear head while we have our discussion. I'll settle for coffee."

Matt filled a coffeemaker with water and freshly ground coffee. Soon the little cabin was perfumed with the fragrance.

After pouring two cups, he turned. Vanessa had already laid out several documents on either side of the wooden table in the center of the room and had her laptop humming.

"Efficient. I like that." He set a steaming cup in front of her and rounded to the other side. "The sooner we talk, the sooner you can get back to civilization."

She nodded. "My thoughts exactly. Especially since the company jet will be returning from Helena to fly me back to Chicago as soon as I'm ready."

"Your wild-animal federation can afford its own jet?"

"Not the federation. But one of the members of the board, Clayton Anderson, made his company jet available, since he was heading on to Helena for business. He'll be back to pick me up in a couple of hours."

"All right, then." Eager to finish the meeting and get

rid of this intrusion on his privacy, Matt took a seat and picked up the first page of the mound of documents. "Let's get to it. My grandmother said you want the Malloy take on the number of wild animals being removed from the government's endangered species list."

"Exactly. The Malloy ranch is successful enough to pack some clout with the officials who set the rules. We're hoping the Malloy name will make a difference."

Matt compressed his lips and decided to keep his thoughts to himself until he'd had more time to see just where this was leading—both with the animals and with this gorgeous woman.

After his father's death, Ash MacKenzie returns home only to settle his family affairs. But a chance encounter with the beautiful woman who was his first love gives him a reason to stay…

Please see the next page
for an excerpt from

THE MAVERICK OF COPPER CREEK

to see where the
Copper Creek Cowboys series began…

Chapter One

Hawk's Wing, Wyoming
Present Day

'Morning, Ash." The fresh-faced banker looked like a high school junior, with wire-rimmed glasses and short-cropped hair. He offered a handshake before indicating the chair across from his desk.

"Jason." Ash shook the young banker's hand and sat, setting his wide-brimmed hat on the chair beside him.

Ash MacKenzie had thought about dressing up for this meeting but decided against it, settling instead for a quick shower and shave. He'd been up before dawn and had already completed a couple of hours of ranch chores. Right now he just wanted to get this nasty business behind him before returning home to face the rest of the day in one round after another of back-breaking work. Work that would all be in vain if he couldn't persuade the bank to increase his loan so he could pay off his debtors, who were snapping at his heels.

"What can I do for you this morning, Ash?"

"I'm here to talk about extending my loan."

The banker's eyes narrowed slightly. "Extending the length of the payback?"

Ash gave a quick shake of his head. "I'd like to borrow more money and have it added to the back end of my original loan."

"You already owe fifty thousand. Why would you want more?"

Ash dug out the documents and passed them across the desk. "My taxes are due, and I just put a new roof on the barn. There was a leak in the irrigation system, flooding the south pasture, and the company that installed it for the prior owner refused to admit that they were at fault. The lowest bid I could get for the repair came to more than thirty thousand."

The young banker blew out a breath. "Wow, Ash. Looks like you got yourself a whole ton of troubles."

Ash had learned at his father's knee to never show fear. His tone was rock-steady. "I can handle them, Jason. I just need a quick infusion of cash, and a little time, and I'll be operating on all cylinders again."

The young banker looked him in the eye. "I'm not authorized to handle something like this. I'll have to take it upstairs."

Ash nodded, knowing that upstairs meant asking permission from Jason's father, Jason Collier III. The Collier family owned the only bank in this tiny town, and they treated every dollar like their own.

"I'd be happy to go with you and present my case."

"That's not the way it's done." Jason pushed back from his desk and walked to the door. "I might be a while."

"Take your time." Ash leaned back and stretched out his long legs, crossing his feet at the ankles, watching the young man's retreating back. Though he looked relaxed, it was only a façade. Inside, his muscles tensed as he thought about the importance of this request.

Since he'd left his family ranch all those years ago, his workload had doubled. But at least now, he was working to please nobody but himself. Though he missed his family with an ache around the heart that would never heal, he didn't miss his father's constantly finding fault with everything he attempted to do.

Mad might have believed that Bear just wanted the best for his sons, but to Ash's way of thinking, it simply meant that he would never be able to please his implacable, rock-headed father, no matter how hard he worked. Now, at least, he was no longer busting his hide for someone else. If he chose to spend his life working like a dog, he had the satisfaction of doing it for himself.

Oh, he'd had years of working on other men's ranches, while he saved every dollar and plotted and planned for his own future. But he had a good piece of land now, and a working ranch, and though his life was lonely without the comfort of family and friends, he was not only surviving but thriving.

He frowned. Not really thriving. More like just barely getting by. But at least he was doing it on his own terms. He just needed one more break, and he could be free of the dark memories of the past.

Ash's musings were interrupted with the return of the young banker.

He made his way to his desk without looking at Ash.

"I'm sorry. The bank just can't take the risk of giving you any more money."

Ash fought to keep his tone level. "I've made every payment on time. I never missed a single one. Besides, if I default, the bank holds my mortgage. The way I see it, you won't be risking a thing."

"We're not in the business of owning ranch land." Jason glanced at the documents before passing them back to Ash. "And from the looks of all this debt, you stand a very good chance of losing yours."

"I'd stand a better chance of holding on if you'd extend my loan."

The young man stood. "Sorry. I tried."

"Mind if I talk to your father?"

"It was my father who said emphatically no." Jason held the door, indicating an end to their meeting. "Unless you agree to ask your father to cosign the loan."

And there it was, out in the open.

"You know how I feel about that."

Jason nodded. "I know. I told my father you've already said you'd never ask your father to cosign."

Without a word Ash left the bank and stalked to his truck. Once inside he turned off the radio and drove the entire distance in silence.

His father.

That was what it all came down to. Even here in Wyoming, it seemed, everyone knew Bear MacKenzie was good for the money. Hell, he could probably hand over a million dollars without even going to the bank. Petty cash for Bear MacKenzie. Chump change, he'd call it.

Ash swore. He'd rather lose the ranch and everything he'd worked for than ask his father for one red cent. It would be an admission of defeat. An admission that these past years had all been a mistake, and now he was ready to crawl home and become the good, docile son his father wanted.

His father. There was no pleasing Bear MacKenzie. Hadn't he spent half his life trying? That part of his life was over.

Come hell or high water he'd make it on his own, or move on and start over yet again, with nothing but the clothes on his back.

MacKenzie Ranch

Bear MacKenzie stood on the banks of Copper Creek, his all-terrain vehicle idling nearby. For the third time he glanced at the threatening storm clouds and swore loudly before walking over and turning off the ignition. The sudden silence was a shock to the system until his ears caught the lowing of cattle, the buzz of insects, the chorus of birdsong. At any other time he would have taken a moment to enjoy the serenity of his land. For as far as the eye could see, this was all his. His little slice of the Scottish Highlands, where his ancestors had ruled. His heaven on earth.

But for now, he was simply annoyed at this waste of his precious time.

He kicked at a stone, sending it spiraling into the creek. While he studied the ripples on the surface, he felt a sudden prickling sensation at the base of his skull, like cold fingers on his spine. Or eyes watching him.

Before he could turn, the sound of a gunshot broke the stillness. Liquid fire seared his veins. His legs failed him and he dropped to the ground. Blood formed a dark, sticky pool around him.

While cattle and birds and insects continued their songs, the life of one man was slowly seeping away.

Willow MacKenzie stopped her pacing when she spotted headlights through the rain-spattered window.

"Finally. Bear had better have a good excuse for being this late for supper." She patted her father-in-law's arm as she hurried past his wheelchair and through the mudroom to throw open the back door of the ranch house.

Instead of her husband, the man striding up the porch steps was Chief Ira Pettigrew, the tall, muscled head of the Copper Creek police force. A force that consisted of three men.

Ira's great-grandfather, Ingram Pettigrew, had been a legendary hunter and trapper in Montana, and he had been a bridge between the Blackfoot tribe of Native Americans and the homesteaders who'd settled the wilderness. Keeping the peace had become a way of life for the men who followed, including Ira's father, Inness, and now, Ira. The father of four, Ira had worked for the state police as a trained marksman before accepting the position of police chief in his hometown. Ira knew every square mile of land in his jurisdiction, and he zealously guarded the people who lived there.

Willow managed a smile, despite the tiny shiver of apprehension that threaded along her spine. "Ira. What brings you out here on a night like this?"

Instead of replying, he whipped his hat from his head and took a moment to hang it on a hook by the door, watching it drip a stream of water on the floor, before laying a hand on hers. "I've got some news, Willow."

He shut the door and led her past the rows of cowboy hats, parkas, and sturdy boots, and into the kitchen. With a nod toward Maddock MacKenzie, he indicated the high-backed kitchen chair beside Mad's wheelchair. "Sit down, please, Willow."

She was about to protest, until she caught a glimpse of the tight, angry look on the police chief's face. Woodenly she sat, stiff-backed, suddenly afraid.

The door was shoved open, and Whit MacKenzie and Brady Storm blew in, shaking rain from their wide-brimmed hats and hanging them on hooks before prying off their mud-caked boots and jackets.

When they spotted the police chief, both men paused.

"Hey, Ira." Whit stepped into the kitchen ahead of Brady.

"Where're you coming from so late?" Ira words were not so much a question as a sharp demand.

Whit frowned at the impertinence of it. "Checking the herd like always."

"And you, Brady?"

The foreman nodded toward Whit. "With him."

"Which pasture?"

Catching the note of tension in the chief's voice, Whit bristled slightly. "North pasture, Ira. What's this about?"

"It's about my reason for this visit." Chief Pettigrew turned his full attention on Willow.

At fifty-one she was still the tall, graceful model she'd been at Montana State, when she'd turned the head of every boy and man on campus, until Bear MacKenzie, ten years her senior and already a seasoned rancher, had claimed her for his own. From the moment he'd set eyes on her, Bear had been head-over-heels smitten, and determined to make her his wife. And who could blame him? Thirty years later she was reed-slender, with a dancer's legs and muscles toned from years of ranch work. With that mane of fine blonde hair and green eyes, even in faded denims and a soiled cotton shirt, and without a lick of makeup, she was still the prettiest woman in town.

"I'm sorry to tell you this, Willow, but Bear's been shot."

"Shot. My God." She was up and darting past him when his hand whipped out, stopping her in midstride.

"Hold on, Willow."

"No. I have to go to him. Where is he, Ira? Did you send for an ambulance?"

"No need." He put his hands on her shoulders and very firmly pressed her back down to the chair. "Willow, honey, you have to listen to me now. There's no easy way to tell you this. Bear's dead."

Time stopped. The utter silence in the room was shattering. No one spoke. No one even seemed to be breathing.

The four faces looking at the police chief revealed a range of intense emotions. Shock. Fury. Denial. And in Maddock MacKenzie's eyes, a grief over the loss of his only son that was too deep for tears.

Except for Willow's hiss of breath, nobody spoke. Nobody moved. They seemed frozen in disbelief.

"How?" This from Bear's son, Whit.

"A bullet to the back."

"Where?" Brady Storm's hand clenched and unclenched, itching to lash out in retaliation.

"On the banks of Copper Creek. North ridge."

"How long ago?" Maddock demanded.

"Couple of hours at least." Ira didn't bother to go into detail about the temperature of the body, or the tests that would be run in the medical examiner's lab in Great Falls, or the amount of days or weeks that would be needed to determine the exact time of death. Copper Creek was too far away from the facilities afforded by big cities. Ira and his three deputies had learned to take care of their own needs. When they couldn't, they knew how to wait. And wait. Small-town crimes in the middle of cattle country were low priority for big-city authorities.

"You said he was shot in the back." Willow's voice nearly broke. She swallowed and tried again. "Do you think Bear would have known the one who shot him if he'd been able to face him?"

"I won't know anything until all the tests are concluded. My guess is that the shooter was a good distance away when the shot was fired. Probably relied on a long-range sight."

Willow's lips quivered and she pressed a hand to her mouth. "So this could have been done by anybody? An enemy? Even a friend?"

"Or someone who calls himself a friend." Mad MacKenzie hadn't just earned his nickname because it was an abbreviation of Maddock. In the blink of an eye, he morphed from grieving father to avenging angel.

Pounding his fist on the arm of his wheelchair in fury and frustration, he looked from Whit to Brady. "We'll find the son of a bitch who did this, lads. And when we do..."

"You'll do the right thing and let me handle it, Mad."

Ira's voice was pure ice. "If any of you learn anything at all, you're to call me immediately. Got that?"

He fixed his glare on Maddock, and the old man returned his look without a word.

Whit gave a barely perceptible nod of his head. "I hear you, Ira."

Finally the chief turned to Brady, who mouthed the word *yes* grudgingly.

Satisfied, Ira turned his attention to the widow, closing a hand over hers. "Willow, I'm sorry that I can't allow you to take possession of Bear's body until the authorities have concluded their tests. I hope you understand."

She blinked twice, the only sign that she was listening. She'd gone somewhere in her mind, locked in her pain and grief.

"Good. Good." Fresh out of words, Ira started toward the door. Then, thinking better about it, he paused and turned. "I can't tell you how sorry I am. You've lost a good husband, son, father, and friend. And the town of Copper Creek has lost a born leader. Bear will be mourned by a lot of people."

He plucked his hat from a hook by the back door and let himself out.

In the kitchen, the only sound was the ticking of the clock on the wall.

The headline in the *Copper Creek Gazette* read:

BEAR MACKENZIE KILLED BY A SINGLE BULLET IN THE BACK

GUNMAN STILL AT LARGE

The news spread like a range fire through the tiny town of Copper Creek, Montana.

The headline and news article were read and discussed in every diner and saloon and ranch, where cowboys and their women speculated on the shooter and the motive for the killing.

And though everyone in the small town claimed to know everyone else, there was the nagging little thought that one of them just might be the vicious gunman who'd ended Bear MacKenzie's fabled life.

Willow's mount was lathered by the time horse and rider topped a ridge and the house and barns came into view. The chestnut gelding had been running full-out across the meadows ever since its rider had left the stables and given him his head. Now, sensing food and shelter, the horse's gait increased until they were fairly flying down the hill.

At the doorway to the barn Willow slid from the saddle and led her mount toward a stall. Snagging a towel from the rail, she removed the saddle and bridle and began wiping him down. After filling the trough with feed, she picked up a pitchfork and began forking dung, even though the stalls had been thoroughly cleaned earlier in the day.

She worked until her arms ached. When she could do no more, she hung the pitchfork on a hook along the wall and dropped down onto a bale of hay. Burying her face in her hands, she began sobbing. Great wrenching sobs were torn from her heart and soul.

"Hey now." Brady Storm stepped out of a back room and crossed to her.

Without another word he wrapped his arms around her

and gathered her close, allowing her to cry until there were no tears left.

When at last she lifted her head, he handed her a handkerchief. She blew her nose and wiped her eyes before saying, "Thanks. Sorry." She ducked her head, avoiding his eyes. "I got your shirt all wet."

"It's okay, Willow."

When she continued staring at her feet he caught her chin and lifted her face until she met his steady look.

Her voice was choked. "I thought I was alone. Don't tell Mad or Whit. I never want them to see me like this."

"It's nothing to be ashamed of. You've got a right to grieve. We're all grieving."

"I know." She stepped back. "But I need..." Her lips trembled and she fretted that she might break down again. "I need to be strong while we sort things out."

He kept his hand on her arm to steady her. "You're the strongest woman I know, Willow."

"I'm not feeling strong right now. I feel..." She looked up at him, and tears shimmered on her lashes. "I feel broken, Brady." She turned away and hugged her arms about herself, as though trying to hold things together by the sheer strength of her will.

The foreman placed a hand on her shoulder in a gesture of tenderness, before quickly withdrawing it and lowering his hand to his side. His voice was gruff. "You stay strong, Willow. What's happened has you down on your knees. I know what it feels like to be that low, when your whole world ends. But each day, you'll find a little more of your strength. And one day, when this is behind you, you'll realize that no matter what life throws at you, nobody and nothing is going to break you."

She turned and pinned him with a look so desolate, it tore at his heart. "What if all my strength really came from Bear? What if I never find any of my own? How do you know it will get better, Brady?"

His words were laced with pain. "Because I've been where you are now. And know this—I'll be here for you whenever you need to lean on someone until your own strength returns."

He turned on his heel and strode from the barn in that loose, purposeful way he had.

Watching him, Willow thought about what he'd just said. It was the most he'd ever revealed about himself.

Though Brady had been in Bear's employ since she first had come here as a bride, she knew little more about him now than she had in the beginning. Whenever she'd asked, Bear had insisted that Brady's past was nobody's business. When pressed, Bear had told her that he would trust his life, and the lives of his family, to Brady Storm, and that should be good enough for all of them. He'd explained that he'd found that one-in-a-million cowboy who he believed would put their interests above his own. When she'd asked how he knew, Bear had said only that Brady'd been through more of life's trials than most men, and he had come out the other side stronger than steel forged in fire.

And now she had to face a fire of her own. She had her doubts that she would morph into a woman of steel. For now, she would settle for the courage to face one more day.

She took in a deep breath, squared her shoulders, and wiped her eyes before making her way to the house.

Fall in Love with Forever Romance

DRAGON FALL
by Katie MacAlister

New York Times bestseller Katie MacAlister returns to her fan-favorite paranormal series. To ensure the survival of his fellow dragons, Kostya needs a mate of true heart and soul before it's too late.

FRISK ME
by Lauren Layne

USA Today bestselling author Lauren Layne brings us the first book in her New York's Finest series. Journalist Ava Sims may be the only woman in NYC who isn't in love with the city's newly minted hero Officer Luc Moretti. That's why she's going after the real story—to find out about the man behind the badge. But the more time she spends around Luc, the more she has to admit there's something about a man in uniform…and she can't wait to get him out of his.

Fall in Love with Forever Romance

THE FORBIDDEN MAN
by Elle Wright

Sydney Williams has forgiven her fiancé, Den, more times than she can count. But his latest betrayal just days before their wedding is too big to ignore. Shocking her friends and family, she walks out on her fiancé… and into the arms of his brother, Morgan. But is their love only a fling or built to last?

THE BLIND
by Shelley Coriell

When art imitates death… As part of the FBI's elite Apostles team, bomb and weapons specialist Evie Jimenez knows playing it safe is *not* an option. Especially when tracking a serial killer. Billionaire philanthropist and art expert Jack Elliott never imagined the instant heat for the fiery Evie would explode his cool and cautious world. But as Evie and Jack get closer to the killer's endgame, they will learn that safety and control are all illusions. For their quarry has set his sight on *Evie* for his final masterpiece…

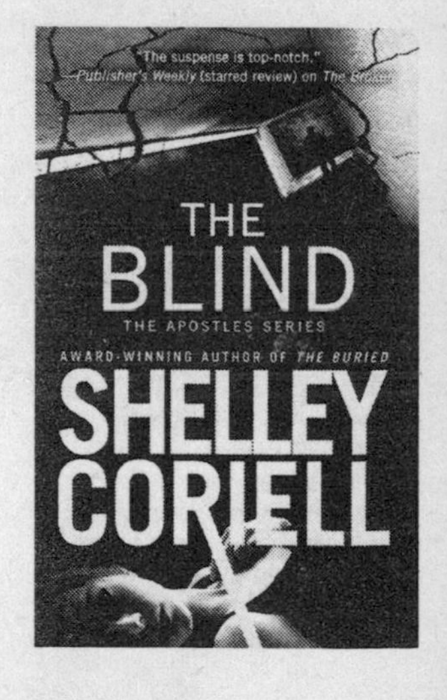

Fall in Love with Forever Romance

THE LEGACY OF COPPER CREEK
by R. C. Ryan

In the *New York Times* bestselling tradition of Linda Lael Miller and Diana Palmer comes the final book in R. C. Ryan's Copper Creek series. When a snowstorm forces together the sexy Whit Mackenzie and the heartbroken Cara Walton, sparks fly. But can Whit show Cara how to love again?

AND THEN HE KISSED ME
by Kim Amos

Bad-boy biker Kieran Callaghan already broke Audrey Tanner's heart once. So what's she supposed to do when she finds out he's her boss—and that he's sexier than ever? Fans of Kristan Higgans, Jill Shalvis, and Lori Wilde will love this second book in the White Pine, Minnesota series.